MW01701656

Break You Down

C. Hazlewood

C. Hazlewood
ROMANCE AUTHOR

C HAZLEWOOD AUTHOR LLC

Book Cover by Zhandre Dex G. (MC Damon)

First edition 2024

To my husband's penis....
Because when I asked him who to dedicate this book to, that was the answer he gave me.
If you like penises as much as my husband likes his, this book might be for you.

Contents

Chapter One

"Hello?" I answered cheerfully, seeing Elias's name appear on my phone. I had just texted him a long message about wishing we could spend the holiday break together and asking him when he would be free to meet up.

I wasn't expecting a call right away. I'd barely snuck out back to answer without my brother noticing.

"Hello? Who the hell is this and why are you texting my husband?"

"Wh-what?" I asked, confused when hearing a venomous woman's voice.

"Listen here, lady. I don't know who you are, but you are clearly not the cleaning lady like you are labeled on my husband's phone. He will not be meeting up with you EVER. Do you understand me? Women like you are pathetic. You see a successful, young, attractive man and all these hussies come out of the woodwork. You are not the only one I have had to deal with, honey, and I'm sure you won't be the last. Leave. My. Husband. Alone."

I was left gawking when the phone suddenly cut off. It took me a moment to find the ability to move again. To even think.

He's married. The bastard told me he was divorced, but he was still married?...

No.... She could be lying.... But....

"Lying, shit-eating, two-timing mother fucker!" I screamed, kicking a pile of snow on the ground. I was still fuming, looking through my tests from the last few days, seeing the short-cryptic one-liners for what they were. I'm such a fucking idiot.

My phone started going off again. It was his number, and I angrily answered with no hesitation.

"Don't fucking worry, lady. I have no plans to see your asshole husband again- "

"Brittany, it's me, "Elias's voice sounded panicked at the other end of the line. Tears burned my eyes, my heart crushed into a million pieces. "Brittany, I'm so sorry. I- "

"Brittany?! Your mistress is named Brittany, huh?" The woman from before yelled from the background.

Anger quickly replaced the sadness inside of me. "I'm sorry, Professor Miles, but I am spending Christmas with my family. I suggest you get back to your wife and family, too."

"Brittany, it's not....It's.... "

A small part of me was hoping he would deny everything that the woman just told me, but I could tell by his hesitation that he couldn't. She was still screaming at him in the background, though it was getting more and more faint.

"Are you still married?" I asked point blank, wanting to get to the root of all this.

"Brittany, I- "

"QUIT SAYING MY FUCKING NAME AND ANSWER ME!" I yelled. "The cleaning lady would like to know if you are still legally married?!"

"Please.... Britt...."

"Yes or no, Professor Miles." I refused to use his first name. "Are you still married?!"

He sighed deeply. "Yes, but I- "

"That's all I needed to know. Your cleaning lady is done," I cut him off, not willing to be the unknowing mistress to my college professor any longer. There were so many red flags leading up to this. He had told me from the start that we were just going to be physical. Nothing more. I let my mind get carried away, deluding myself into thinking he might change his mind.

He won't. He has a wife. I was always just going to be the affair partner. I can see that now.

"Brittany, this conversation is not over. You are misunderstanding and do not interrupt me ag- "

"Excuse you!?" I scoffed. "No, this conversation is over. I'm done. So done. And don't you worry. I didn't get attached, since you were just looking for a physical relationship, anyway." The steady beeping from the call waiting let me know I had someone on the other line trying to get through. I pulled my phone away for a brief second, huffing at the irony that Chris was choosing this moment to call me. "I'm so unattached. I kept a secret from you, too. He's calling me now, so I have got to go. Wish your wife a Merry Christmas for me, and I hope you choke on your eggnog."

"Brittany, don't you- "

I let out a furious growl as I hung up the phone, shrieking into the chilly night air. Angry tears were running down my face. Chris was still calling me, but I would not answer. I said what I said out of anger, not because I was going to give in to my drunken, grief-driven hook-up from months ago. Chris is my brother's friend. Not someone I should have ever slept with in the first place, and I would not use him now.

No. I really am done with this whole thing. I need to talk to Missy. I think it's time to move back home.

***

Four Months Later.....

Professor Dickhead:| Call me.

Professor Dickhead:| Brittany, answer the phone

Professor Dickhead:| It was just a misunderstanding

Professor Dickhead:| Please, just let me explain

I grimaced at the thread of unread messages on the lock screen on my phone. I knew there would be a lot when I felt it going off while I was helping Adrian load the boxes I needed in the back of his truck, but I didn't expect there to be this many. I'm glad I didn't check it then, because I wouldn't have been able to hide the contempt on my face. I had just unblocked the prick, and he was already starting up. I haven't opened a single text, a single email, a single anything from him since Christmas day. I will not start now.

Professor Dickhead:| She was lying, Brittany. It was a lie. Just answer your phone! I......

I rolled my eyes, chucking my phone onto the bed, not wanting to read any more of his lies in the previews of each text message. I'll delete them later without opening them again.

It happened on Christmas day. Fucking Christmas. I don't believe for a second that she just was with him on the biggest holiday of the year that was meant to be spent with family and only the closest of friends and just happened to see his phone. One of them is lying, and considering he has a track record for it, and I hadn't even heard of her before, it's easy to conclude who the liar really is.

"All packed up?" Missy asked, stepping onto the camper where I have lived the past couple of months, ever since Christmas, when I decided to move back home from school, which was in Oregon. My brother- and sister-in-law have been letting me crash in the camper stored in their garage shed in exchange for free babysitting when they need it. Missy told me to stay as long as I needed to, even without the offer of babysitting, but moving back in with family after being on my own in college for the last few years is hard to adjust to. My brother is too nosy and involved. Plus, seeing him chasing Missy's tail all the time makes me want to barf. You would think Adrian would have cooled it over the years, especially with a newborn in the house, baby number three, but he was as bad as ever. I don't know how Missy puts up with him.

"I got the last of what I need," I nodded to a duffel bag on the ground near the door. "I'll get the rest when the house is finished. Are you sure you don't mind storing my stuff here?"

"Of course not," Missy waved her hand. "You know, you could stay here until the house is completely finished. We really don't mind."

"I know," I smiled thankfully. "I'm eager to get started with my life, you know. I just want to be in some kind of normal without my brother having to wheel my home away to empty the septic tank every week."

"Yeah," Missy sighed. "He does get a bit annoying when he does it."

Adrian goes on and on for the rest of the day about how stinky my shit is and stuff. It could smell like freaking roses and Adrian would still give me crap.

My phone buzzed against the bare bed, vibrating loud enough to cause both of us to look. I groaned, and Missy scowled.

"Why don't you just change your number? Or block him?"

"I can't change my number. I'd have to update it with school and too many people since graduation is coming soon. And I did block him. He ended up calling me from the school's phone and I kept answering, thinking it was something to do with my diploma. I unblocked him just so he would stop doing that."

"I could just tell your brother and he would take care of the guy for you," Missy muttered, picking up my phone and examining the screen when I made no movements to check it. A smirk then spread across her face. "Or maybe we could just move on to this guy instead." She turned the phone around, showing me who it was.

I rolled my eyes and fell back on the bed, regret filling me all over again. I never should have slept with Chris Finley. No matter how depressed and heart-broken I was feeling, jumping into bed with my brother's childhood friend was not the answer to my problem, and the dude has been a headache ever since.

Missy giggled and crawled onto the bed beside me. "What's your excuse for not blocking him?"

I frowned at her. "He'll just show up here. That's why."

"Psh," she waved her hand dismissively. "He shows up for my cooking. Not your company."

"Bull shit." He shows up, just begging to get his ass kicked. Not for food, no matter how good of a cook my sister-in-law is. I'm surprised Adrian hasn't caught on yet. My brother is usually observant.

"I guess that is one good thing about moving. Chris can't persistently stalk you by inviting himself over for dinner with Adrian after work every day. He'll have to get creative," she giggled. "No one has persistence like Chris. Weaponized persistence. That's what he has."

"I don't even want to imagine what he is going to come up with," I snorted. As annoying as it is, it is flattering that his persistence is focused on me. It's unwanted, but it helps my ego after the crappy mistress situation Elias put me in. I feel wanted at least.

My phone vibrated in Missy's hand again. She looked at the screen and then scowled. When I saw her press the answer button, my heart stopped.

"Hello?" she answered in a leveled voice.

"What are you doing?!" I hissed.

I heard the rush of words from Elias at the other end. "Brittany? Finally, I-"

"Guess again, professor. Brittany is busy and will be busy for the foreseeable future. I would really appreciate it if you would stop harassing her. I would hate to get a restraining order in place. It surely wouldn't look good for a married man to be served a restraining order while working, especially since it would come from a current student. Do me and yourself a favor and leave my sister alone. She is not interested in lying, married men, and you've about gotten on my last nerve."

With that, she hung up, not giving him a chance to respond.

"MISSY!" I huffed, stealing the phone back from her.

"There. Problem solved."

"Not problem solved! Missy! You could get him fired!"

"So?!" She lifted her chin stubbornly. "He is the one who cheated on his wife with an unsuspecting student of his. He deserves to get fired at this point. If not you, it will be a new student. I'm tempted to report him, anyway."

"He told me he was getting a divorce."

She scoffed, rolling her eyes. "No. He told you he was divorced. Big difference."

"Still...." Looking back, there were signs. I thought he was being cautious because of his job and me being a student. Not because he was still married.

I'm a fucking idiot.

"They all say that they're divorced or getting divorced. He's not worth it. Don't worry about getting him in trouble. He is bringing it on himself. Men like him are all the same."

I know enough about Missy's parents to understand why she is so up in arms over Elias, but....

I did love the man. I'm an idiot for falling for him, especially when he told me we would never be more than physical partners, and I know he deserves to have his world crashing down. I just don't want to be the reason for it. I would rather just move on with my life and hope he does the same....

I clutched my phone in my hand, noticing more and more how it wasn't ringing anymore. Maybe Missy scared him for good.

I don't know how I feel about that....

"Hey you two," Adrian stuck his head in the camper. "We're all loaded up and waiting in the car."

Missy plopped back down on the bed. "Good job, daddy. Just give us a call when you're done unloading the boxes, too. We're gonna stay here and take a nap."

"Oh, no ma'am. You don't take naps without me." Adrian got one of those sleazy grins on his face that instantly made me want to gag. He prowled his way to Missy, grabbing her sides and making her giggle.

I took that as my cue to leave. "I'll be waiting in the car too, you sickos."

My brother was whispering bull shit nonsense in Missy's ear, grinding his body into hers as she laughed uncontrollably. It made me sick but jealous at the same time.

That's what I wanted. The whole time I was hooking up with Elias Miles, I was wishing for a relationship like this, where we could make others sick with the magnitude of our love. Elias always kept me at arm's length, only showing vulnerability when we were in bed.

Now that chapter is over, and I need to move on with my life.

When my phone vibrated again in my hand, I couldn't help myself from feeling that familiar bubble of excitement as I checked it. That bubble burst when Chris's name showed on the screen.

They came out after what felt like two hours later because of Landon's whining and Quinton being fussy, but it was probably only ten minutes. Missy's hair was a mess, and my brother had that stupid grin on his face. He got lucky in some sort of way, I'm sure.

"Would you like another reason I am not living with you two a moment longer?" I asked, sliding out of Adrian's back seat where I was sitting with the boys, trying to keep them calm.

"Because your brother is just too sexy and Missy can't keep her hands off me?" Adrian smirked, slapping Missy's ass.

"Gross." Hailey stuck her tongue out in disgust. "Can I move with you, Aunt Brit?"

"Of course you can, sweetie." I bent to kiss her nose through the open window of the passenger seat. "I should report them for child abuse, making you see that kind of crap every day."

"That's okay," Hailey giggled. "Daddy said he was going to give me a room at your house so I can just live with you."

"Did he now?" I looked at Missy and winked.

I asked my brother- and sister-in-law to give me a spare room for Hailey when they told me they were buying me a house so I could get all my aunt and niece bonding time with her on the weekends. I may have missed Hailey more than anyone else while living away from home for college. I love my nephews too, but Hailey and I have a special bond, and I've always been protective of her. Old habits die hard. With all the bullshit we faced because of Hailey's biological mother, I tried to fill that void the best way I could until Missy came along and swept our whole family off our feet. She was the mother Hailey needed and the partner my brother deserved. I will always have that special bond with Hailey, though.

"Wanna start with a sleepover tonight?!" I asked Hailey excitedly.

"YES!" Hailey threw her hands up in the air.

Adrian drove the kids, and I drove Missy and me in my car. I was excited about my new home. I had always planned on moving back home to live with dad, but then he and Roseanne got married just after Christmas at the courthouse and she moved in with him. I could have gotten an apartment or even lived in the camper longer, but Missy didn't give me a choice in the matter. She said if I didn't want the house in the long run she could keep it as an investment property and let me live in it rent free in exchange for babysitting and helping with the kids. It's her go-to trade for any kind of financial help. She rarely, if ever, actually asks me for help with anything. I just give it when I see the need, which I would do anyway, even without the house or any other help.

Missy and Adrian are both fiercely protective and supportive of our family. It makes taking the offer of this house so much easier, because I know her intention and the mindset she has behind it. I'm just as much her family as Hailey, Landon, Quinton, Adrian, and my dad. This gift is from the heart and out of the love she has for me.

My dad and brother have been fixing up this house for a few months now. It is close to the school where I will teach starting in the fall. For a three-bedroom, it is actually really cozy. It has a wrap-around porch my brother has been waiting to re-do because of the snow. It has a garden in the back that Missy was eager to get her hands in. The inside was gutted after they bought it. Adrian got a bathroom and the two extra bedrooms finished. He still needs to finish the master bedroom and the master bath. The kitchen was remodeled and is just waiting for the marble countertops and the ovens. The microwave and fridge are there, so I can make do until those get finished. I don't cook much, anyway.

Dad was already at the new house waiting when we pulled in. He wasn't alone....

"Oh, my," Missy giggled, giving me a side-eye to catch my reaction. "Looks like we got some extra help getting the four boxes and your suitcase and duffle bags into the house."

"Looks like it," I muttered, pulling into the driveway with a scowl.

"We may not have been able to manage without the extra set of hands. Lucky you."

"Lucky, lucky me," I mumbled, scowling at Chris Finley who was leaning on the back of my dad's truck with an eager grin on his face.

Chapter Two

"Aunt Brit, what's he doing?" Hailey asked, watching Chris pacing outside of my house. He had a single rose in his hand. The stem was looking mangled from him gripping it so tightly while pacing and biting his nails.

"I don't know, baby girl, but get out of the window before he sees you." I then muttered to myself, "I'm going to need to get pest control soon."

"Can I tell him to come in? He looks sad," she asked, turning the blades of the blinds back in place.

"No. No, you can't," I said flatly. "He can stay sad outside."

Hailey giggled. "You're funny, Aunt Brit. You get grumpy every time Mr. Chris is around. You were mean to him earlier, too."

"That's because he doesn't know when to quit," I mumbled.

Earlier, when we were unloading my stuff from Adrian's truck, Chris tried to take half my crap into the house on his own on one trip. He had both arms hooked in the straps of two large duffel bags, then rolled both of my suitcases to the stairs where he fumbled to get them up. I put all my books in the suitcases since they would be heaviest and I could roll them around. Watching Chris struggle was amusing, but aggravating at the same time. Adrian was watching him like he had a few screws loose, and Dad was staring at me and my reaction the whole time.

Stupid Chris. Dad was too observant for him to be acting like that.

When everything was unloaded into the house, Chris cornered me in my temporary bedroom and offered to stay and help unpack. I refused bluntly. A little too bluntly. I said, "No, you freak. I don't want my underwear to go missing," not knowing that my niece was just behind him. She laughed and said Chris couldn't fit in my underwear, and that his butt was too big. I thought that was the end of it when he left with my dad, but now he is back here on his own after everyone else left, pacing outside like a weirdo.

"Josh Donalds brought me a flower to school yesterday," Hailey told me proudly while plopping herself onto the single loveseat in the living room. "He was nervous about giving me my flower, too."

"Who's Josh Donalds?"

She shrugged. "My boyfriend."

Oh, my brother is going to love this. "Does your daddy know about Josh Donalds?"

Hailey gave me a 'what do you think' look that made me laugh more. "I told mom, and she said we could just be friends."

"Then he can't be your boyfriend."

"Yes, he can. He's a boy and my friend. Boyfriend." She looked at me accusingly. "You aren't going to tell daddy, are you?"

I laughed at her expression. "No. Just don't tell your daddy about Chris and we can be even."

"Deal," she grinned, flipping over the cover of her iPad to open her messenger app. I'm going to have to look at that app later, just to be sure Joshy-boy was nothing to worry about. They're eight, so I'm sure everything is still pretty innocent, but as her aunt, I'm still going to check. I'll be working at her school soon, and can keep a better eye on her then. I'll play the cool aunt now and turn into crazy stalker aunt when she's not looking.

I was in the kitchen, trying to figure out where to put a coffee maker without kitchen counters, when I heard a knock at the door. I rolled my eyes. Seems he got the nerve to finally get rejected again and get out of here. The man just doesn't take no for an answer.

"Door!" Hailey yelled, not looking up from her iPad.

"Don't worry. I'll get it," I said sarcastically.

She giggled at me. "I don't think it's for me, Aunt Brit."

"Yeah," I murmured to myself. "Me neither."

I opened the door in a huff, but was surprised to see that Chris wasn't alone on the other side. Missy was standing there too, with a plentiful smile on her face. Chris had a big cooler in his arms and a sheepish expression, while Missy was now holding the man-handled rose.

"We brought you dinner," she said, her voice full of amusement.

"We?" I lifted my eyes at Chris. He now had the proudest smile on his face.

"I'm helping carry it."

He walked past me into the living room saying, "Hey squirt!"

"Where's the flower?" Hailey asked, eyeing the cooler.

I turned an accusing glare on Missy. She was biting her bottom lip to restrain her smile. She lifted the flower towards me. "I think this is for you."

I yanked it from her hands and tossed it in the bush beside my door. "Are you the one that asked him to come back here?"

"Oh, no. That was just a happy coincidence," she laughed.

"Happy for who?!" I hissed quietly, trying not to raise my voice while Chirs was inside with Hailey.

"Hmm, for me?" She said it like it was a question. "The boys passed out when we got home, so Adrian stayed back to watch them. I liked not having to carry that heavy cooler."

"I could have carried it!"

"Why when Chris was willing to help?" She bit back her laughter. I'm glad she is finding this all so amusing. I basically have a stalker and she is encouraging him now.

I suddenly felt heat radiating behind me. When I turned to look back, Chris was right there, not four inches away from me, close enough where I could smell his cologne mixed with the musky natural scent he usually had from being a blue-collar worker. That scent still gets to me. It makes me remember that night. If it wasn't for that damn scent, it would have been easier to be close to him. The memories involved with a single scent can be so heavy sometimes. So binding.

So fucking frustrating.

"Anything else, Missy?" Chris asked, his voice rough but cheery, as usual.

"There's a bag for Hailey in my passenger seat. Do you mind getting it?"

"Not at all," he smiled, gently brushing past me, his hand barely grazing the small of my back like he was trying to steady me.

"Idiot," I muttered, feeling a heat traveling up my spine. If he heard me, he didn't let it show.

Damn it, Missy. I don't know why she helps him worm his way into my space. She knows how disarming he can be....

"Mama, what did you make?!" Hailey called to her from inside, trying to unfasten the latch to the YETI cooler.

"Fried chicken and cheesy potatoes," Missy answered, patting me on the shoulder with playful sympathy before going inside, closing the door behind her. There was a smirk on her face. She's being too obvious with her intentions.You would think with her history with Chris, she wouldn't be playing this game right now.

I stood exasperated, with a scowl on my face, staring at Chris as he made his way back to the porch. Noticing his muscled arms with his shirt sleeves rolled up, and his rough, rugged hands gripping Hailey's small pink backpack made my scowl deepen. Is he so smug because he knows he's attractive? Is he just not used to being told the word 'no'?

"You're not invited to dinner," I informed him, blocking his entry with my hand planted firmly against the door frame.

"Why, yes, I was. Missy invited me herself. It's my reward for all my help today."

"So, you just helped for free food? I'll give you ten dollars to spend at the diner right now."

"Come on, Brittany," he leaned in and husked deeply in my ear. He still had that bright smile on his face, while I was still frowning. "You know why I really helped."

"Weaponized persistence?" I muttered.

He chuckled deeply, making me want to squirm and punch him at the same time. I stood stiffly as he slid the backpack up my arms and onto my shoulders. He somehow made the action seem sexual with that sleazy smug smile on his stubble-ridden face. "Why let something that was so good go?"

"Because no means no," I seethed in a whisper.

"Does it?" he tilted his head. "I remember you saying no a lot that night too, but it was followed by 'don't stop'. Said it so much that it must have stuck." He pressed his lips next to my ear. "I don't think you really want me to stop now, either."

I closed my eyes, not letting his hot breath tickling my neck make me move away. I'm standing my ground. "Why do you think that?"

"Because you never stop me from doing this," he said, right before his mouth came down on mine.

Damn it.

***

Chris

Damn it, she tastes good. I know I keep pushing my luck, but every time she lets down her guard enough for me to kiss her, the reward is too great for me to give this up.

Her breath hitches as I run my tongue over the seam of her lips, giving me the opening I crave. The sweetest tasting furious moan leaves her, making my lips smile against hers.

She might tell me no every time I ask her on a date, or every time I call her just wanting to hear her voice, but when I get the chance to kiss her, 'no' never leaves those sweet lips. It makes it impossible to give her up, no matter how much she fights me.

She's not fighting me now. She was clenching her hands at her side, like she was refusing to touch me, but she didn't stop me from touching her. Her skin felt so soft as my hands spanned her waist. Her shirt rode up, and the chilly air was making her flesh cool to the touch. Man, what I would do for a chance to thoroughly heat her body up, but that really would be pushing it right now.

Baby steps. I'll be content with sneaky kisses for now. Now that she has moved back home and is on her own, I'll break down the rest of her defenses until I make her mine.

"Stop," she whispered, but then her mouth molded to mine again. It's like this every time. It's like she is starved for lovin'. I wish she wouldn't fight me so much, because I would give her all the lovin' she could ever want or need.

The door suddenly opened behind her, startling her and making her stumble back as our lips broke apart. My hold on her waist was the only thing preventing her from falling backward into Missy.

"I'm sorry, I-" Missy froze, her eyes widening and a slow grin lifting her face. "My, my, my. I did not mean to interrupt."

"You didn't," Brittany said venomously, pushing me away and stumbling against the doorjamb. I reached out to help her, but she slapped my hands away, stumbled a bit, then let out a frustrated growl before retreating into the house. "Stupid, persistent, infuriating bastard," she mumbled, dropping the backpack on the ground and bending to pick up a beer off the floor, walking toward the kitchen.

"We got to work on our pet names for each other, sweetheart!" I yelled after her. She flipped me off without turning around, disappearing around the corner.

"Look at you," Missy giggled. "You are just asking for a black eye, aren't you?"

"She would never," I shrugged, barely containing my joyous smile.

"She would and so would her brother, so watch it." Missy stabbed me in the chest with her finger. "Hailey might keep secrets, and so will I, for now. I'm betting on you too," she made a bit of a face. "You have been the distraction she needed. Just don't let anyone else see you making out with her on her front porch. This is a small, gossipy town. Adrian does occasionally sign your paychecks."

"Good thing my boss's boss is betting on me," I said, feeling pretty smug.

"Your boss's boss can't stop him from killing you," she laughed. Missy then patted my cheek. "Thanks for the hand. Enjoy the fried chicken. I packed extra," she winked at me before turning to leave.

I waved goodbye to my boss's boss, then let myself in. I closed the door behind me, and that's when Brittany yelled out, "Hurry and lock that, Hailey, before he comes back."

Hailey looked over at me, grinning as I pressed my finger to my lips. She nodded at me, then yelled back, "Okay, Aunt Brit!"

I quietly crept into the kitchen, stifling my laugh at seeing Brittany fumbling frustratedly with a bottle opener and her beer.

"Persistent, arrogant, no-good, prick of a-"

"Let me get that for you, sweetheart," I surprised her, wrapping my arms around her from behind and catching the beer when she accidentally tossed it to the side.

"You asshole!" She gasped, stomping her foot over my steel boot, then turning to threaten me with the beer opener. "I thought you left!"

"Weaponized persistence, remember?" I grinned, carefully taking the bottle opener from her hand and opening her beer. I took a big swig of it before handing it back to her. She narrowed her eyes at me, giving me a cute little glare. I chuckled and quickly pecked the tip of her nose, then jumped back before she could land a swing at me.

"Get out!"

"Can't," I grinned. "I'm hungry."

"Then go to the diner."

"I'd rather eat here with you," I said, taking a step towards her. "I would rather eat, well, you, but I'll settle for fried chicken for now."

She rolled her eyes but didn't make any movements to stop me. Not until her phone, which was wedged in an exposed kitchen drawer with no counter overtop, vibrated loudly. She looked down at the screen and her face changed completely. There was anger there, but it was mixed with some level of pain I hadn't seen since that night. The night we slept together.

She dropped the call, then tossed the phone at me.

"You know what? Fine. Stay for dinner," she muttered before taking a long swig of her beer. "I could use the distraction," she muttered to herself, combing her fingers through her blonde hair. "Just don't let me answer that tonight."

Chapter Three

Brittany

"Your school is calling again," Chris said around a big bite of cheesy potatoes. My phone was in one hand and his paper plate in the other.

"Just ignore it," I told him for the hundredth time. "They'll stop calling, eventually."

"What about 'Professor Dickhead'? Will he stop calling eventually too?"

"Beep!" Hailey said from the couch, censoring bad words like she usually does, thanks to my brother.

"Sorry," Chris muttered. "Professor Penis-head is calling you now. You want me to ignore that, too?"

"Yep," I scowled, then tore off a chunk of fried chicken from the bone with a little too much force with my teeth. Professor Dickhead is what Missy changed Elias's name to, and I liked it much more than the 'Professor <3' I had named him before, so I left it.

"Alrighty then," Chris pressed the off button on the side of my phone and slid it back into his jean pocket. He smiled at me with a mouth full of food, and despite myself, I couldn't help but to crack a small smile too at how ridiculous he looked, and how ridiculous this whole situation was. When I was leaving my brother and Missy's house, if you had told me I would finish my day eating fried chicken on the floor with Chris, I would have said you were crazy.

Being with him all evening has done wonders to keep my mind off Professor Dickhead. Even with Elias calling so much again, it's not pissing me off like it was this morning. It's annoying still, but Chris is giving me a whole new set of problems to focus on. Like....

"Mr. Chris? Are you spending the night too?" Hailey reached over his shoulder to take a fresh drumstick from his hands that had just lifted from the foil pan. He acted offended about her stealing his food, and she giggled while taking a bite.

Chris chuckled at her antics. "I don't know, honey. Should I spend the night?" He then looked over and winked at me.

"There are not enough beds. You would have to sleep on the couch, but you're tall."

"Maybe someone might want to share their bed?" Chris said, giving me the side eye again.

"Not me," Hailey gagged, sticking her tongue out in disgust. "Daddy said you have to be married to share a bed with a boy."

I choked on my beer, laughing at my brother's hypocrisy. He had Missy pregnant with Landon months before they said 'I do'.

"How bout it, Brit? Hailey said we had to get hitched."

"I don't think that's what she was saying at all," I snorted.

"That's what I heard."

"You should get your hearing checked."

"My hearing is perfectly fine. We can go get it checked together tomorrow after we get up if you're that concerned, sweetheart."

I narrowed my eyes at him, resisting the urge to smile. "You're not spending the night. You're leaving the moment you're done eating."

Chris had the nerve to pout his lips, looking ridiculous. The smile broke free on my face as he made a show of taking the smallest bites possible of his next piece of fried chicken. My phone must have vibrated in his pocket again. He took it out and grimaced at it, but just dropped the call and slid it back in.

He hasn't asked me about why I'm not taking those calls once. I like that about Chris. He doesn't ask questions. His persistence seems to only apply to his love life. Anything else going on, he's the shoulder shrugging, 'it will work itself out' kind of guy. I think that's why he and Adrian could stay friends for so long. Adrian is no bullshit and Chris doesn't get wrapped up in this town's drama, either.

After Hailey finished eating, she asked us to paint our nails. I just went with Missy for manicures and pedicures, but that didn't matter. I happily let Hailey take off my fresh nude nail polish and replace it with every color of the rainbow. We took turns between letting the paint dry, putting smiley faces and hearts on each other's nails with a nail polish pen. Chris even got his toes painted, but claimed his fingers were too busy slowly eating his chicken to be done. He was taking his sweet time finishing his food.

After nails, she picked out a movie to watch together. We sat on the floor in her room and watched it on the TV Adrian brought over for her. Chris followed us back on Hailey's invitation, still with a fried drumstick in his hand. He was barely taking nibbles off of it now. Only when I said something about it, would he keep up with the pretense that he was still eating. Hailey thought it was hilarious. I was having a hard time resisting the urge to smile every time he played it up like he was still starving, too.

"Aunt Brit. I'm getting sleepy," Hailey said, leaning against my shoulder with her hooded eyes. We were only about halfway through the Goonies, but I was losing interest too. It was hard to focus when Chris was sitting right next to me and his foodless hand kept brushing against my leg.

"Wanna finish this up tomorrow?" I asked her.

"Yeah," she yawned, stretching and making her way to the bathroom to brush her teeth.

"Need help?" Chris asked as I started pulling the covers down for her to get into her bed.

"Not with a half-eaten chicken carcass still in your hands," I smirked at the cold, discolored, gnawed-on bone gripped between his greasy fingers.

He looked down at his hand and smiled. "Oops. I, uh, guess I can be done now."

I lifted my brows sarcastically as I fluffed a pillow. "I think you've been done for a while."

"I'm still starving," he claimed. "Think I'll just go toss this and grab me another one."

"I think it's time for bed and you should-"

"Oh, I can eat in bed," he gave me a suggestive look. "You know that."

I rolled my eyes and looked away, trying not to show my embarrassment. Yeah, I know that. Once drunk, I can get pretty demanding, and he answered every one of my demands to the fullest. I was starved for that kind of affection. I tried to remain selfless whenever Elias and I met because I didn't want to overstep his boundaries or ruin our fragile relationship. Then I went back home, went out to get a few drinks to drown my sorrows when Elias told me our relationship would always only be physical. I was so low and so deprived and needy that I demanded the only man there not scared enough of my brother to talk to me to fill every unmet need I had been trying to repress for the past several months.

Chris didn't disappoint, but I always knew it would be a onetime thing. He just didn't get that memo. No, he probably got it shredded it, disregarding it completely. I've been pretty obvious with my intentions towards the incident. I wanted to pretend that it had never happened. Chris just was not on board with that.

Stupid Elias. He would drip feed me hope and I clung to it like a lifeline. When I got back to school from break after that time with Chris, he apologized for the way he left things, giving me a vague, "I care about you and didn't want to hurt you," but that meant nothing in the end. He was just stringing me along as his unsuspecting mistress, oblivious to the wife he secretly had at home. I adamantly pushed Chris away because of the small chance things might change when I graduated with Elias. I was a fucking idiot.

If that was the only reason I pushed Chris away all this time, then why am I still building up that wall between us?

....My brother. Adrian would pop a vein if he knew I had drunkenly hooked up with his friend. A friend that he employs at his contracting firm. Adrian would kill Chris, or at the very least, fire him. Adrian never wanted me to be with a man from this town. He wanted me to be with someone smart and dignified. Someone who he thought could fully support me. Chris was not someone he would approve of, especially with how things had happened between Chris and me already. If I selfishly used Chris any more than I already had just because I have needs and I know he can fill them, it could hurt Chris in the long run. I don't want that. This is a small fucking town. If word gets out about a single hook-up, people would whisper for weeks, but if word got out that Chris and I were hooking up on the regular..... It could ruin both of our lives.

Chris came back in with Hailey on his back, no chicken leg in sight. She was giggling as he twirled her in circles before flopping back and dropping her on her bed.

"You're almost as strong as daddy."

"Oh, I'm way stronger than your dad."

"Bull shit," I scoffed, watching with my arms folded and a smirk in place.

"Beep, Aunt Brit." I rolled my eyes at my niece, censoring my curse.

Chris pulled up his sleeve and flexed, giving me a sideways grin. "How bout them apples?"

"Looks mushy and unripe to me," I teased him, even though that was far from the truth. He was impressive, but I always have been and always will under the assumption that my brother is the toughest guy in the world. He told me that enough times when we were growing up that I really can't imagine otherwise.

I tucked Hailey in and kissed her nose while Chris playfully scowled at me, rubbing his arms like he was confirming they weren't mushy. "Night, pretty girl. I'll see you in the morning."

Is Mr. Chris staying over?" she asked me again.

"Nope," I looked up at him before continuing, "He finished all his food, so he is ready to go home now."

"Okay," she looked at Chris with a small smile, and then he winked at her. He's been good with Hailey all evening and I smiled at their exchange. "Can you put on a show for me? Mama lets me watch TV until I fall asleep on the weekends."

"Sure," I clicked on Courage The Cowardly Dog, since it was one I knew she enjoyed falling asleep too. I then wished her goodnight one more time before I pushed Chris out of her room so she could go to sleep.

"Alright, mushy man. Time for you to go home so I can go to bed too."

***

Chris

"Ah, I'm not full yet," I whined, putting on the breaks once her pretty little hands pushed me out to the living room. "There's still two pieces of chicken left."

She looked down at the bowl and grimaced. "They're old and gross. If you eat those, you're going to get sick."

"Now, I wasn't talking about the chicken," I wiggled my eyebrows, pulling on those hands that were pushing me moments ago and bringing her against my chest. She let out the cutest little huff, then scowled up at me.

"Chris, I told you no. I've told you no in every way imaginable. Just grab your salmonella chicken and take it to go."

"But I want a sleepover too," I said softly, moving my face closer to hers. She didn't flinch away. She never moves away from me when I get close to her. She stands her ground, then gives in when I just....

"Don't you dare," she brought her hand up to my lips before I could kiss her. "I'm not doing this with you. Hailey is going to sleep in the next room."

I kissed the tips of her fingers, smiling when it made her gasp so softly before she narrowed her eyes. "So does that mean if she wasn't here, you would let me kiss you?" I puckered my lips against her fingers once more. "Kiss you again, I mean."

"If you just wanted kisses, then that wouldn't be the problem."

Oh, I know. We had already started things backward, so of course she thinks all I want from her is sex, but I don't think she really realizes I want much more.

"One date. Agree to go on a date with me and I'll leave for tonight without a fight."

She pursed her pretty lips. The little humming sound she made while she was thinking was driving me crazy.

"No," she stubbornly said. "My brother-"

"Your brother isn't your daddy, Brittany. You're an adult. Dre can't control you."

She frowned. "No, but he can control you. Chris, this town is too small to casually date someone without consequences. You know that."

I groaned, hating this excuse. Yeah, it's a small town, but she's Brittany Brewer. No one that knows her would ever think in their right mind that she would just be sleeping around or casually dating anyone. She's the diamond in this rough mountain town, untouchable for all her adult life because no one wanted to anger her brother to get to her. I was the exception, and now that I had got to touch the rarest jewel, I didn't want to let anyone else come in and snatch her from me.

"Let me stay for one more beer, then. One more beer and then I'll go."

She huffed, the smallest, faintest groan leaving her with her heavy sigh. "Fine. One more beer and then it's time for you to go."

"Yes!" I pumped my hand in the air.

"Just. One," she held her finger up.

I smiled, mirroring her with my finger, then following her to the cooler to grab another Coors Light.

I took my time, sipping my beer slowly, laughing at Brittany as she tried to figure out what to do with the rest of the leftovers while chugging down her own beer. It was maybe her fourth one, and when she grabbed her fifth while I was still nursing my one, I could tell she was getting a little tipsy. She plopped her skinny booty down beside me on the loveseat, giving up on the food. Her kitchen was a mess, half finished with most of her boxes of kitchen goods still in her brother's barn or her dad's garage. I started telling her about all Adrian was having us do to her house to finish the kitchen this week before we started on the master when she grabbed her sixth beer.

Her eyes were getting glossy, and her laughter was more abundant. This was the same Brittany from the bar that night we hooked up. She was teasing me, but not in that annoying flirty way most of the bar bunnies do. She was like just another one of the guys with the way she talked, but she was gorgeous, so it had thrown me for a loop back then and it was charming the laughter right out of me tonight too.

Pressing my luck one more time, I brushed the hair off her shoulder as I asked, "You sure you don't want me to have a sleepover too? I can make a mean eggo waffle in the morning."

She laughed, so carefree and beautiful at me that my hope started to rise. "Nope." she poked my nose with her finger. "Not going to happen, mushy man."

I groaned at the new nickname. "Come on. I can wake up early and go get you coffee and donuts, then help you unpack?"

"Nope. Nice try," she said, then finished her beer. She got up to toss it in the trash before grabbing another, the last one in the cooler. "Your beer is all gone and looks like we have no more. Too bad. Now, you gotta go and I gotta shower," she said with a giddy voice, her words aggregated a bit.

I sighed, knowing I should give up for today. I was still planning on showing up in the morning with donuts and coffee. Waiting a few hours to see her again wouldn't kill me.

I tossed my beer, and she ushered me to the door. Before heading out, I leaned against the doorframe, towering over her, enjoying the gleam in her eyes and the tipsy smirk on her moist lips. I couldn't stop myself. I leaned down and tasted them, groaning lustfully, when she kissed me back.

After pulling away, I rested my forehead on hers. "Goodnight, Brittany."

"Night, mushy man," she giggled, watching me as I walked back down her sidewalk to my truck.

I looked back just in time to see her close the door, swinging that bottle to her lips. Damn, she looked good drinking a beer. She looked good all the time, but seeing her lips on the end of a bottle made my mind go to dirty places.

I had just gotten my keys in the ignition when my pocket buzzed. Shit. I almost left with her phone. I pulled it out and frowned when it was her school calling her again. It was after nine at night. What the hell?

Without thinking much about it, I answered her phone, half expecting it to be some sort of school emergency. I wouldn't know what kind of school emergency would entail a phone call this late, but I was still curious.

"Ye-ellow?"

The phone line was silent.

"Hello?" I repeated. I was about to hang up, thinking it must be one of those automated calls, when a man's voice finally spoke.

"Hello? Is.... Is this Brittany, uh, Brewer's...."

"Brit? Yeah, she's getting in the shower. Can I take a message?"

"She's.... She's in the shower?" the voice repeated in disbelief. "I'm sorry. Who are you?"

"Uh, who are you?" I said sarcastically, not liking his tone. "Wait, let me guess. Professor Dickhead?"

"I beg your pardon?" he practically growled. "Who the hell are you, asshole?"

"Hey, hey, hey. Don't get mad at me. We were talking about a Professor Dickhead earlier and I was just curious. Don't get your panties twisted. If you want, you can give me a message to give to Brit. If not, I'm hanging up."

There was a loud crash at the other end before the phone line cut off. Guess he didn't have a message for her. That was weird. The weirdest phone call I've ever had, to be honest. I'm more confused about what that was about than before I answered. I still didn't know why her school kept calling her.

I pulled my keys back out of the ignition, then started walking back to her front door, shutting off her phone so she didn't accidentally answer it drunk. I know Hailey has a phone, so hopefully, if Missy or Adrian need to call, they will call their daughters when Brittany's doesn't work.

I knocked on Brittany's door, and only two and a half knocks in it swung wide open. Before I can say anything, Brittany throws her arms around my neck and pulls me down to kiss her. I was surprised for about two seconds before melting into her beer-tasting lips.

"I thought you were really about to leave," she whispered in a rough, whiney voice.

I groaned, kissing her senseless again before picking her up and carrying her back to the other bedroom, so fucking thankful it's two doors down from Hailey's, whose TV was still on, and even more thankful for that weird phone call.

***

Elias

"DAMN IT!" I yelled, tossing the entire landline phone across the room, making it break against my office wall. "Damn it," I said in a more broken tone, leaning back against my bookshelf before falling to the floor.

Damn everything. Damn the school for granting her this early graduation. Damn Lindsey for her stunt on Christmas. Damn fucking everything, including the asshole with her right now, showering and taking messages for her.

If she would just talk to me, just for a second, I could explain. I could tell her everything I was planning on telling her anyway the second she graduated.

Now, she is showering with some hick back in her hometown, talking about me and calling me insults that are deserved, but not for the reasons she thinks.

I should have been honest with her from the start. I thought I was protecting myself and her but keeping her at a distance for now, but if I knew this was going to happen, I would have told her everything the moment I knew I had more than just lust for the young woman.

I wanted her. Brittany was a breath of fresh air, like pure oxygen, after I'd been suffocated in the toxic filth of my life before I met her.

Now that my oxygen is gone, I don't know how to breathe again. I don't know how to survive or function without her here.

She was my escape, but now she has escaped from me. She's showering and joking about me with some common-hick joe, and I'm unable to breathe.

Damn it, I'm not going to just wallow here any longer. I need to do something. Everything is almost done. I was going to wait until the final arrangements went through to do something, but now I realize I don't have the luxury of time.

Brittany, my sweet flower, exuding clarity and beauty, providing me with life's most basic needs. I will not stay still while some other man takes you from me. I won't let a misunderstanding cause me to lose everything.

Chapter Four

Brittany

"Ugh," I wiggled in agitation, feeling Hailey's dog, Hunter's tongue, licking on my neck. "Go away, you stupid puppy," I groaned, rolling over to get away.

The deep chuckling that followed made me confused, the grogginess fading from my mind. I rolled back over, forcing open one eye. My heart beat wildly when I saw Chris instead of that dumb dog.

"What the hell?" I looked around, disoriented, in the unfamiliar room. It took my brain another few seconds to remember I had moved into my house yesterday. Then, the memories from last night hit me all at once. "Crap," I groaned, covering my face with my hands. Why, oh why, did I drink so much last night?

"Good morning to you too, sunshine," Chris laughed softly, not put off by my pissy, regretful mood. He pulled my naked body close to his and nuzzled his nose against my face.

"I told you to go," I grumbled.

"Hmm, I remember you telling me to cum several times last night."

My gosh. I didn't even drink that much. Just enough to lower my guard. What's worse is, I remember everything that happened. I can't even blame Chris. I remember this overwhelming sense of loneliness coming over me the moment he walked out the door, and when he came back, I didn't think about the reasons for pushing him away. All I could think about was how good it felt to be kissed by this man.

"What time is it?" I mumbled, rolling over to grab my phone. Only, I had no idea where my phone was.

"Whatcha lookin' for?" Chris asked, rubbing his hands up my arm when I leaned up to look around.

"My phone."

"Oh," he said unenthusiastically. He rolled to grab something off the floor, then handed it to me.

That's right. I gave it to him last night. It was off, so I hit the power button, hoping it wasn't dead. I don't know where I put my charger yet. Luckily, it still had a third power left.

"I had to turn it off because your school kept calling again," Chris mumbled. He didn't look too happy about it. The calls must have been coming nonstop.

I looked at the call log and my stomach dropped, seeing the top line black as the others were all red. "You answered it?!"

Christ shrugged. "I thought it might be important."

Fuck. "Wh-what did you.... What did he....?"

"He, meaning professor dickhead?" Chris raised his eyebrows.

I bit my bottom lip and nodded once.

"Professor Dickhead asked for you, and I simply told him you were unavailable. When I tried to take a message, he hung up. Nothing exciting."

"Good," I sighed. The call log showed they only talked for 46 seconds. Not much can be said in 46 seconds.

"I may have said something about you being in the shower. He sounded a bit pissed over that."

"Oh, gosh," I groaned, throwing my head back and covering my face. Leave it to Chris to not only answer that call but also say some shit like that.

"Professor Dickhead has a temper," Chris said in a pouty voice.

I stared at his solemn expression for a moment, then burst out laughing. He looked perplexed for a second, then started chuckling too.

"What? What's so funny?"

"He does have a temper," I choked out through bursts of giggles. "And you're you."

"I'm me?! What does that mean?"

"You're just funny." I wiped tears from my eyes. "My gosh, I can just picture that conversation." I could see them having a conversation now in my head. Elias would be all stiff and gruff, using big words or complex phrases, while Chris just acted like Chris, never being serious and being simple and sarcastic. They're the total opposite of one another, and I still feel like Chris would somehow use his simple straightforwardness to win any argument.

"Is that a good or a bad thing?" Chris narrowed his eyes at me, "because mama always told me I'm a catch."

"I'm sure she did," I giggled, rolling to stare at him. "She probably told you you're special, too."

"How'd you guess?" He smiled proudly, which made me laugh even harder.

When he pulled me towards him, I didn't stop him. I giggled until he had my body lying on top of his. Then, I pressed my lips together, staring at his scruffy face, liking the way his smile lines wrinkled his eyes and somehow made his mouth more attractive. I couldn't stop myself from tracing those lines with my fingers. When they grazed the corner of his lips, he turned and kissed my fingertips.

It's morning and I'm no longer drunk. I have no excuses to cover for my attraction to this man.

"You can kiss me if you want. I won't stop you."

"My breath probably stinks."

"Eh," she shrugged, not denying it, but acting like it wasn't a big deal.

"Your breath probably stinks," I scoffed.

"We can stink it up in here then."

I giggled at his logic. He leaned in and bad breath was the last thing on my mind when he kissed me. His knees pushed between mine, forcing my legs apart and up, then he grabbed my thighs and had me straddling him. His firmness was pressing into my naked center in a delicious way.

The sun wasn't even all the way up in the sky and we were about to do this again. I knew Hailey would still be asleep for another few hours, and I couldn't think of any other reasons any longer to resist. When he started to grind against me, gripping my ass to move me back and forth against him, I wanted more.

"Mmh, I hate to stop for anything, but I used every condom I had last night," Chris groaned, nuzzling my face. He stopped rocking his body underneath mine with regretful restraint.

I lifted my chin, giving him access to my neck. "No need to stop," I whispered. "I'm on the pill."

"Fuck yes," he moaned, then rolled us over so he had me pinned underneath him. He suckled my chest, his tongue lapping around my pebbled nipple. I was growing wetter and wetter by the second. "You have the most perfect tits," he groaned, biting down on the fatty flesh. I was going to have marks all over my breasts by the time he was done. I fucking love my chest being played with. He must have caught on to that, because he was relentless.

"Fuck me, Chris," I begged.

I felt his smile against my skin. "I thought you wanted me to go?"

I groaned in frustration. "Fuck me or I'm kicking you out myself."

"Cumming it is," he said with a cocky smirk, then thrust himself inside of me. My back arched and eyes closed at the sweet invasion. "You have the most perfect pussy, too."

"Shut up," I moaned, trying to focus on the aching pleasure pulling at my core.

"So fucking good, Brittany," he cooed roughly in my ear, dipping his head to suck on my breasts once more. "You're so damn tight," he said around my nipple."

"Chris!" I jerked my head down to stare at him, a smile on my face. "Shut up!"

"Yes ma'am," he smirked, then really started to pound into me. He was still murmuring simple nothings to me, praises and kinky shit, but I was getting lost in the tingling building between my legs. If I listened too much to the things Chris was saying, it was going to start going to my head. He was talking like you would to a girlfriend, not a one-night stand or random hook-up, which I'm still assuming that's all this is.

When I felt the damn about to break, Chris cupped my face between his hands, forcing me to look at him. He was staring down at me with an expression I was scared of. It was so tender and so heartfelt. It was like he was lost in my world and never wanted to break free.

"So beautiful," he whispered, his voice as tender as his face.

When he kissed me, I gasped, my orgasm breaking free. He sailed right through my guttural cries, making my toes curl and scrape down his legs. When his legs went stiff and tense, I felt a gush of warmth rushing inside of me.

His groans were so sexy, and the pure gratification on his scruffy, handsome face had my chest swelling with satisfaction. I bit my lip, feeling sated and content. Chris planted gentle kisses all over my face, nuzzling his nose against mine, and whispering words of affirmation in my ear. Being treated so affectionately is not something I am used to. I close my eyes tightly to stop my emotions from showing. It's embarrassing how much this is affecting me.

When Chris slid out of me, rolling over to pull my body against his, I sank into his warmth. This was also something I wasn't used to. The tender cuddles after sex. My throat felt clogged and my eyes burned, the sweetest getting to me.

"Get some more sleep, beautiful. I'll wake you up with something you'll really like soon."

I choked on a laugh, that statement not fitting with the tender mood. If it wasn't for this man's mouth....

"Okay," I just said, sinking my face into the crevice of his arm, still feeling the effects from before he opened his mouth. I would not let my walls drop so easily, but that doesn't mean I don't feel content in Chris's arms.

***

Chris

It took about ten minutes for Brittany's muffled snoring to start again, and I knew she was out. She went wild last night, so I knew she had to be exhausted. I didn't mean to wake her this morning when I started kissing her, but she had the cutest, sexiest, yummiest looking freckle on the back of her neck and I couldn't stop myself from nibbling on it a bit.

I kissed her temple, praying she wouldn't wake up. When she didn't, I gently rolled her to the other side and made sure she was good and tucked in, then kissed her freckled temple one last time before slipping out of bed.

Damn, I didn't want to, but I also didn't want to disappoint her when she woke up again and I didn't have what I was already planning on going to get.

Her phone was tangled up in the bed, and fell on the floor when I rolled off. I grimaced at it before picking it up and setting it on the little bedside table. She didn't have any notifications, thank the sweet baby Jesus, but I still felt a little sour about the whole Professor Dickhead nonsense.

Who the hell was the guy and why was he calling her so many stinking times? She acted weird when I mentioned him, too.

Her little fit of giggles was adorable when I mentioned my conversation with him last night, though. Damn, I love how she throws her entire body into her laughs. She holds nothing back. At least with her laughs, she doesn't. Her guard is still up and rock solid ninety percent of the time. That ten percent when she lets herself be vulnerable though..... She's fucking gorgeous. Like a pure ray of sunshine. I can't believe it took a drunken night at the bar for me to fully notice.

I eyed her phone for a few more seconds, then took it with me. Not because I was worried about Professor Dickhead calling again, but because I wanted her to sleep. It was for totally selfless reasons. She told me to watch her phone for her, anyway. I'm just carrying out the task I was given. Nothing more.

I had to get one more kiss right on her lips before slinking out of the room. It made her snore catch in her throat, and I held my breath, waiting for her to mumble for the stupid dog to go away again, but she made a little snorting sound after a few seconds and went back to her cute snoring again.

When I got out to the hallway, I slowly closed the door, careful it didn't make a sound before turning to face the hallway. When I got to the end, I almost leaped out of my pants, seeing Hailey lying on the couch, her iPad in her hands, while cartoons silently played on her screen.

Crap. I thought the kid would still be asleep.

"Uh, hey kiddo. Whatchu doin' up so early?"

Hailey let out the heaviest little sigh I've ever heard, dropped her iPad in her lap, then turned to look at me. "Watching Tool Time." She looked me over for a second, then a slow smile formed on her little face. "What are you doing here so early, Mr. Chris? I thought Aunt Brit told you to go home?"

My whole body seemed to freeze over. "I was, uh, just.... I was coming to bring you guys breakfast!" I blurted. It was kind of the truth. I was about to head out to pick something up before Brit woke back up.

Hailey made a point of looking at my empty hands, then back at me. "I don't see no breakfast."

"That's because I haven't gotten it yet," I said sheepishly.

She looked like the old hussies at the coffee shop when they discovered new juicy secrets about someone they were looking forward to turning into hot gossip.

"Mama is going to be so happy," she said in a gleeful tone.

I knitted my brows, tilting my head in confusion. "What do you mean by that?"

"Oh, you know, because mama said she likes you better than the other guy. We're supposed to be rooting for you and not telling dad."

"What other guy?"

Hailey shrugged. "Mama didn't tell me that. She just said there was a bad guy and a good guy, and you were the good guy, so we have to root for you."

"Did she now?" I'm wracking my brain, trying to figure out who this bad guy could be. Was it the same douchebag that was calling her on repeat last night? Professor Dickhead? Is that why she left school early? Was a professor harassing her?

I felt for the phone in my pocket, happy I decided to bring it with me.

"Can I come with you to get breakfast?" Hailey asked, jumping up from the couch."

"Uh, sure kid," I said, still thinking about who this bad guy could be.

Chapter Five

Brittany

Damn, that was the best sleep of my life. My insides were still tingly and my muscles still felt like jello, and I didn't want to wake up or get out of bed. "What time is it?" I stretched and grumbled, reaching out next to me for a warm body, but finding the spot cold.

This intense sense of loneliness and déjà vu swells inside me. I'm very familiar with the feeling of a cold spot next to me after a night of sex. Maybe Chris really was just looking for a lay.

"Asshole," I grumbled, tossing the pillow he used across the room. I can smell him on it. I can spell his cheap cologne and musky natural scent everywhere on this bed, which is pissing me off.

I don't know why I am letting myself feel disappointed by waking up alone. It's not like I let him in, like I tried to let in Elias. This was nothing but a one-night-stand to begin with.

"Where the hell did he put my phone?" I searched the nightstand and the floor, not finding it anywhere. After making the bed, I didn't find it in the sheets either. Did he drop it under the bed? I couldn't find it anywhere.

I gave up after I had the entire room, which was still pretty bare after the move, completely cleaned and still didn't find it. I'll use Hailey's phone to find it later.

After putting on my robe, I slipped on some shorts and slippers and went out to see what Hailey was doing. It had to be getting close to eight, maybe even nine. She had to be up by now. I guess I should be grateful to Chris for leaving before she woke up.

"Hailey?" I looked in her room and found her bed empty. Her pajamas were on the floor, so I knew she had already gotten dressed. She wasn't in the living room or the kitchen either. "Hailey?! Hailey!"

Shit! Why the hell didn't I wake up sooner? I looked for my phone even harder, needing to call Missy, call Adrian, call someone, but it wasn't anywhere in the house. I couldn't even find Hailey's. I only found her iPad sitting on the couch.

"Shit, shit, shit!" I fumbled to unlock it, knowing I could use it to call someone. I could at the very least FaceTime her parents.

They're never going to let her spend the night again, and for good reason. First, I slept in because I was up all night fucking a man that didn't have the decency to stay to say bye in the morning, and now I lost their kid. They're never going to forgive me. I'm never going to forgive myself.

I was just about to press the FaceTime button for Missy, feeling sick on the inside, when the front door started to rattle and Chris walked in with Hailey in tow.

"Why does this donut box feel so much lighter, little lady? Did you swipe one when I wasn't lookin'?"

"No," Hailey giggled, chocolate icing all over her lips.

"Hailey!" I ran over to her, pulling her away from Chris and into my arms. I knelt on the ground, checking to make sure she was okay. "I was worried to death! What the... what were you..." My anger was boiling over, turning into fiery rage. A tremor ran over me, and I glared up at Chris. "You."

"What?" Chris had a stupid look on his face, like he had no idea why I was pissed.

"What?! Are you that fucking dense?!"

"Aunt Brit, we were just getting donuts." Hailey tugged at the sleeve of my robe. Her little face was pure anxiety. It calmed me enough to realize yelling in front of her wouldn't be okay.

"You," I pointed at Chris, "outside. Now." My voice was cold but steady.

He frowned, his brows knitting. "Let me just put these down in the- " he started walking towards the kitchen.

"OUTSIDE!" I stopped him before he took two steps.

He scowled, nodded, then started heading for the door. My heart hammered with anxiety when Hailey hurried to follow him and I almost stopped her, but she just took the box of donuts from him and the drink carrier from his hands.

"I'll put it in the kitchen for you, Mr. Chris," she told him softly.

His scowl softened to a grateful smile. "Thank you, squirt." He messed her hair, then gently poked her nose before heading out the door.

Hailey watched after him, then turned accusing eyes to me. "I'm rooting for Mr. Chris, Aunt Britt. You gotta be nice." She held the box and cardboard drink carrier up in the air. "He got me donuts."

"Hailey," I pinched the bridge of my nose. "Donuts doesn't excuse taking you without permission. Go sit in your room and wait for me. You're in trouble too."

Hailey made a sassy grumbling sound, then stomped her way to her room, taking the donuts and drinks with her.

"Brittany, I... I don't know why you are so worked up. I just-" Chris said after I went outside.

"You just took my niece without even telling me!" I pushed both my hands against his chest, making him stumble back a little. "Do you have any idea how scared I fucking was?!"

"We were just gone for a bit! I wanted to get you breakfast, and she wanted to go with me."

"You should have told me!"

"I was trying to let you get some sleep." He looked at the ground, making a bashful expression. "I didn't really let you sleep much last night."

My face turned bright red. From anger or embarrassment, I didn't know, but I decided the best course of action at this point was to just start slapping and beating on him wildly, letting all my frustration out with my hands. "You gave me a freaking heart attack, you asshole!"

"Hey, hey, hey! I was just tryin' to do somethin' nice!"

I growled furiously. "Something nice would have been to tell me before you kidnapped my niece while I was fucking sleeping! I didn't even have my phone to call and find out where she was! I couldn't find it anywhere!"

His face looked guilty, so I cocked my head to the side, giving him that look like he needed to spill whatever it was he was feeling guilty about before I beat it out of him.

"I, uh, might have taken it with me," he reached into his pocket and pulled out my phone.

A calm rage settled over me for a split second, then burst forth as I started slapping the shit out of him again. "What the fuck!"

"You told me to hold on to it for you, Brittany! Ow!" He quickly grabbed one of my hands before it made contact with his shoulder again. "Your little hands sting! Stop!"

"You stop!" I snapped, yanking my phone away from him. "Stop being such an idiot!"

"You told me to hold on to it!" He argued in a whiny voice.

"Last night! Don't you think I might need my phone if you are going to kidnap my niece from me?!"

"I didn't kidnap her! She asked if she could go and I agreed. If it didn't take the kid an hour to get ready, we would have been back long before you got up."

"Well, you weren't!" I slapped his arm once more.

"Brittany," he tried to pull me towards him by the arm, saying my name in a soothing manner.

I slapped his chest with the phone in my hand, making him grunt. "Don't. Go home, Chris."

"But my coffee is inside."

"That sucks for you," I scowled, trying to yank my arm free from his hold.

"And I want a donut."

"We can't all get what we want," I said with malice. "I didn't want to wake up and have a freaking panic attack." I didn't want to wake up in a cold bed. I didn't want to be reminded again of how lonely I was, and then have that sinking feeling of helplessness overtake me when I couldn't find Hailey. There are so many things I want and didn't get, and that I got but didn't want. Chris can survive without his damn coffee and donut.

"Britt," his voice was deep, full of regret.

"Go home Chris," I said once again, all the fight leaving me. I just felt tired now. "Just go home."

I walked back inside, not looking back. I could feel his eyes on me, but he didn't open that big mouth of his to argue any more and just let me go. I shut and locked the door, then took a deep breath to collect myself. Regret and guilt hit me, with the sense that I may have gone overboard just now. But he took Hailey without telling me. That fear of losing my niece was like a monster tearing me up on the inside.

This was probably just the universe telling me that this couldn't happen again. What the hell was I thinking, getting drunk and letting a one-night-stand stay the night with my niece over here? I wasn't thinking. That seems to be the trend for me concerning men.

Last night can't happen again, even if Hailey isn't spending the night. This was a sign. A sign to get my head out of my ass and focus on myself. Focus on my family.

No more men. No more Chris.

***

Chris

I sat in my truck at the curb for a long time, staring at the wheel while running through what had just happened with Britt.

Everything was so fucking perfect this morning before I got out of bed. I should have just stayed there and held on to her for as long as I could. Trying to do something nice backfired right in my face.

Maybe taking Hailey without saying anything to Britt wasn't the best idea, but I really thought we would be back before Britt woke up. I didn't want to wake her. I was trying to be considerate. I could have left a freaking note or something, though. I guess I really am an idiot. It didn't even cross my mind. I have nieces and nephews, but I've never tried taking care of them before.

And the stupid phone. That was all on me. I got this pit in my stomach thinking about that guy from last night calling her again. I know the excuses I made were just to cover up my anxiety. There is this wall between me and Brittany I just can't seem to break down. There are holes in the wall when she shows her vulnerability in bed, but those walls are iron clad the rest of the time.

"Damn it, Chris," I hit the side of my head. "Why didn't you leave a note?!"

KNOCK KNOCK

"Ah!" I jumped in my seat, hitting my head on the ceiling of my truck when someone startled me by knocking on my window. "Damn it," I rubbed my head.

"You're here early," Adrian was staring in through the glass.

Damn it.

I quickly rolled the window down, trying to keep the guilt on my face by focusing on the throbbing in my head. "Hey, Adrian," I said, a little too enthusiastically.

"I told the crew to get here at nine. Why are you here so early?"

"Nine," I repeated, looking at my clock. "Uh, I, uh, thought you said eight?"

He studied me for a second, then shrugged. "Lucky me. I got a trailer full of granite. You can help me unload."

"Sure thing, boss," I laughed nervously, rolling up the window and reaching for my work gloves on the center console

Chapter Six

Brittany

"Aunt Brit?" Hailey looked at me with those big, inquisitive eyes of hers. "You're here again?"

"Coffee," I muttered, walking past her into their house. "I need the coffee."

Hailey giggled and followed me inside. "Mama! Aunt Brit's here again!"

"It's not even nine yet!" Missy yelled from somewhere down the hall.

No. It's not nine. It's freaking 7:36. Too freaking early to be up and out without coffee and a full night's sleep under my belt. I tossed and turned all night, restless for so many reasons, then got too paranoid to stay in bed any longer. I got dressed and ready early and headed over here again because of one person.

Chris.

That stubborn, heavy-hanging jackass is going to get caught if he keeps his crap up. Three days ago, someone showed up at 8:30 with coffee and flowers. I freaked out at him, calling him a flipping idiot and shooing him away before he got us caught. Adrian could have shown up early and both of us would have been screwed. That was the first day I left my house to come over here and hide, making the excuse of wanting to get out of the workers' hair.

So, then Christ took that as a sign to get to my house even earlier. Two days ago, at eight sharp, he was knocking at the door, spamming my phone to let him in. I showered with music blasting to ignore his persistent banging on the door. I then slipped past him the moment another crew member showed up, leaving to hide at Missy's. When he asked where I was going, I stiffly said I was helping with the kids.

Yesterday, my phone rang at 7:30. When I checked it, Chris left a message saying he had stopped to get breakfast from the diner and was on his way, so to let him in. I grabbed all my stuff, my clothes, bag and keys, and peeled out of my driveway so fast. I narrowly missed him, and Missy stopped believing I was just coming over to get out of the construction zone.

This is day three. I wasn't taking any chances. I left my house at 7:15. Chris is probably there right now, looking all smug and ridiculous with his meager offerings of food after not taking a hint. Not taking several hints. I don't know how to make it any more clear I'm not doing anything with him again.

As I stumbled to the coffeepot, my hobo bag stung over my shoulder with my clothes for the day and my laptop, my ringer went off. I groaned, dropping the bag on the counter, planning on just ignoring it.

"Who's that?" Missy had Quinton on her arm, still in her pajamas. She went straight for my bag as she walked in the kitchen, fishing my phone out of it. She laughed as she stared at the screen. "Aw, poor Chris."

"Don't start, you traitor," I grumbled, taking my first sip of the life liquid in my hands. "This is all your fault."

"How so?" She blinked her big eyes all innocently.

"You know how."

"Oh, I'm sorry for stripping you both down and forcing you in bed together."

"Missy!" I looked around anxiously for signs of my brother.

"Oh, relax. He's not here. Adrian left at seven to pick up materials at the shop."

"What about Hailey?" I mumbled, darting my eyes pointedly at Hailey sitting on the couch with her iPad in her hands.

"Dad says worse," Hailey said without even looking up.

Poor kid. I can only imagine the torture of living with my infatuated brother and the object of his obsession. Missy's probably pregnant again already.

"Yes, he beeping does," Missy grimaced. She leaned in and whispered, "He seriously told Hailey to close our door after she woke us up this morning so he could get in his morning cardio."

"Gross."

"I know," Missy sighed. "It was quite the messy workout."

"Missy!"

"What?!" she laughed, adjusting my nephew so he could turn his head to see me.

"Jeez. My brother is rubbing off on you too much."

"Hmm." she whispered low, "It's probably from all the rubbing together we do."

"Okay, no." I gingerly took my newest nephew from her. "You're grounded from talking until I get more caffeine in me and some baby love in."

"Fine," she laughed, tossing her burp cloth at me and walking back toward the hallway. "I have to get Landon ready to go to Roseanne's anyway."

"Roseanne's?"

"Yeah. She's taking her grandkids to the shop today to make cookies. She asked if Hailey and Landon wanted to come too."

"That sounds like fun," I smiled at Quinton in my arms. He's smiling at everything now, and it's the cutest thing ever. Landon was always a grumpy baby, only wanting Missy and her buttermilk boobs. Quinton is a sweetheart. He must take after his mama more.

"You should come, Aunt Brit! Mama can't come because she has to work with grandpa."

"I should, huh?" I don't have anything better to do today. Quinton will be going with Missy, since he's only breastfed right now. I didn't really want to go to the shop and chance running into Chris, and there was nothing to do in town. Normally, I would just stay here at their house and lounge around, but Roseanne makes the best cookies.

"Don't you want to hang out with me?" Hailey flashed me a cheesy grin. "I'm your favorite."

"Okay, you convinced me. Watch your brother while I get ready."

My phone rang again as I was getting my clothes out of my bag, but I ignored the call before walking off to get ready.

***

"Welcome! Welcome!" Roseanne said as I wrestled Landon to the door Hailey was holding for us. "Brittany! I didn't expect to see you here too! Are you joining us?"

"If that's okay," I said to my dad's new wife. It's still weird thinking of her as my step mom. I love her with dad though. He's been so much happier since they got together.

"Of course it's okay," she waved me in, taking Landon's other hand to direct him towards the back. "It must be 'bring your aunt or uncle to work day' for the kids, because Mike's brother brought the boys too."

I stopped walking as the blood drained from my face.

"Mike's brother?" There are three boys in the Brewer family. It could be the other brother she was talking about.

"Yeah. Chris," Roseanne stared back at me with concern.

"Hey squirt!" I heard that all too familiar voice call out as Hailey walked ahead, pushing open the heavy swinging door to the kitchen.

Hailey bit her little lips, looking back at me with childish amusement. I could see what she was thinking, and the wheels turning in her head.

"Hi, Mr. Chris," Hailey said teasingly, still staring at me. "Are you making cookies too?"

"Cookies?!" London tugged on my hand, finally wanting to move on his own. He was throwing a tantrum to stay in Missy's van to watch his cartoons on the TV, but now he's moving with a purpose for the kitchen.

"Pull up a stool," Roseanne said. "Chris is just measuring out the portions for us, then we can get started."

Chris was standing on the other side of the stainless steel island, a huge container of flour in front of him that he was shifting into measuring bowls. He had this lazy smirk, like he had a secret, as he looked me up and down. I scowled, not liking the way his smug face made my stomach tighten up.

Josie and Ethan, Isabelle and Mike's kids, were standing on chairs on either side of him. Josie had a spatula in one hand, looking eagerly at the chocolate chips in a large bowl on the counter, and Ethan was unwrapping sticks of butter, dumping them in a bowl.

"Hey Ethan!" Hailey went to wash her hands and join him. They were in the same class at school a few times and got along well.

Chris was giving me a look that made me want to squirm. It was like he won some small victory, and he wanted one thing as his prize.

Fat freaking chance. He kidnapped my niece the last time I gave him an opening. It's not worth the problems that come with it, no matter how good the sex is.

"Aunt Bit!" Landon pulled on my pant leg, breaking the staring match I had with Chris. "Want chips!" He was pointing a chubby toddler finger at the chocolate chips.

"I want them too!" Josie said in her sweet voice.

"Oh!" Roseanne jumped and grabbed her face like she just remembered something. "I forgot to get the M&M's out of my car. I'll be right back."

"I can go get them," I offered, not wanting to be alone with Chris and the kids. He wouldn't care what these kids overheard.

"No, no. You go help Chris measure. He's still got to do the sugar."

"Come help me get some sugar," Chris said tauntingly.

I frowned, now alone with him, except for the miniature people, because Roseanne just grabbed her purse and left.

I was thinking about making a run for it, but then Landon tugged on my leg again. "Aunt Bit! Chips!" He made the same face my brother makes when someone's denying him food. "Want chips!"

"Come on, little man," Chris waved his hand to call him over. "It won't hurt anyone for you to have a couple."

"Roseanne didn't say they could," I argued.

"Ah, she won't care. Why do you think she's getting the candy from her car? She's planning on filling them up with sugar before sending them back to their parents, like any good grandma would." He gave me what I can only assume was an attempt at a seductive look. "I can fill you up with sugar too, if you'd like."

"I'm good." I moved a chair to the table for Landon to stand on, then scooped two small measuring cups of chocolate chips for the kids.

"Ah, come on, Brit. I didn't mean to freak you out the other day with Hailey. I was just trying to get you breakfast. I was doing something nice."

"The panic attack I had first thing in the morning was nice," I muttered.

"I'm sorry! Let me apologize. You won't even talk to me."

"Fine." I jutted my chin out stubbornly. "I forgive you. Can we drop it now?"

"Well, I don't know. Can we go to dinner this Friday so I can at least make it up to you?"

"Nope. I'm busy." Fridays are family dinner nights at the diner. Even if it wasn't, I would still find another excuse to be busy.

"Saturday?"

"I'm busy that day, too."

"Then go to church with me on Sunday. Mom hasn't seen you since you got back from school. Come, say hi and go eat with us after the service."

"No, thanks. I can nap at home."

"You can't nap at church, Miss Brittany," Ethan said. "Mom swats me right here when I fall asleep." He pointed to a spot on the back of his head.

"Who does what now?" Roseanne asked, coming back in with several large bags of candy in her hands. Chris walked quickly over to relieve her, dropping the bags on the counter. Josie and Landon's eyes went wide, seeing all the new candy to sample. They still weren't halfway done with their current sweets and had melted chocolate mustaches.

"Ethan said his mama hits the back of his head when he falls asleep in church," Hailey informed Roseanne.

"She does not! I'll have to have a talking with that daughter of mine. It wasn't too long ago she was the one nodding off during a service."

"Was she really?" Ethan asked, a curious grin on his face.

"Sure was. I tell you what. She won't be trying any of these yummy cookies we're making for forgetting that. We better make them extra delicious so she doesn't know what she's missing."

Roseanne was a great grandma to all the kids. She helped each one mix and form their own kind of cookie. She reminded me of Missy a bit. I didn't really have much to help with.

Because of that, I had a lot of idle time to watch from the back as they worked. So did someone else. I tried my hardest to ignore him, but he didn't make it easy for me.

When Roseanne took the kids to the walk-in to pick out their colors of ready-made frosting, Chris's comments became more bold.

"I got some milk for the cookies if you want me to bring it over later," he whispered suggestively in my ear.

"I'm going to make you choke on a cookie if you don't stop."

"Your cookie?" Damn it, the way his breath was fanning over my neck was making goosebumps rise up on my skin. "I wouldn't mind being smothered with your cookie."

"You're so gross."

"You offered."

"I did not." I spun my head towards him, which was a mistake. Our lips were almost touching.

My eyes were locked on his, and I could taste his breath. It was like chocolate and brown sugar, and I could imagine how sweet his mouth would taste.

"We got it!" Roseanne cheered before coming back into the room with the kids. "We got the frosting!" She had each kid carrying two piping bags with their colors, wrangling the two youngest to walk in the right direction as they licked the ends of their bags.

I quickly jerked away from Chris, taking a step to the side to give myself some space to breathe. His deep chuckle made my inside dance. I hated how my body just reacted to him automatically, even though my brain was screaming that if I kept this up with him, nothing good could come out of it.

"You two doing okay?" Roseanne asked us. "You can go get yourself some drinks in the front if you want."

"Thanks. I think I'll do that," I said, grasping the excuse to escape.

"Me too."

My eyes rolled in the back of my head when Chris followed me out the heavy swinging door.

"You're a real pain in the ass. You know that, right?" I said when I was sure we were out of earshot of the back room. I turned to glare at him.

Suddenly, he was grabbing my face, pulling me in for that kiss.

I was right. His mouth was really, really sweet..

Chapter Seven

"Hey, kids!" Missy said enthusiastically as Hailey and Landon ran ahead of me into the house. Her voice was coming from the kitchen. "Where's your aunt?"

"Here," I walked slowly, still halfway in a daze. Lethargy was weighing me down. Or maybe I was still stunned because of a certain jerk.

Chris just doesn't know how to take a freaking hint...

But why do I keep accepting him when he finally gets me to break?

That asshole. He kissed me. No warning or anything. He just kissed me in the open front of the bakery, where anyone could have seen.

And I kissed him back. I don't know what came over me. I wasn't just taking part in the kiss. I was hungry for it. I don't know if it was the adrenaline or what, but I just gripped my fists in the front of his shirt, pushing my body up on my toes. The kiss was like a fight between us. Only, it was fighting with our lips.

I don't know who the heck won afterward, but for some reason, I think it was him. He had that cheesy Chris smile on his face, staring at me in that way that made butterflies flutter in my chest. He casually reached into the fridge beside me and got me a soda, popping the top, then giving me one more brief kiss before he handed it to me.

I didn't even react. I was still in shock over my own reaction. I stood there in a daze as he turned around and walked back into the prep room with a giant, shit-eating grin on his face. It took me a few minutes of pressing my finger to my lips and resting my hand over my racing heart to fully comprehend that Chris had just forced a kiss on me again, and again, I played right into his hands.

He was smug for the rest of the visit. He even managed to put his arm around me when Roseanne asked to take a picture of everyone and left it there far longer than necessary. I had to shrug him off, but it didn't detour his good mood at all.

Josie and Ethan were staying with their grandmother for the rest of the day, so when it was time for me and my niece and nephew to leave, Chris walked us out. He chatted away as I fought to ignore him, but Hailey, being the devil's advocate, talked to him in my stead. She was enjoying herself too much in her little scheme. I knew what she was doing.

After I got Landon buckled in his seat and Hailey was in hers, I closed the doors to find Chris still waiting by the driver's side, his hand on the handle to open it for me.

"Don't you have somewhere you need to be?" I asked him.

"Nah. Why? You offering something?"

I scoffed, trying to get around him to get into the car, but his hand was still on the handle, and he was not budging at all. When I huffed and looked up at him, ready to tell him to go play in traffic or something, he did it again. He kissed me right off of the main street at the busiest time of the day.

And just like before, I didn't stop him. I kissed him back, our lips moving together in a familiar dance. It wasn't until he pulled away with that same grin as before that I realized where we were standing and what we had just done. I knew that someone had to have seen it.

Chris didn't seem to care. Of course, he didn't. He's just asking for my brother to kick his ass. He just walked away smugly with his hands in his pockets, whistling some upbeat tune.

Hailey was all giggles and grins the entire way back to their house. She is overly smiley now, and I know she's getting ready to spill some tea by the way she keeps looking at me from the corner of her eye. I shook my head subtly at her, but I knew she didn't have any loyalty towards me on this topic. She was going to tell Missy everything.

Missy gave me a curious look, and I could see on her face by the small smile playing on her lips that she knew something. This traitor. Did she know Chris would be there?

"Did you guys have fun making cookies?!" Missy turned her attention back to her toddler and daughter.

"Mine!" Landon jerked back his takeaway box when Missy tried to look inside.

He pouted his lips and looked apologetic when Missy gave him one of her mom looks. He moved the box back between them, and she could not keep her smile off her face. It was one of those smiles mom's fight to not show how their kid's bad attitude is amusing them. The kid was cute in his tantrums.

"I'm not going to take them from you, baby. Thank you for letting me see."

"Mine," Landon pouted still when Missy peeked in the box.

That kid. He's my brother's spitting image. Possessive of food with a soft spot only for Missy.

"Mama! Guess what! Mr. Chris was there!" Hailey looked at me with that secretive smile, ready to spill all to her mom at last. Her words were rushed, like she was trying to beat me to speaking first.

"Oh, was he?" Missy didn't look surprised at all.

I narrowed my eyes. "Coincidence, huh? Did Roseanne not mention that when she invited the kids to come hang out?"

"No," Missy bit back a grin. "But I may have gotten a few pictures."

"Of course you did," I sighed, plopping down on a stool.

"Mama! Mama!" Hailey tugged at her sleeve. "Mr. Chris kissed her!"

"Really?" The glint in Missy's eye at hearing this grated on me.

"Yeah! It was a gross kiss, too. Like you and daddy."

"Oh, my." Missy pressed her lips together. "Where did this happen?"

"Outside," Hailey said proudly, like the queen of gossip. "They kissed for like ten Mississippi right by the car."

"Like, on Main Street?!" Missy looked at me in shock.

"Maybe," I groaned, "The asshole has no sense of place or timing. Adrian is going to find out."

"So?" Missy scoffed. "I can handle your brother. That's not the issue. You kissed him too? Like, you kissed him?"

I grimaced, not willing to confirm, but also unable to deny it either.

Landon had taken his box of cookies to the living room, hiding behind the couch as he picked candy off the frosting, but Missy didn't notice. She was still too engrossed in the Chris drama with me.

"Brittany! This is huge!"

"No, it's not," I sighed, dropping my head in my hands. "It's just a freaking hook-up. I don't know why he is getting so attached."

"I don't think he's the only one getting attached." Missy raised her eyebrows.

No. I don't think Chris is either. I can still feel his lips against mine, and the heat of his body as he pressed into me. I still get those butterflies when I think about it.

I'm trying so hard to close myself off to Chris. Why is he making it so hard?

"Mama?"

"Yes, Hailey?"

"What's a hook-up?"

***

Chris

"You look like you're in a good mood," my brother, Mike, said as I got out of my truck, a little extra pep in my step. "Did you eat all Roseanne's cookies or something?"

"Nah, I left those for the kids," I dropped into an old, beat-up swivel chair in his office, kicking up my feet onto his desk. He grabbed a ruler off his desk and pushed my boots back, so my feet fell loudly to the ground.

"Make yourself at home, why don't you?"

"I'm trying."

"Punk," Mike huffed with a small smirk. "Seriously, what's got you all happy? You looked pretty glum when you left with the kids this morning."

"Eh," I shrugged. "Maybe I just enjoyed spending time with my niece and nephew."

"Bull shit. You argued with me for ten minutes when I called and asked you for that favor."

Yeah, I argued with him, but that was just because I didn't want to miss a chance to see Brittany while working on her new house. She's been avoiding me since the last night we spent together. If it wasn't for the kids having a day off from school and my brother being called into the shop because of an accident, I would have missed the opportunity to spend most of the day by her side.

"Some things just work out, you know," I shrugged.

"Huh?" Mike looked at me like I was crazy. "Spill it or get out. I've got work to do and I don't want to deal with your good mood right now."

"Jeez. Who spit in your coffee?" My brother looked more annoyed than usual. I was in such a good mood from Brittany that I didn't notice.

Mike sighed, pulling one of his rough hands down his face. "I just had to deal with a shitty customer, is all."

"What kind of shitty customer?"

"Some stuck up prick got a stick up his ass. Chewed out my mechanic for not having his tires in stock. I had to drive all the fucking way to Redding and back to get them. Izzy's doing a double shift today too, so I'm fucking beat."

"I'm sorry, man." I rubbed the back of my head, thinking of some way I could help. Roseanne has the kids for the night, so he doesn't have to go home to take care of the kids at least. "I wish I could help. Wanna go out for a drink tonight or something?"

"What I wish is for you to come work for me," Mike grumbled. "Why the hell would you pick the Brewers over your own brother?"

"I have my reasons."

When my brother bought the repair shop a while back, I quit my previous job to go in on the business with him. I only planned on working with Adrian for extra cash, but then Brittany happened. Now

I'm working for Adrian full time and only helping Mike when he needs me.

Since his current mechanic is looking to retire, Mike is needing me more and more lately. I just don't want to give up my only excuse to run into Brit.

"If you don't tell me those reasons, I might just get you fired myself." Mike smirked.

"How the hell are you going to do that?"

"I have my ways," Mike snickered. "I might have pictures of our texts from before he and his wife got together."

My blood drained from my face. "You wouldn't."

"I might. It'd be worth it to see you get your ass kicked," Mike snickered. "Ah, that might lift my mood. Maybe I should send him those pics now."

"Fuck, you're annoying," I growled, kicking his desk hard, so it shoved up against his chest. He grunted, then threw an air filter at my head.

I don't give a shit about Adrian seeing those ancient texts from years ago about Missy. He knew I liked her. Yeah, they may have been a bit raunchy, but it was fucking guy talk with my brother. I'm not embarrassed about that. I just don't want Brittany to see them. I don't harbor any feelings towards Missy now. Her cooking, maybe, but sure as heck not towards her.

The only Brewer I have feelings for is Brittany.

"You're annoying," Mike grumbled. "You're not a construction worker, Chris. Why the hell would you rather do that than come work with me? You love working with cars. This was our fucking dream."

Yeah. It was our dream, but now that dream has changed. It's grown to include a certain blonde woman with sugary lips and huggable hips.

I was silent for a long time, staring at my brother begrudgingly, and he stared expectantly back at me.

"I like Brittany," I admitted. "I like Brittany Brewer."

Mike's eyes went wide, then his brows knit. "Are you joking?"

I laughed humorlessly, shaking my head. "No. I'm not. I think she might like me too."

Mike was staring at me like I had just confessed to shitting lollipops or something. It was like he couldn't comprehend me and Brittany. "You're serious?"

"As a damn heart attack."

"Wow," Mike rubbed his chin. "And she likes you too?"

I couldn't keep the smug grin from lifting my face, remembering how she had kissed me back at the bakery. Not once, but twice. "I think so."

"And Adrian?" Mike lifted a brow. "Does he know?"

My silence was enough of an answer, making my brother laugh.

"I can deal with Adrian later. I'm just focused on getting Brittany to like me enough to take a chance with me right now."

"Oh, I can't wait to see how you deal with that protective brother of hers. You know, there's a fucking reason no one in this town ever messed with his sister, right?"

"I'm not messing with his sister," I grumbled. "Well, it depends on what you mean by messing," that caused Mike to snicker, "but I'm serious about Brittany. I really, really like her, Mike."

"Okay, okay. You don't have to convince me," he laughed. "You like Adrian's sister. Wow! Ha, everything makes sense now."

"What does?"

"Oh, nothing. Something I heard Izzy saying to Missy last time we got together."

I grinned widely. "Missy's rooting for me," I stated proudly.

"Good. She can keep her husband from killing you." He signed, looking around his office. "I guess I should get this place set up to have another desk soon."

"Why?" I looked around, confused by the change of topic.

"Because Adrian's going to fire your ass soon."

Chapter Eight

Elias

"Checking in?" An old woman wearing too much cheap perfume asked behind the sad excuse for a reception counter when I entered the only lodging in this small town. This place couldn't even be counted as a hotel. It stated it was an inn on the sign, but it was nothing more than a motel.

"Yes, please," I smiled tightly, pulling my wallet from my back pocket after taking off my driving gloves. "Room for one."

"We only have rooms with double beds. Is that going to be okay for you, sugar?"

"Well, I guess it will have to be, won't it?" I said with barely restrained annoyance.

This whole town is a nightmare. How could Brittany, in all her brilliance, ever be happy in a dump like this?

I paid for my room, a meager seventy dollars, then took my key. A regular key on a large wooden cut out of a tree key ring.

"How... appropriate," I muttered, then smiled tightly again, nodding at the old woman before leaving. I sighed heavily as I stepped back out to the parking lot, looking at mountains and trees around as I readied myself to see whatever nightmare of a room was waiting for me.

The town may be a dump, but the view was one for the books.

After checking the number on the key, I walked to the other end of the inn where my room was located. The paint was chipping off the door, and the film on the windows had trapped moisture in between it and the glass. These were already foreboding signs.

I was surprised when I turned the key and the door swung in to reveal a very well-kept room. The outside of the inn looked like the rest of the town, but the inside of the room looked refurbished and new. The two double beds had stark white sheets and a duvet with a protective cover. The pillows were stuffed inward and wrinkle-free. I expected some forty-year-old mattress with a worn thread-bare blanket and yellow pillows.

Upon further inspection, I found the bathroom to be up to my standards, too. The rooms must have been refurbished. Why they would just fix up the inside of the inn and not the outside is beyond me.

I moved my car to be closer to my room, so I could monitor it. After waiting for the better part of the day for the tires to be replaced in that miserable excuse for a mechanic's shop, I was nervous about leaving it just parked off the main street of this dumpy town. I might wake up to the windows smashed and my radio missing.

Throwing my weekend bag on the free bed, I fished my phone from my jacket pocket. The 76 previous failed calls didn't deter me from trying again. Again, I was met with a message that my call was unable to be connected.

I mouthed the words along with the prerecording. I have heard it too many times today already. Every call, every text, every attempt I make to reach out fails.

A call comes in, making my phone vibrate in my hands right as I'm about to put it away. I hurriedly checked the screen, letting hope arise…

But then disappointment hits me like a blow to the chest. It was not the woman I wanted to hear from. It was the one that lose Brittany in the first place, and I'm not going to humor her by answering.

I'd hoped to find Brittany early enough to convince her to go out to eat with me, so we could talk and I could explain everything. It was too late for that now. The only address I had for her was the home of her father, and from what she has told me, she doesn't live with him anymore.

In a town this small, I would most likely just run into her. After a good night's rest, and a long shower to get the grease smell off me, I'll try again in the morning.

I took my time in the shower, trying to let the hot water ease my tension. The more I thought about Brittany, the more stiff I felt. Everywhere. I had to take my time relieving my other body tensions as well.

It had been so long since I'd felt her warmth. Since I've held her in my arms. With every passing day, the restlessness inside me grew.

I should have been honest with her from the beginning. The second I knew it was more than just a lustful attraction for me, I should have told her everything. All my circumstances. I thought I was protecting her by keeping quiet. By keeping her at arm's length, I told myself I was keeping her safe.

I can admit now that it was fear for myself.

With my head pressed against the shower wall, I closed my eyes and imagined a time of having her in my arms. Her writhing body. Her needy blue eyes. Those sun-kissed cheeks flushed over as she gasped and moaned.

I imagined the feel of her body sucking me in, her hands clinging to me desperately as I drove my name from her lips.

Those lips.... She was always so eager to please me with those lips. Nothing was sweeter than devouring her while she devoured me.

My tongue glided across my teeth as I pumped my fist, keeping the picture of her pleasing me in the front of my mind. The hollowed pull of her cheeks as her ass twitched and her perfect breasts bounced with every movement.

She was my sun. My air. My reprieve in the chaos of my life. I needed her. I still need her.

"Professor," I imagined our first time together. How timid and shy she was. Until we got in bed, then 'professor' felt like a dirty word, screamed from her lips every time she reached her climax.

She would call me professor in class after that, and I'd be ruined the rest of the day. I had her call me by name after that when we were alone, but those first few times when she called me professor were ingrained in my head.

I want to hear it again. I want to hear all her desperate cries and names for me again.

With a deep groan, I opened my eyes from the daydream to see my desperation wash down the drain.

I was still tense and pent-up. More so than before.

I begrudgingly got dressed again, knowing rest would not come for me anytime soon. I grabbed my keys and wallet, planning on going to a liquor store, but my only option was the grocery store or gas station. I couldn't imagine the options either of those places would have.

I passed a bar while driving around and decided it was my best option. Pulling in, the stares I was getting, I already knew I wasn't going to fit in. Fitting in with a bunch of roughnecks is not something I strive for, so I walked in with confidence. I took a seat on a beat-up bar stool right at the center of the bar, and when the bartender tossed a dishrag over his shoulder to stare at me, I ordered.

"Whiskey. Neat. Top shelf."

He gruffly continued to stare as he poured the drink, setting it in front of me like he was daring me to find something wrong with his Crown Royal. I resisted wiping the rim of the glass, maintaining his stare as I took the first long sip and hissed in satisfaction. I downed the rest of the glass, then pushed it towards him.

"Another."

He pursed his lips and nodded, seeming satisfied. He poured me one more glass, then went to attend to others.

I sat in peace for about ten minutes, just sipping slowly on the burning amber liquor. Locals were quietly mumbling around me. The usual musings when a stranger walks into a place like this, I'm sure. Easy to ignore.

Then the bar suddenly got loud, and I turned to see what the sudden ruckus was.

The owner of the mechanics' shop, the one who defended his incompetent worker instead of reprimanding him for the discord, was coming in with another man. They looked so similar. I was sure they were brothers, but who knows in a hick town like this?

"How you gonna go from his wife to his sister like that?!" The mechanic owner, Mike, if I recall, laughed loudly, messing up the other man's hair.

"Stop talking so loud, you asshole," the other guy pushed him off.

"Ah, don't want to get caught yet? Not eager for that ass beating, are you?"

"Why does everyone think he can kick my ass? I can hold my fucking own."

"Sure you can," Mike snorted.

A crowd of people were eagerly greeting and teasing the two men as they walked to the bar. When the mechanic guy saw me, he grimaced a bit, nodded, then went back to joking and talking with the others.

"Hey, Chris," a Hispanic man leaned over the bar towards the guy Mike came in with. "I saw something interesting driving through town today. Right outside Roseanne's."

Mike started hooting, slapping the other guy on the back. "So it begins."

"Jose, if you know what's good for you, you will keep your damn mouth shut," the Chris guy said.

My interest peaked the more they talked. I tried not to make it obvious I was listening, but small town drama was the perfect distraction. Hearing the teasing about this Chris liking his boss's wife, and now going after his sister was like listening to a soap opera, only it was real life.

Then the men went silent. Eerily so. I turned to see why, and their eyes were all on the door. Truck lights were shining through the window, high off the ground. The deep rumbling of a diesel could be heard now that the guys beside me had quieted down.

"That truck sounds awfully familiar," the Hispanic man grinned, elbowing the Chris guy.

"Shut up!" He hissed, panic on his face.

The truck's engine stopped, and seconds later a tall, rough man with a scratchy beard and a beat-up hat walked in. He had on paint-stained jeans and a shirt that said "BREWER CONTRACTING" on the front.

I perked up reading the name 'Brewer'.

"Dre!" A group of men sitting near the door cheered, lifting their beers in the air. "What's up, boss man?"

"Where's Mrs. Boss Lady?"

The new guy sighed with a scowl. "None of your business."

"Oh, did someone get in trouble? You knock her up again?"

The guy scoffed. "Not yet. I'm working on it."

"Adrian!" The Hispanic man yelled, waving wildly from the bar.

The Chris guy elbowed him in the side, and the mechanic snickered behind his beer.

Adrian Brewer. I recognized the name instantly. That was the name of my Brittany's older brother.

The man, Adrian, narrowed his eyes at Chris. "You skipped work today to go drinking?"

Chris sputtered, "Wha- what?! No! I told you, Mike, here, had a crisis at work."

"What kind of crisis?" Adrian sided up the bar, and the bartender handed him a Coors without even asking.

The mechanic side-eyed me, and I tried to keep my face friendly and innocent as I looked anywhere but at him.

"We had an unruly customer that demanded tires we didn't have in stock. I had to drive to Redding to get 'em."

"Jeez. I hope you charged him out the ass for them."

"Oh, I made sure we were compensated for the hassle," Mike scoffed, sending me another tense glance.

I snorted to myself. I thought the price seemed a bit high, but I was frustrated and furious and would not argue with the owner when he offered to go retrieve the tires himself. I agreed to whatever price it took to get out of that place sooner rather than later. I wasn't going to leave my car in that dump and be stranded overnight while waiting for a delivery service.

"So," the Chris guy said nervously. "What are you doing here tonight?"

"Is it that weird for me to go out to have a fucking drink?"

"Yes," all three men said in unison.

"You cling to your wife like a leech," Mike snickered.

"Well, have you seen my wife?! Can you fucking blame me?"

"No, which is why we're asking," the Hispanic man said.

Adrian leaned against the bar and grumbled gruffly, "Missy and Britt kicked me out. Said they were having a girls' night and to give them a few hours, so here I am."

Bingo. This man was, in fact, my Brittany's brother.

His eyes met mine as he caught me staring. I put on a mask of friendliness, hoping my earlier confrontation with the mechanic wouldn't ruin my first encounter with Brittany's brother.

I lifted my glass in greeting, smiling as I nodded my head.

"You're a new face," the man said.

"Indeed, I am. Elias Miles," I introduced myself.

"Adrian," he reached over to shake my hand. "Nice to meet you, Elias."

"Oh, no. The pleasure is all mine."

Chapter Nine

Chris

"Elias?" I tested out the stranger's name. I didn't like it. Sounded stuffy and stiff. Just like the man himself looked. "What's someone with a name like Elias Miles doing in our small town?"

Mr. Stiffy frowned at me. Mike snickered, trying to hide his smirk behind a beer bottle. Mike's been giving the guy next to us at the bar the stink eye since we got here. It piqued my curiosity enough to finally ask.

"Well," he looked at my brother, "first, I had to stop to have my tires replaced."

I choked on my beer, and I swear I saw beer fly out of Adrian's nose.

"You should have had them switched out before leaving the cold," Mike said stiffly. "I'm pretty sure it's too warm, even in Oregon, for fucking snow tires."

"Indeed," the out of towner smiled tightly.

"Oh, damn." Adrian reached over the bar for a rag to wipe his face. "I needed a good laugh."

"Glad to oblige," the guy said, waving for the bartender. "Let me get you another beer."

Something about this guy was just plum irritating. Maybe it was the fake smile or the out-of-place outfit. Or maybe it was his voice. Listening to him talk to Adrian, I can't help but think that I've heard his voice somewhere.

"Now that your tires are fixed, you heading out soon?" I asked, interrupting whatever bullshit small talk he was saying about the weather or some shit.

The prick grimaced at me, clearly not enjoying being interrupted. Everyone was staring at him for an answer, so he couldn't just ignore me.

"Not yet," he said with hesitation. "I'm here to find someone."

"Well, who?" Adrian perked up. "We know everyone. I'm sure one of us could help."

He stared at me for a few seconds, clearly irritated by my question. Then he sighed, and said "I'm trying to find one of my, uh, well, a former student of my school who lives here. I need to find her to discuss some things."

Jose asked, "Where's your school, my dude? You talking Middle, High School?..."

"No," he shook his head with a humorless scoff. "No, I teach at a university."

"A professor, huh?" Adrian took a swig of his beer. "Which one? I know Wendy Trout just graduated from Pacific Union."

"No," the dude made an expression like he was offended.

"He's got Oregon plates," Mikey said.

"Oregon?" Adrian's brows pulled down. He pieced it together just as the rest of us did. "Oregon University?!"

"That would be the one," the prick smiled, looking a little smug.

"You here to speak with a Brittany Brewer by any chance?" Jose asked, looking fully entertained.

The corner of the dude's lips lifted smugly. "Would you happen to know where I can find her?"

Mike and Jose were laughing behind their beer bottles, looking at Adrian. I wasn't finding this as funny as they were. Neither was Adrian.

"Why are you looking for her?" Adrian asked, his friendly demeanor gone.

The dude could see that and suddenly looked less confident. "It's over a matter concerning her early graduation."

"So you drove here instead of just calling her?"

Calling her...

"Shit." I set down my beer, staring at him in disbelief. I had heard his voice before. "Professor Dickhead?"

He looked taken aback for a second, his eyes going wide.

"Why are you calling him that, like you know him?" Adrian asked.

"We've spoken," I grumbled.

I knew I didn't like this guy. He was the professor harassing Brit. What kind of stalker bull shit is this for him to show up here because Britt won't answer him?

"When?" Adrian was staring at me like I was the problem here. It wasn't until I heard Mike and Jose snickering that I realized why.

I shrugged nonchalantly. "I answered her phone for her when we were helping move her into her new place."

"Why?" Adrian didn't seem suspicious, just dumbstruck about why I would have Brittany's phone.

"She, uh, told me to hold on to it for a sec."

"Was that all she asked you to hold?" Jose mumbled.

"Shut the fuck up," Adrian threw the towel at Jose. "That's my fucking sister. Not even funny, dude."

"My bad," Jose snickered. "You're right. It's not cool at all to mess with someone's sister."

"So you are her brother?" Professor Dickhead asked. I had almost forgotten about him in my brief panic.

"Yeah," Adrian leaned against the counter, seemingly casual, but I knew him well enough to know that he was anything but relaxed right now. Dickhead was one wrong line away from getting his snobby ass thrown out the door. "What is it you want with my sister? According to her, all her graduation shit has been worked out."

"I just need to speak with her," he said softly, treading that fine line. On one side, he wouldn't get his ass beat. On the other, he would have Adrian taking him to meet Brittany personally.

I was cheering for the ass beating.

"About?" Adrian pressed.

The dickhead seemed uncomfortable now. I was even wondering what he wanted with my girl, even though I had a good guess.

"You're awfully young looking for being a professor," I commented. "Really young."

"What's a young professor doing looking for one of his students in her hometown for?" Mike added fuel to the impending fire.

The dude looked me straight in the eyes, his hard gaze unwavering. "It's as you are suggesting," he said plainly, making my smile vanish. "I fell in love with Brittany Brewer, and after a very regrettable misunderstanding, I'm here to see if I can win her back."

"You're fucking shitting me," Adrian growled.

"No," Dickhead looked at him. "I'm not shitting you. Not at all." He then looked back at me. "I'm man enough to declare my intentions towards Miss Brewer, even to her brother. That's how serious I am."

That was like a kick in the fucking guts.

"Bull shit," I sneered, clenching my beer in my hand.

The dickhead smirked. "Does my interest in Miss Brewer offend you for some reason? Mr....."

"Chris," I snapped. "Yeah, it fucking offends me. You stalked her all the way to her hometown."

"It's not stalking. I have yet to meet with her, or even see her." He squared his shoulders, then leaned slightly forward. "Did you see Brittany today, Mr. Chris?"

Fuck.

"None of your fucking business," I muttered.

He sat back and smiled, picking up his glass. "That's what I thought."

Fuck. Fuck, fuck, fuck.

Adrian was giving both of us odd looks, while Mike and Jose were staring with wide eyes, like they were waiting for the shit to click in Adrian's head.

I wasn't going to wait around for that to happen. I needed to see Brittany. Now.

I set my beer on the counter, then turned angrily for the door.

"Where are you going?" Adrian asked.

"Don't fucking worry about it," I snapped.

I was going to pay for that later. Especially since he was liable to find me at his house before the night was over.

***

Brittany

"You tramp!" Missy slapped my knee, staring down at her phone. "I just got another text asking if I knew about you and Chris."

I leaned my head back on the couch and groaned. It was just a matter of time before my brother found out. Chris would be fired, and I would permanently be labeled as one of the town whores.

"Aunt Bitt?" Landon slapped my other knee. "What a tamp?"

I narrowed my eyes at Missy. "He better be asking me what a tramp is and not calling me one."

She was too busy laughing her ass off to care about the threat in my tone.

"What a tamp, Aunt Britt?!" Landon asked more forcefully.

"It's a dog," I answered dryly. "Like Lady and The Tramp."

"I've seen that movie, and I don't think that's what it means," Hailey said, playing with her dog on the floor.

"Hush it, traitor."

"Oh, relax," Missy said, wiping tears from her eyes. "Your brother needed to know, eventually. It will be fine."

"No, it won't!" I groaned, reaching for the wine bottle. "He's not even serious, Missy. This is just Chris being Chris. He's going to cause all sorts of drama, and it's just going to be the same shit like it was with you."

"Beep!" Hailey looked at me as I cursed.

"Mind your beeping business," I made a face at her. She stuck her tongue out back at me, then giggled.

"It's not the same," Missy insisted. "He stopped coming after me the second I told him to stop. You've told him to stop a million times, and he's still coming at you hard."

"It's his weaponized art of persistence," I muttered. "And the fact that I keep giving in to him when he pushes me far enough."

"He's wearing you down," Missy laughed.

"He's just annoying the crap out of me now."

"Yeah, yeah. That's why you kissed him on Main Street," Missy snickered.

"And in Grandma Roseanne's bakery!" Hailey had to remind everyone.

"Can we talk about something else?" I begged. "All night, all you've wanted to talk about is Chris."

"Well, yeah." Missy took a sip of her sparkling cider. She didn't want to drink while breastfeeding. "Why do you think I sent my husband to the bar?"

"To prevent baby number four?" I saw the predatory look in my brother's eye when he got home from work.

"That too," she giggled, then sighed. "I'm going to have to get on birth control this time. I know they say you can't get pregnant while breastfeeding, but it's like Adrian is trying to beat those odds."

"Ew! I don't want to hear that!" I waved my hand at the kids. "Hailey is right there!"

"It's okay, Aunt Britt. Dad says worse."

Missy nodded and shrugged. So I knew it was true.

The baby started fussing on the baby monitor. Brittany got up, but I set down my wine and muttered, "I got it," before she could. Quinton was the only person in this house not pestering me about Chris or calling me a tramp. He was my official favorite.

"Peggy just texted me!" Missy yelled out. "You know Chris's mom is going to be the next one to message me, right?"

Oh, lord. I can just imagine what that woman would say about the tramp making out with her christian son in the middle of town. She'd probably tar and feather me if she could. She was more sore than Chris when Missy rejected her son. A good virgin girl with a christian upbringing and inherited wealth. Missy was her dream daughter-in-law. I'm just a returned townie with a basic education degree and student loan debt.

Stupid Chris. I'm just another Missy. Not even a Missy. I'm just the current obsession. When another girl rolls into town with better credentials than me, he will be onto the next.

Thinking about it is driving me crazy. He drives me crazy. Why can't I just refuse him? Why do I always let him get me like he did today?

"Hey, baby," I crooned, picking up my youngest nephew. "You're the only man Auntie Britt needs. Yes, you are."

"I can hear you!" Missy yelled.

"Good," I smiled down at my wide-awake nephew. "Quinton's Aunt Brittany's favorite in the entire house. Yes, you are. Yes, you are!"

He crooned back to me, smiling ear to ear, making all my anger melt away.

The doorbell rang seconds later, just as I was changing his diaper on the changing table.

"Who could that be?" I asked softly to no one in particular. I was just talking to calm the squirming baby.

"Chris?" I heard Missy's surprised outburst through the open door. "What are you doing here? Adrian's not-"

"Where's Brittany?"

"The hell?" I muttered, quickly fastening a new diaper in place.

I picked Quinton up and started walking down the hall as Chris came barreling in, asking again where I was. When his eyes landed on me, he stilled for a second. He looked irritated, and maybe a bit shaken.

Oh no.

"Adrian knows?" I gasped, dread settling in my chest.

"What?" his brows pulled down. "No. Well, maybe by now, but that's not.... Damn it," he muttered, coming towards me. "I need to talk to you."

"Um, no!" I took a step back, cradling Quinton in my arms. "Not here!"

"Here," he was panting. "Right now. This can't wait."

He was right in front of me, staring down at me with such a serious expression, it sent anxiety running through me.

"I'll take him," Missy said calmly, relieving me of the baby. "Why don't both of you go out to the backyard?"

"Yeah," Chris didn't wait for my agreement, taking my hand and dragging me through the house to the back doors with him.

"Hey, Mr. Chris!" Hailey yelled when we walked by.

"Hey squirt," he murmured.

Hailey looked concerned for a second, then gave me a thumbs up. That little traitor.

Chris opened the back door, then pulled me through it. Missy was there right behind us, closing the door with a curious expression. She didn't look concerned at all. She looked excited as Chris dragged me with him to the workshop.

"What the hell is wrong with you?" I pulled against Chris's grip when we got inside. "Why are you acting more like a freak than normal?"

He was seething. His stare was so angry that it sent a chill through my body. He's never looked at me like this before.

"I just met Professor Dickhead," he eventually said.

"What?" My heart stopped when it fully registered what he meant. "Elias?"

Chris scoffed, taking his hat off as he paced away. He ran his hands through his hair a few times before putting his hat back on and walking back towards me.

"I'm going to ask you this once, Brittany, and I want you to be fucking honest with me."

"Chris," I tried to cover his mouth with my hands to stop the question from coming out. I had questions of my own, like where the hell did he see Elias? But I wasn't ready for this conversation. It made me feel dirty and used to just think about it.

Chris gently, but firmly, took my fingers in his hand, gripping them tight and bringing our hands between us. He stared down at them as he asked, "Just once, Brittany. Just for fucking once, be completely honest with me. Did you have a thing with your professor?"

"Chris, I didn't-"

"Were you dating your professor?" He asked bluntly, cutting off my denial.

I hesitated, then whispered in a broken voice. "No. No, we were never dating. I was.... I mean, he told me we were never going to be serious."

This answer didn't satisfy him. "Why?!" he urged, shaking our hands.

I stared up at him, waiting for the judgment that was to come. "I didn't know. I didn't know he was married."

"Damn," he murmured, his brows pulling down. "So you were just fucking him?"

Tears filled my eyes, and I nodded as I looked away. I couldn't handle the shame and seeing the look on Chris's face. "I didn't know he was married," I said again. "The second I found out, it stopped."

"Shit," Chris spat out, dropping my hands and pacing away from me.

I stood frozen as he paced back and forth alongside the trailer. I didn't know what to do. If I hadn't been drinking, I would have just gone home. Maybe I could just lock myself in the trailer and hide from it all. Hide from Chris and the shame of being caught as the mistress to my married professor.

Before I could make my escape plan, Chris stopped pacing, just turning back to stare at me. His fuming gaze made my heart sink further in my chest. It was like I could breathe as our eyes were locked.

Then he let out a frustrated growl and stalked towards me, taking my face in his hands. He pushed me back against the trailer and kissed me so deeply; it stole what little breath I had left. I gasped, and he took the opening to force his tongue into my mouth. Soon, as I always did, I melted into him, my body molding against his.

Desperation coursed through me as I clung to Chris's shirt, clawing my hands up to grip behind his neck.

"I'm not letting anyone take you from me," Chris groaned, his mouth skimming along my jaw. "Never."

I didn't know what he was talking about, and at that moment, I didn't care. I was losing myself in him again, just like I always did. I was pinned between him and the hard exterior of the trailer, and at the moment, that was exactly where I wanted to be. All thoughts of running away were gone.

"You're mine," Chris growled, lifting my legs and wrapping them around his waist.

I moaned into his mouth as his center started to grind against mine. Everything else began to fade away but him.

Until I heard my brother's voice.

"What the fuck are you doing to my sister?"

Chapter Ten

Chris

"What the fuck are you doing to my sister?"

Shit.

Everything inside of me froze. I just got caught not just kissing his sister, but practically dry humping her on the side of his camper. This will not end well.

I was so heated, so fucking desperate, I forgot where we were. Seeing that devastated, broken look on Brittany's face, seeing so much raw emotion in her that she had never shown before at the mention of that dickhead professor, made my rage and jealousy spike.

I wasn't backing down for that prick. That married, piece of shit, cheating son of a bitch could go drive off a cliff. Brittany was mine. No one could change that.

Not even her overprotective brother.

My body was still frozen from the sound of Adrian's voice, the shock of being caught making my mind work slowly. Brittany was pushing against my chest, trying to get down. I let her legs fall to the ground, but I didn't give her any room to escape me. Knowing her, she would run away to another fucking state to avoid this discussion. I wouldn't let her run away from me anymore. My fingers dug into the soft flesh of her waist, keeping her against me.

"I'm not going to ask you again," Adrian's voice sounded lethal.

Fuck.

"Yeah, can you give us a few minutes?" I stupidly asked. "We were, uh, just talking."

"Talking?!" Adrian burst out, yelling like a fucking banshee.

"Chris," Brittany hissed, tapping against my chest, staring up at me with big, worried eyes. "He's going to kill you."

"I'm not scared of your brother," I hissed back, even though my hands were clamming up as I held her in my grip.

"Ho, boy," Adrian circled his neck, popping his knuckles. "Let's fix that."

Instead of pushing me away, Brittany gripped my shirt and turned our bodies like she was trying to plant herself between us.

"Adrian!" Missy snapped, suddenly coming in behind her husband as he moved forward like a predator about to pounce. She grabbed his arm, stopping him. "Leave them alone and get inside!"

She had a baby on her hip, and Landon was yelling at her from somewhere outside, but she looked just as deadly as her husband at that moment.

"You want me to leave them alone? The.... The... The fuck I will! Do you know what they were just doing?!"

"I can imagine. I'm sure it was a lot less than what you did to me when we were dating." She flashed us a look, then turned that cold stare back on Adrian.

"They're not fucking dating!"

"Oh, yes, they are. Even if they weren't, your sister is a grown adult. Get your butt inside."

"What the hell!" He paced around in a circle like he was steaming in the ears, "You knew about this shit?!" He started to get in Missy's face, but she raised her chin, and he backed right the fuck off.

"You really want to yell at me right now?" She raised an eyebrow.

Hailey walked in, holding her brother's hand. She looked at her parents with concern, then took one look at Brittany and me before a cheesy grin spread across her face. "Did you finally get caught, Mr. Chris?"

Adrian's face stormed over, his eyes going impossibly wider as his tensed arms flailed everywhere in disbelief.

"Are you fucking kidding me?!" He waved a hand at his oldest.

"No, sir," Missy snapped, then pushed her baby towards him. "Get your beeping butt inside, Adrian. You're not doing this right now."

"Yeah, dad. What's the big deal? We like Mr. Chris."

"The fuck we do!"

"Adrian!" Missy pointed a finger in his face. "You're one more beeping word away from sleeping on the couch."

He turned that anger back to me. "This isn't over, you son of a bitch. You just wait till I- OWW!"

Missy grabbed and twisted his ear. "Inside!"

"Fine! I'll sleep on the fucking couch!" He held his baby against his chest, the little human staring up at him with fascination as Adrian grumbled while storming outside.

"Holy moly, thank goodness Hailey saw him pull in." Missy took a deep breath, holding her chest. "He didn't even come inside."

"Landon heard his truck. You didn't because you were too busy watching out the back window," Hailey said, swinging her brother's hand.

"Big tuck!" Landon said proudly.

Missy's face turned red, like she had been caught. "I was just checking the porch lights," she said as an excuse. "Why don't you go get Aunt Britt's bag from inside for her, so she doesn't have to see your dad again."

Hailey shrugged, then walked off to do what her mom said. Landon followed behind her, still babbling about big trucks.

Brittany took a deep, shaking breath, her hands still knotted in my shirt. "Crap, I thought he was going to kill him."

"He still might," Missy laughed humorlessly. "What happened?" She looked at me for answers. "Did someone at the bar tell him?"

"Maybe," I grumbled. "I think everyone except him knew when I left."

"Is that why you came here like you did?"

Brittany stiffened at her sister-in-law's question.

Adrian had nothing to do with it. Imagining Professor Dickhead getting to my woman before I could had lit a fire under my ass. I ran out of there with no other thought than to get to Brittany. I needed to touch her, see her, taste her, or I never would have been able to calm down. I needed the physical reassurance that she was still mine. Even if she denies it, her lips, her body, the little noises she makes as she clings to me could never lie.

Brittany was mine.

I stayed silent, not knowing if I should tell Missy all that. Brittany, being the affair partner of one of her college professors, wasn't something I wanted to be common knowledge around town. That sleezy fucker took advantage of her. That was clear to me. I don't know if others would feel the same, or who else knows. I wasn't going to be the one to say shit.

"Elias was at the bar," Brittany told Missy, a grave look on her face. Missy's eyes went wide. She knew.

My heart stopped. Brittany told Missy. Of course she did. They were too close for Missy not to know.

Still, I stared at Brittany and couldn't keep the pain from showing on my face. She wouldn't even meet my eyes.

Why? Was there more she wasn't telling me?

My brain worked in overdrive. Then something occurred to me.

Brittany was graduating early, and that decision was made after Christmas. We slept together for the first time long before that....

Did we overlap?...

I don't know if I have a right to be angry or hurt. We weren't together. It was a hook-up after a night of drinking, no talk of commitment after that point. Even now, Brittany won't commit to me. Was it because she still held feelings for him? She said she stopped it after she found out he was married, but if she never found out, would she still be....

I gritted my teeth just imagining that bastard touching her. He used her. That was clear. But she had to have feelings for him. She's not the type of woman that would get into that situation if feelings weren't involved.

I was getting angrier and angrier the more I thought about things.

He came here to get her back. That adulterous asshole still thinks he has a chance with her.

Does he?

If she saw him again, would she go back to him?

She's mine. I won't give him the opportunity to find out.

***

Brittany

"Mom, dad's yelling a lot. I think he's on the phone with grandpa," Hailey said when she came back out with my bag.

"Now dad knows too?" I muttered under my breath.

Missy sighed, taking my bag from her daughter. "Why don't you go watch your brothers for me? I'll be right there."

"What about Mr. Chris and Aunt Britt?"

Missy looked at us from the corner of her eye. "I think Mr. Chris should drive your aunt home for now."

"Aww, you said Aunt Britt is having a sleepover. Can't Mr. Chris just stay over too?"

I scoffed, just imagining how that would go.

"Maybe another time," Missy calmly said, then directed Hailey back outside before turning towards us. She pinched the bridge of her nose, looking exhausted. "That man is going to be such a headache tonight. You realize I might end up pregnant again because of this?"

Chris snorted. "He should thank me then."

"Shut up," I pushed his chest. He was still holding onto my waist and barely even moved.

"What? I'm just saying."

Missy stared at me, silent communication passing between us. She was worried about me. I knew she was, and I also knew it wasn't because of Chris.

"So, your professor was at the bar?"

I looked at Chris for confirmation, then regretted it instantly. His eyes were cold and tense.

"Professor Dickhead was there alright. That asshole even had the fucking nerve to tell Adrian he was here for Brittany."

"Jeez, what a mess," Missy sighed. "Good thing you two are dating now. Maybe he will just go the beep away. If Adrian kills him, the lawyer's fees will be atrocious. I love him, but I'm not helping him bury a body."

I froze when she said me and Chris were dating.

"Uh, we're not, Missy."

"Not what? Burying him? Burying a body doesn't sound fun, does it? I guess we can pay Larry at the morgue to cremate him. It might be cheaper than the lawyers."

"No!" I snapped. "Missy, Chris and I aren't dating."

"Yes, you are," she said. At the same time, Chris said, "Yes, we are."

"No! We're not!" I twisted my body until I finally got free from Chris's vice grip on my waist.

"You are," Missy said firmly. "Brittany, I just told your brother you were."

"Oh, okay. Then, sure," I scoffed. "That magically makes us a couple."

"Brittany," Missy gave me a disapproving look, then moved her eyes to Chris with concern on her face.

I looked back at him, and he really looked hurt. My heart sunk in my chest, my words choking in my throat.

"Chris, we... we aren't-"

"You will fuck me, but won't date me?" He sounded so broken, so hurt. I wanted to wrap my arms around his waist and make that smug smile of his return.

Instead, I clenched my hands at my sides, resisting the urge. "Chris, I don't think you actually like me. This is just infatuation. Like what you had for Missy."

His eyebrows pulled down. He was getting pissed. "It's not. That was a small damn crush years ago that died as soon as it started. With you, it's completely different." He looked furious now. "So fucking different."

I wanted to believe him. I did, but at the same time, I was scared to.

Then there was the shit with Elias showing up. How could he want to date me now after knowing all that happened between me and my professor?

I'm dirty. A fucking mess. I was a mistress, sleeping with my married professor, and now he knows. If I give in to Chris now, what happens when the dust settles, and he realizes how far I am from his ideal woman? I'm not some pure, innocent girl like Missy was. I'm damaged goods. Not exactly a woman that his mom would be happy parading around church.

He's so persistent, it's hard to tell what's genuine and what was just typical Chris Finley stubbornness.

I'll admit, I have felt something for him. That's probably why I'm avoiding him the way I am. It's why I run away every time he tries to get close. Because I know if I give in to Chris and this ends up not being the real deal, it might break me more than Elias ever could.

Elias told me from the beginning not to expect a relationship. This is different. It will be a different kind of pain. Chris is Chris. He gets me so mixed up; I don't know what to expect. I have to keep my guard up all the time with him.

"Why don't you two talk about this at your house, Britt?" Missy said, breaking the intensity between me and Chris. We had been standing there, staring at one another for so long, I almost forgot she was here. "Adrian might come back out."

"Yeah. You're right. Let's go," Chris grabbed my hand and pulled me towards the door. "Thanks, Missy. Let your grumpy-ass husband know that I'll turn in my two-weeks on Monday."

"You don't have to do that. He'll calm down eventually," Missy tried to say.

"It's fine," he muttered, still dragging me towards his truck.

Shit. I caused Chris to lose his job, too. Why would he want me when it's this complicated? This damaging?

I didn't even fight him. The wine, learning about Elias, my brother finding out about all aspects of my sex-life, and then this shit with Chris has me too exhausted to resist. He opened the passenger door, then turned to stare down at me. His eyes were intense, a mixture of so many emotions. It made my sinking heart beat rapidly, my stomach churning with anxiety.

"Don't run from this, Brittany," he said in a low, deep voice. "Please get in."

"Okay," I said hoarsely, my voice caught in my throat.

Before he closed the door, he took an extra few seconds to stare more, making all kinds of feelings churn inside me. The burning in my chest from my nerves was getting painful.

That was, until he leaned in and whispered roughly, "I meant what I said, honey. You're mine. I'm not going to keep letting you get away."

Then his mouth met mine, and like all the times before, I melted, those walls inside me breaking a little bit more. He was chiseling away at my walls, a little bit at a time.

I was scared. So scared of what would happen when he finally made my walls come tumbling down.

Chapter Eleven

Missy

Tonight was going to be a mess. I could hear Adrian yelling from inside the house as I walked to the backdoor. Adrian was pacing. I could see his outline moving along the drawn shades of the back windows.

I cringed when Chris started his truck. These men and their diesels. Why do they have to be so loud?

Adrian heard Chris's truck, too. He stopped pacing and started walking towards the back door. Right as I got to it, he threw it open, looking ready for a fight with his phone in one hand, his other hand clenched in a fist.

"Uh, uh. No, sir. Get your butt back in the house," I pushed him back inside.

"Where's Brittany!?" he demanded.

"None of your business. Get inside."

"How the hell is it none of my business?!"

He was seething, but it registered about two seconds too late that he was barking up the wrong tree. I raised my eyebrows at him, and his shoulders sagged. He wiped a hand down his face, then asked in a calmer tone, "Missy. Where the hell is my sister?"

"That is none of your business. She is a grown adult, Adrian, and so are you. If you keep acting like a child, I'm going to treat you like one."

"Daddy, go time out?!" Landon giggled, munching on a cookie from Roseanne's. One of Hailey's cookies, by the looks of it.

I had to fight to keep the smirk off my face. When Landon broke off a piece of his cookie and tried to feed it to Pickles sleeping on the headrest of the couch, my face broke out in an all-out grin. It wasn't the time or the place, but seeing my greedy son willing to share food with the cat when he wouldn't share with anyone else was sweet enough to break the tension inside of me.

"There's nothing funny here, Missy," Adrian snapped. "If she left with that asshole, I'm really going to kill him."

"HELLO?!" a voice called out from his phone. It was still on, and it wasn't Rick. It was Mike's name, sprawled out on the caller ID.

"Your phone." I raised my eyebrows at Adrian.

He looked down at the device in his hand, scowling, then yelled at the receiver, "If your fucking brother even breathes on my sister, he's fucking dead!" Then he clicked off the phone and threw it across the room. It landed on one of the kid's bean bags, but still made a loud smacking sound when it hit.

I sighed, realizing this talk shouldn't take place in front of the kids. Adrian was still too heated.

"Hailey?" I looked at our oldest, who was already sitting with the baby on a blanket on the floor. She had the remote in her hands, scrolling to find a show for Landon.

"I know, mama. I'll watch the boys."

"Thank you, baby," I smiled at her, then dropped that smile when I stared up at my seething husband. I grabbed the front of his shirt and started dragging him with me to our bedroom.

"Mama!" Landon yelled in a commanding tone. "I come?!"

"No, baby. Mama has to put daddy in time out."

"Bull shit," Adrian hissed, even though he wasn't fighting my hold on him as I pulled him behind me.

"Keep it up, and I'll swat your butt too," I whispered so low that only he could hear.

"Don't threaten me with a good time," he grumbled. "This is bull-shit. How could my wife and daughter keep this shit from me? You're both a couple of traitors-MMPH."

The second I pushed him into our room, I grabbed his face, then kissed him deeply, cutting off all rants and tirades. He was stiff for only half a second, but he couldn't resist for long. He wrapped his arms around my waist, lifting me so my legs circled around his waist. He deepened the kiss, carnal desire taking over. His tongue felt hot and demanding in my mouth. I moaned deeply in response.

"Fuck," he growled as he sat down on the edge of our bed. "You pissed me off."

"Deal with it," I snapped back, tossing his hat to the floor and jerking his head back with my fingers knotted in the back of his hair. "You should be less concerned with your sister's love life and more concerned with your own."

"And why's that?" There was a challenge in his eyes, daring me to give him a reason he couldn't be in charge of both.

"Because," I grinned, grinding my warm center against the seam of his pants, making him hiss. "You aren't going to have much of a love life sleeping on the couch."

"Are you threatening me with sex?" he scoffed.

"I very much am." I lifted my chin.

I almost had him. I could see the defeat rising on his expression, but then in half a second, that fury returned. He grabbed my waist, locking me in place.

"You lied to me."

I rolled my eyes. "I did not. I kept your sister's private life private."

"You knew," he said darkly, a vein ticking on his forehead. "Hailey knew. How long?"

I shrugged. "A while. Brittany was trying to figure things out. That's why no one wanted to risk telling you yet."

"So you both chose to lie to me instead?"

"No one freaking lied to you, Adrian!" I pushed against his chest, trying to get off his lap, but he was still holding me in place. "Look at how you're acting right now. We all knew you would act like this. That's why no one wanted to tell you."

"Then what about Brittany and her professor?" His eyes turned cold. "Did you know about him, too?"

I bit my bottom lip, looking away. I couldn't meet his eyes. I wanted to tell Adrian about that professor when I found out he was married, and he was just using Brittany, but I knew my husband well enough to know what he would do. He would have caused Brittany to lose her chance at graduating. He would have really killed the guy.

"You knew." Adrian sounded more hurt than mad.

"Adrian..."

"No," he shook his head, moving my body to sit on the bed as he slowly stood up. "Missy, that's not fucking okay."

"It's not my business to tell anyone. Even you. I was helping her through it. Why do you think she's graduating early?"

"Because of him?" Adrian scoffed. "Why? Because they broke up? She left college early because of dumping some dipshit?"

"No. That's not exactly what happened," I murmured.

Should I tell Adrian this? Would I be able to keep him from killing the adultering jerkoff, at least until Brittany gets her diploma?

"Then what the hell happened?"

He's going to find out, eventually. Soon. If that professor is in town, then maybe Adrian does need to know.

I was just about to tell him, but then he scoffed loudly, shaking his head. "You know what? Fine. You all want to keep your little secrets, so fucking be it." He picked his hat up off the ground and turned for the door.

"Where are you going?" I hopped up and followed him.

"That's none of your damn business," he growled, throwing my words from earlier back at me.

It hurt, but fear overtook the brief pain, thinking he might be going to do something crazy. "You better not mess with Brittany or Chris, Adrian." I followed him as he headed for the front door. He detoured in the kitchen, getting his keys from the counter. Both older kids looked up and stared as he stormed past.

"Adrian! I'm serious! Leave them alone!"

He didn't say a word. He just stormed out the front door, slamming it behind him. I was stunned, tears burning the back of my eyes.

"Daddy need 'nother time out," Landon said from the couch.

He needs more than a timeout.

I opened the door just as he was starting his truck. He didn't look back at the house once as he drove off.

"Shit," I cursed under my breath.

That was not how I expected that to go.

I went back inside, going for my phone in the living room. I tried calling Adrian first, but dread washed over me when his phone started ringing from the bean bag across the room.

"Uh, oh." Hailey looked at it, then back at me with wide eyes. "You better call Mr. Chris."

***

Brittany

"Yeah? Okay.... Yeah, I got it. No, we'll go somewhere else for now.... Thanks for letting me know.... Bye."

I stared at Chris as he drove along the curvy mountain road towards town. I saw Missy's name pop up on his phone, but could hear her side of the conversation.

"Change of plans," Chris muttered. "We're not going back to your place tonight."

"What? Why?"

"Well," he scratched the back of his head. "I guess Missy couldn't calm your brother down. He just left, and she doesn't know where he is headed. Left his phone at home, too."

"Shit," I murmured, a wave of anxiety traveling over me, making my skin feel like pin-pricks.

"It's okay," Chris smiled, reaching over to grab my hand. I didn't resist. My fight was gone. "I know somewhere we can go instead."

"I'm not going to your mom's house," I said in a low tone.

"No," he shook his head. "Not mom's house."

I didn't have the energy to nag him to find out where he was driving us. I knew his mom was in the opposite direction of where we were driving now, and that's all I cared about. As much as I didn't want to watch my brother kill Chriss, I didn't want to feel the condemning stare of Chris's mom in the morning, either.

I stared mindlessly out the window as the dark silhouettes of the forest sped around us. Minutes later, it was the town that passed us by.

"You're not going to sleep on me, are you?" Chris broke the silence.

"Not yet."

His fingers rubbed against the back of my hand. "We're almost there."

"Where's there?" I asked, not from genuine curiosity, but just to fill the silence now that it was broken. I didn't want to sit in awkwardness.

"The shop. My brother has an apartment above the office we've been fixing up for me to use soon."

"Why would you need an apartment in your brother's shop?"

He shrugged. "I'll be working there soon. Why not? It's also closer to the girl that I like." he squeezed my hand. A warmth spread over my cheeks.

"You're going to work for your brother?" I asked, trying not to dwell too much on the comment about me.

"Not for him. With him. We were supposed to go into business together, but then I got feelings for my boss's sister and decided to wait a bit."

"Seriously?" My mouth dropped. "You stayed working for Adrian all this time to be closer to me?"

"Is that so hard to believe?" he asked sheepishly as he pulled up outside of his brother's shop. "Not like you were giving me many chances beyond that."

"Because it was a one-night-stand, Chris," I whispered.

He shook his head. "Not for me, it wasn't."

The sincerity written on his face was hard to dispute. He was serious.

"What was it then?"

He brought my hand to his lips, kissing the back of it tenderly. His gaze was so soft, so full of affection that it made me want to crawl over the center console and feel the full force of that affection.

"It was the beginning of us."

"Us?" I got weird butterflies floating around in my chest.

"Us," he nodded, then kissed my hand again. "The us where I no longer just saw you as my friend's younger sister. The taboo had been lifted," he chuckled. "Drinking with you, laughing with you, hearing you bull shit with the guys and insulting anyone that pissed you off. Even before we got in the back of my truck, I was falling for you, Brittany. Falling for you hard."

"You... You still like me? Even knowing... Knowing everything you do?"

"I still like you," he said with a firmness in his tone. "All that did was just made me realize I needed to up my game, because no way in hell was I going to lose you to anyone else."

Fuck it.

I crawled over the console, straddling Chris as our lips met in a hungry, raw kiss. I was frenzied, trying to melt our bodies together. He was holding me tight, letting me lead, but supporting me all the same. It wasn't until I rocked my body against his that he stopped me.

"Wait, wait, wait," he gasped.

"I don't want to," I mumbled, raking my teeth over his bottom lip.

"Let's get inside," Britt," he pointed to the building. "It's not that late yet. We don't want to give everyone anything else to talk about so soon."

Chapter Twelve

"Wow," I murmured, looking around the cluttered space. "This looks...."

"I know, I know," Chris chuckled, clearing off a space for me to sit on an old sofa. "Out here is a mess. We just redid the bathroom and bedroom. Haven't touched this space yet."

I coughed as he smacked the dust from the old couch cushion, and it went flying up around us.

"You are going to live here?"

He shrugged. "Most likely. Why?" A broad, wicked smile spread on his face as he wiggled his eyebrows. "You offering other accommodations?"

"Yeah," I scoffed. "My brother would love that." The house they gave me was entirely a gift. A gift from Missy, no less, so Adrian really can't get a stick in the ass about it too much, but that won't stop him from blowing up like he did today.

"Speaking of your dipshit brother, I think I should move my truck in the garage just to be safe. Wait right here for a second. I'll be right back."

While Chris went back down the stairs to the shop, I took a moment to really look around the cluttered space. It was a small living area, which was probably why it looked so cluttered. There was a small kitchenette area with a two-burner stove and a half-sized fridge. That area was the only place not cluttered in this space. It looked like it had been used regularly. There was a dish towel on the sink and dishes on a drying rack.

I got curious about the bedroom and bathroom. There was only one other door in the space besides the one that opened to the narrow stairs. That had to be it.

Cracking open the door, I was shocked by the night and day appearance of the room compared to the living space. It was almost empty, except for a bed and a dresser. The bed wasn't even fully made. It was a brand new mattress still in the plastic cover.

The walls were freshly painted, and from growing up with my dad and brother, I knew the walls were new, too. The drywall was smooth and textured differently from the walls out in the living space. It would have been the first thing my brother would have pointed out.

There were two doors in the bedroom. Both were open, and one was clearly meant to be a closet. It was a small confined space, but it just didn't have the hardware hanging off the walls yet. The other was dark, but when I switched on the light, I found a cute bathroom, basic but updated.

"There you are," Chris said, coming into the bedroom. "I thought you ran away for a second."

"I'd have to run right past you. I don't think I'd get very far."

"That's true. I'm sure I can run faster than you."

"Ha. Yeah, right."

He laughed, "What? You think you could beat me in a race?"

"I was on track," I smirked.

"So was I."

"No, you weren't!" I choked on a laugh, knowing beyond a doubt that he wasn't.

"I could have been," he said stubbornly.

"Only you weren't."

"I'll race you right now," he lifted his chin.

"Oh, now you want me to run away from you?"

"Please," he scoffed. "You couldn't even make it out of this room."

This competitive need rushed over me, and my eyes flashed to the door. A sneaky grin lifted my lips, and then I bolted for it, only to be caught within seconds by two large hands.

I squealed, yelling, "No!"

Chris just laughed, pulling me to his chest. "See. I'm faster."

I laughed, still trying to wiggle free, until I wiggled around and was facing him.

Was he always so much taller than me? His chest and arms felt so strong, so hard, as he pressed me in. His mouth was stuck in a cocky grin, but his lips still looked so soft and tempting.

"You're staring awfully hard," he said, his voice deep and rough.

I pressed my lips together, looking away. "No, I'm not."

"Sure," he laughed softly. "Was there something you wanted?"

"Nope. Not a thing."

"You sure?"

No. I'm not sure, but instead of telling him that, I continued to stare everywhere except his face.

"The bed doesn't have sheets," I mumbled, staring at the fabric covering it.

Chris chuckled, his thumbs skimming my bare back where my shirt had ridden up. "Not yet. I bought some when I bought the bed. Want me to go find them?"

"If we're sleeping here, you probably should."

"That's cute," he rested his forehead on mine. "You think you're getting any sleep tonight?"

I slapped his chest. "Go find the sheets!"

"Okay, okay," he laughed, kissing my cheek before letting me go.

I stood there, dazed for a moment, rubbing my cheek. Who knew Chris Finley could be so swoon-worthy? My heart is still racing.

"Found them," he came in a minute later. He had a big plastic bag with bedding inside. Your typical bed-in-a-bag. Jet black. I almost laughed. It was bachelor bedding for sure. "Seven-piece set. Everything's here."

"What about the pillows?" I raised an eyebrow.

His smile dropped. "Shit."

I laughed, suspecting as much. Adrian went up until he moved in with Missy with just a singular pillow on his bed, and it was the one he had stolen from me. Guys don't think about that stuff.

"Good thing we're not sleeping tonight anyway," I snickered.

"You're right," he shrugged. "You'll be passing out on top of me like you usually do. You don't need no damn pillow."

My mouth dropped. "Excuse you?"

"I said," he grinned devilishly, slowly unzipping his bedding, "You'll be passing out on top of me. It's kinda our thing."

"What the hell?!" I fought back a smile. "That's not a thing."

"It's your thing," he smirked. "Riding me until you pass out. Happens every time."

"Nuh uh," I said stubbornly.

"Watch. I'll bet you breakfast in the morning you do it again."

"You're on," I was determined to prove him wrong, even though some nagging feeling inside me said that I wouldn't. But I was excitedly looking forward to seeing myself fail.

***

Chris

After Brittany helped get the bed made, something I couldn't manage to do on my own, I went hunting in the little kitchen for something to drink.

Who the hell designed fitted sheets to go on the bed a certain way? It should fit no matter what corner you start with. Brittany stood back, watching with barely suppressed laughter as I tried repeatedly to force the fitted sheet to fit sideways.

Eventually, when I was contemplating burning the thing and sleeping on a bare mattress, she had mercy on me and showed me the tag that had 'BOTTOM' written on it in bold letters.

Now that the bed was made, Brittany was washing up in the bathroom. She asked to take a shower to calm down after her brother made her sweat up a storm. I was more than happy to let her get naked here. I even found her an extra shop shirt to change into afterward in my brother's office. This place wasn't really ready to be lived in, so we'll have to make do with what we can find for tonight.

I wasn't thinking much more than I didn't want to face off with Adrian again tonight when I thought of bringing her here. I'm not entirely sure what's all in the kitchen. I know Mike uses it. This space is more of his retreat right now than a future apartment for me. When we talked about buying the place, it was always the plan to make this my apartment, so someone could be at the shop at all times, but then Brittany happened and that delayed my plans to move in. Mike still insisted on fixing it up though.

He even takes showers up here when he's really greasy and doesn't want Izzy to flip out on him tracking it in their house. The bathroom was equipped with clean towels and a bottle of Irish Springs.

I let him know while I was hiding my truck in the garage that I was here. He had called my phone half a dozen times. I guess Adrian called him to chew him out too, right as Brittany and I left. He was worried about me. Said something about not touching a hair on Brittany's head, or I might die.

I let him know I was touching all of her several times over tonight, but I would try to steer clear of her hair if it made him feel better before hanging up.

Adrian can't hurt me. Well, he might be able to hurt me, but he wouldn't kill me. He wouldn't want to do the jail time and be away from Missy or his kids.

I needed to let Mike know that I had quit sometime tomorrow. That would perk him up. Now's as good a time as it gets to hand in my resignation to Adrian. Continuing to work for Adrian will be hazardous to my health.

Opening the fridge, I didn't find much. Just endless bottles of beer and a questionable container with brown mush inside that must have once been leftovers from Mike's home or something.

I grabbed two beers, then dug around for a bottle opener. I didn't find one, but I found my brother's stash of junk food. There were half-eaten bags of chips, pop tarts, and loads of beef jerky. After using the edge of the counter to pop off the tops of the beer, I grabbed some of everything and carried my load back to the bedroom.

"You okay in there?" I knocked on the door after setting my bounty on the dresser.

"Yeah, but.... I can't figure out how to turn the water warm."

We haven't marked the nob yet to distinguish between hot and cold, and it turns in complete circles, which makes it harder to figure out. I tested the doorknob, finding it was unlocked, so I went ahead and let myself in.

"You could have knocked." Brittany eyed me, pulling her towel tighter around her body. It made her boobs push up and spill out of it, having the opposite effect of what I'm sure she was going for.

"Nice towel."

"Shut up and help me work this," she huffed, though a blush moved across her cheeks and down her neck. Her hair was tied up, giving me a clear view of all of it.

I reached around her, turning the nod to that sweet spot and showing her the almost invisible arrow of the nob that needed to point at a perfect 45-degree angle to the left. The shower was new, but the plumbing was still in the original layout, so it's the opposite of the norm.

As she tested the water with her hand, satisfied when it got hot, I peeled my clothes from my body.

"What are you doing?" She stopped to stare at me.

"Taking a shower."

"Can't you wait until I'm done?"

"Nope," I grinned, kicking off my pants. "It's a small water heater. It will only last about ten minutes." It would last near twenty or thirty, but I'm okay with telling this small lie.

"Then give me five minutes and I'll be done."

"Hmm," I pondered something, turning to walk out of the bathroom with only my boxers on.

"Finally," Brittany muttered, and I heard the shower curtain moving around.

I smiled to myself, grabbing both the beers from the dresser, then walked back in. I startled her when I pulled the shower curtain back and got in behind her.

"What the fuck?!"

"Shower beers," I handed her the second glass bottle.

She stared at me in disbelief, then her beautiful face contorted as she tried to resist laughing. She snorted instead, taking the bottle from my hand.

"Weaponized persistence," she muttered before taking her first drink.

"I don't know what you are talking about," I mumbled, taking in her entire naked body and I knocked back my drink. I was drinking her in too.

I will never tire of seeing her like this.

With a little more persistence, I got her to let me wash her beautiful body, lathering her up in the manly smelling body wash. I paid extra attention to every inch of her body, being very meticulous with the excuse of working one-handed.

I could see she was frustrated by the time I was through washing her. I smirked while she watched me slowly clean myself with the same meticulous handling.

"You're annoying," she groaned, staring down at my erect and happy member.

"Thanks," I chuckled. "I like you too. Now, let me get under that water to rinse off."

She moved around me, letting me have the direct path of water. I set my now empty beer off to the side as I turned around to block her view. As I was rinsing off my face, I felt small hands graze against my back. I stood stock still as they glided across my waist, her body pressing up behind mine. Her hands moved down my happy trail, gripping my dick firmly and making me hiss.

"What're you doing?" I whispered.

"Making sure you get all the soap off," she said, her voice a sultry whisper.

"Fuck," I groaned, opening my eyes to stare down at her petite hands move up and down me, squeezing me tight with every pump.

"I think you're clean," she laughed as I got harder in her hands.

"Not for long," I growled, turning around and kissing her.

She gasped into my mouth. My fingers found her wet entrance and slid right inside of her as my mouth furiously devoured hers. She was slick, ready for me.

I wanted her. Now.

"Turn around," I groaned in her ear.

She smirked, a playful glint in her eyes. "Make me."

Fuck me, she was playing with fire right now. I wanted her too badly to not take her up on that offer.

"Gladly."

I made her hiss as I grabbed the back of her hair, tugging it back and using it as leverage to make her turn her ass towards me. She moaned, her pussy getting more wet around my fingers. Her ass was grinding against me as she arched her back, ready and waiting.

With the water still pouring down over us, I lifted her leg and rammed myself inside of her. An icy shiver moved through my legs from the exhilarating feeling of being inside of her.

"This pussy was made for me," I pressed my lips against her neck. "She's all mine."

"Prove it," Brittany challenged in an airy, needy voice.

Fuck, I love a challenge. I rammed into her repeatedly, as my fingers rubbed against her sensitive clit. Her mangled cries of, "Yes!" and "Fuck," were riling me up more. Her ass was backing into me, meeting me thrust for thrust.

Soon, I felt her tight tunnel quivering around me, making my balls tighten as I reached that finish line right after her.

This was just the start. With no pillows and a fridge full of beer, we had all night to claim one another.

"The water's still hot," she murmured, resting her head against the shower wall. "I thought it would only last ten minutes."

"Maybe twenty," I smirked, messaging her back before pulling her back against me. We were very much dirty again, but I like her smelling like sex more than my brother's soap. She was only going to get dirty as the night wore on.

"We have a bet to settle," she stared back at me with a stated expression.

I chuckled, "I look forward to you buying me breakfast in the morning."

Chapter Thirteen

My face hurt. It legitimately hurt from smiling so much.

"I told you I would win," I whispered into Brittany's hair, mixing kisses in with her golden strands.

She couldn't hear me. She was dead ass asleep. Just like I told her she would, she passed out on top of me. I'm so proud that I can't help but gloat, even if she couldn't hear me.

I strained to reach for my phone on the nightstand to snap a picture. I knew I wouldn't be able to stay like this holding her all night, so I needed some kind of proof that I won.

Plus, having this picture on my phone just to gloat on my own later would be great.

I snapped the picture, making sure to capture her drool in the photo while I threw a thumbs up and a goofy grin. I couldn't help myself.

Then I started taking pictures of her sleeping face, just for me. I wouldn't use these to gloat. I just wanted evidence of this intimate victory for my satisfaction.

But what good is a victory if no one else knows you won?

The more I thought about it, the more this nagged at me.

Brittany might be pissed, but there was one thing I just had to do.

I snapped a few more pictures, making sure Brittany was covered by the sheet, but also making sure it was obvious what had just taken place between us.

After gently rolling her off me to lie on her own on the bed beside me, I slipped out from under her and started looking for her phone. I knew Professor Dickhead was that prick from the bar. I also knew I wasn't letting him go another night, thinking he had a chance with my woman.

It took me a second to find his number on her list of contacts. She changed his name from Professor Dickhead to just Dickhead. That had me snorting to myself. It was like the last bit of recognition she had for that man just vanished with the disappearance of his title as her professor. He was nothing more than a dickhead to her now.

I quickly took his number and entered it into my phone, then made sure he was blocked on her phone. I didn't want him reaching out to her after I acted a bit like a dickhead myself. If he wanted to talk to her, he could through me.

One more petty move, and I was out of her phone. I had to change the contact name one more time, then the contact name for myself. Then I put her phone back in her pants pocket. She would be none the wiser for now.

I went through all the pictures on my phone I had taken of us until I found the perfect one, then sent it with a snarky as shit message.

ME:| Take your snooty ass back to Eugene, to your wife. Leave my girl alone. She's taken care of.

I then sent several obscene emojis to enforce my little message. The shiver of adrenaline as I pressed send made me nervous for a second, but I still did it. This immense feeling of satisfaction overtook me soon after. Especially when the 'read' receipt came through.

The picture was fucking perfect. Brittany was drooling onto my chest. The sheet pulled up to her neck. You could see just enough of one shoulder to know she was naked beneath the sheets. I was sprawled out proudly beneath her, looking smug as shit, with my arm wrapped around her and the other holding up the phone for the picture. My arms were flexed perfectly, too.

Damn, I was one good looking mother fucker. Brittany really brings out the best in me. The sex hair and hickeys on my neck were a nice touch.

After getting back under the blankets with Brittany, I stayed up another twenty minutes, waiting for him to reply. He never did. I saw the text bubbles pop up a few times, but he never sent anything back.

Chicken-shit mother fucker. He and his snow tires could fuck off back to Oregon and never come back.

After a long time of no text bubbles, I figured he was really too much of a shit head to respond. I pulled Brittany close, nestling her in my arms in place of a pillow, and drifted to sleep. I had a lot of teasing to do when we both woke up. I need to be well rested.

***

Elias

Sitting on the edge of the bed in the hotel room, I just stared blankly at my phone. The picture and text disappeared long ago as my phone went into rest mode, but I was still too frozen with despair to move to unlock it again.

She really was sleeping with that backwoods hillbilly. Some small part of me was still holding out hope that she wasn't, and that maybe everything had been a misunderstanding on that part too, but there was no denying what I saw in that picture.

Never, not once, did I get to see her sleeping face like that. I always had to hurry home not to arouse suspicion. Not for the reason she is thinking now, judging by that comment about my wife. I was never two-timing her. Not really. I just couldn't be caught.

Yes. I have a wife. I had a wife while I was seeing Brittany, but the term wife is a very loose reference to what that woman really was to me.

She was a shackle. A mistake of my youth I had been trying to unbind myself from since before Brittany ever became my student.

The divorce had become complicated and messy, and to avoid losing my job and everything I had worked for, I had to play my wife's games for far too long. Her father, a politician and an elite member of the school board who had the highest donations made each year, gave me an ultimatum. Play nice with his daughter for now until after his election, and he would ensure I made tenure. If I didn't, I could kiss my job goodbye.

It seemed easy enough at the time. Lindsey was a nightmare to live with, but her explorations outside of our marriage had become more frequent, and I rarely had to tolerate her presence. I figured I would just bide my time until after the elections, as her father told me to do, then go forth with the divorce proceedings again.

But then Brittany happened.

She was my sunshine on the darkest of days. She would light up my existence whenever she was near. After living on autopilot for so long, her strong will and brilliant responses during all the classroom discussions broke me from my monotone prison.

I know my wife had become more suspicious that I was stepping out of our marriage too, but I worked hard convincing her it was just her projecting. Our married life had long ended, so I didn't think she would notice or care, but that wasn't the case. She was spiteful to the end.

I had to be careful after that. I told Brittany countless times that our relationship was strictly physical and to not expect more. I was putting up those walls to protect both of us. If Lindsey's father could hurt me, a professor, I had no idea what he would do to a student. I didn't know the storm that was to come, though.

As November came and went, the election season came to pass and I started the divorce proceedings again, but she suddenly fought me about it. I had to be even more secretive with Brittany because of how much Lindsey was complicating our divorce.

Then there was her father, who still expected us to show a united front in public until the divorce was settled. He wanted to keep appearances with the early months of his newly won office, just for a time. I couldn't escape her family and the public events we had together just yet, even though I was long checked out and biding my time.

I wanted Brittany. I knew I loved her by that time, but I still had to protect us both.

Lindsey got suspicious near the holidays. At Thanksgiving, seeing me immersed in my phone instead of acting the part of a perfect husband as I should have been was what first caught her attention. She watched me like a hawk and eventually hired someone to follow me.

That was how she found out about Brittany.

Then Christmas happened. Christmas night was the worst night of my life.

Or I thought it was. Getting that text and picture tonight, after meeting Brittany's brother at the hick bar, would be hard to beat now. I thought her brother might actually hit me at one point, but even that would have been less of a gut punch than this picture.

The divorce was almost completed. I'm almost free, but my sunshine has gone to shine over someone else. Someone surely less deserving. He could never match her brilliance or beauty.

But there she was. I clicked on my phone again to stab myself in the heart. Her relaxed beauty, sleeping while lying on the chest of another man, broke me.

I should have come here sooner. I'm scared I might actually lose her.

Not that I'm ready to back down. I know I have much more to offer her than this hillbilly ever could, and I'm sure her brother will see that.

One thing that can put me ahead of this hick in her brother's eyes has to be that I confessed from the beginning my intentions with his sister. What deflected Adrian Brewer from me tonight was his greater anger at realizing his friend had rushed off to find Brittany confessing nothing.

***

Adrian

"Hey," the deep, gruff voice of my old man woke me as he kicked the corner of the couch. "You wet-eared little punk. Wake up," he kicked the couch again, making me roll and fall to the floor.

"Dad," I groaned, pushing myself up. "What the hell?! What are you doing here?"

"What the hell are you doing here?" He glared down at me as I tried to push my aching body up off the floor. I was stiff and sore from the worst night's sleep I had ever had in my life. "Why the hell are you in your sister's house?"

I rubbed my hands down my face, like I could wipe away the shame and pounding headache from last night. "Did Missy call you?"

The shame hit me full blast at the mention of my wife's name.

"Missy. Hailey. Mike was even calling Rose to see if you were with us. He almost came to get the kids."

Shit, I fucked up last night. I knew I did the second I opened the door to Brittany's house and saw no one was there. I looked for my phone to call her, then realized I had left it at home. At home with my probably pissed-off little wife. I couldn't even call or text Missy to apologize.

I grabbed a beer from Brittany's fridge, deciding to wait for her to show up instead of going home right away. I already fucked up. I was ready to commit to the fuck up and at least feel better by the time I went home. Just one punch in Chris's face and I could say it was all worth it. The fight with Missy. Pissing off my sister. All of it.

One beer turned to two, then three, and then four. Eventually, I realized Britt and that mother fucker would never come, and I was too drunk at that point to go home.

"Fuck, what time is it?" I asked, looking around for my phone again like an idiot, until I realized once again that I had left it.

"Nine. You're late for work. I had to send Jose to watch over the job site for today. Get your ass cleaned up for now." He kicked a bag towards me, and a pile of clothes fell out. My clothes.

"I need to get home to Missy." I grabbed my keys off the make-shift table, which was essentially just a cooler with a box on top of it. I ignored the bag completely.

"Missy isn't home," Dad scoffed.

Red flags started going off in my head. I slowly turned to look at him. "What do you mean, Missy isn't home?"

"Exactly what I said. She left this morning after I stopped by to check on her. Here," he pulled my phone from his pocket. "You might need this."

I frantically grabbed my phone from his hand, turning it on to call my wife to see where exactly she had gone. I didn't like my dad's tone of telling me she wasn't home where she should be.

As soon as I turned on my phone, there was a text waiting for me.

> **Sugar Mama:|** My sweetest father-in-law did me the favor of changing the locks on our house. He's handy like that. Let's play a little game, since you decided to act so childish last night. Your children and I are hiding somewhere. We needed a little escape. We're close enough for you to find, and I'll reward your effort with the new keys if you can find us.

> Also, we have the camper, so even if it takes you days, we will be fine.

Right after the first texts, there was another that had me wanting to chuck my phone at the wall.

> **Sugar Mama:**| If you can find us by tonight, I might not even make you sleep on the couch. I'll be turning off all our phones and devices until you do! Happy hunting, you big baby. Enjoy the adult diaper I packed you instead of boxers. Jerk.

I slowly looked up from my phone, glaring at my dad. "You changed the locks on my fucking house?"

"Nope. My boss commissioned me to change the locks on her house. Seems her husband was acting like a real ass last night. She wanted to teach him a lesson."

"By locking me out of my house!?" I was seething now. I know I fucked up, but this was fucking petty. "You know I can just drill through the locks, don't you?"

"Ah, that I do. But I also know you won't."

"How do you know that?" I scoffed.

He smirked, turning to the door. "Because you already pissed your wife off enough. You won't dig yourself in any deeper."

"Me?!" Anger welled inside of me again. "Do you even know what fucking happened last night?"

He stopped to stare back at me with a look on his face I hadn't seen since high school.

"You mean what you told me about Chris Finley? Boy, everyone in town knew. I've noticed for months the man had his eye on my daughter. He's a good kid at the core, so I let it go. A little loose in the jaw for my taste, but it's not my choice who your sister dates. Not yours either. She's a grown woman now, and I hardly think her dating life is anything for you to ruin your marriage over."

"But Missy knew!"

"Of course she did!" Dad wiped a hand down his face in exasperation. "Adrian. Brittany found in Missy what she could never have in you or anyone else."

When I kept quiet, just continuing to glare, he continued on.

"Brittany finally has a confidant that she never had in this town before. Your mother left us when she was still a toddler. She never had another woman to rely on before you wife moved here. Missy healed her as much as she healed you, and I'm fucking proud that your wife has kept Brittany's trust. Especially in matters that are none of your fucking concern. Those girls need that in each other, and if you try to take that from them or shame your wife for it, then I hate to say it, but I'm disappointed in you."

He gave me a look that made me feel like an eighteen-year-old kid again, confessing to my old man that I had got some girl pregnant that I didn't even like. I felt that same level of disappointment.

"Fix it," he said firmly. "You're not your sister's keeper. She's my daughter. If I feel something needs handling, I'll do it. You worry about your own wife and kids. Unless told otherwise, that's the only place to stick your nose."

Then dad left the house, and I felt two feet tall. I was ready to dig out that adult diaper from the bag, crawl into a fetal position, and not move until I recovered from the verbal lashing I just got.

Damn, that old man did me in. I need to find my wife and kids.

As I left the house, locking the door behind me, Brittany and Chris, and even that bullshit with her old professor were the furthest things from my mind.

Missy. I somehow knew that was her plan, but I was too worried about finding her to care.

Chapter Fourteen

Brittany

"Quit smirking," I muttered under my breath as we walked together to the coffee shop.

"He, he. I can't help it." Chris wrapped an arm around my shoulders. "I like winning."

"So do I, so quit rubbing it in," I said sourly, but I still placed my arm around him as well.

He kissed the side of my face, then whispered in my ear, "You're probably sore enough as is. Don't be a sore loser, too."

"I swear, I'm going to- "

I swung my free hand at him, but before I could even finish my threat, Chris grabbed that arm and pulled me in for a kiss. A deep, tummy-tingling kiss that drained all the fight right out of me.

When I was breathless and melted into him, he broke the kiss with a crooked grin. "My girlfriend is a feisty one. I like that."

"Masochist," I rasped half-heartedly.

"Mmh, yeah, but only with you."

I laughed softly. "I'll beat you any time you'd like."

"Except for last night," he reminded me with a cheesy grin. "Because I totally won."

I tried not to smile, but his mood was infectious. I laughed and leaned up on my tiptoes to kiss his lips one more time.

"Let's go get you your victory breakfast. I need coffee if I'm going to keep up with your energy this morning."

"Yeah, we definitely got to do something about your energy and stamina," he teased, pulling me along with him down the sidewalk.

"My stamina?! I did half the work!"

"Yeah, but you passed out," he smirked while reminding me. "I was nowhere near finished with you."

"Bull shit."

We went for what felt like hours. There was no issue with my stamina. His stamina was just too high last night.

"Too bad my brother got to the shop so early, or I could show you," he joked. "You'd be taking me out for lunch instead of breakfast."

I pinched his side, making him hiss and then laugh. He just pulled me against him and kissed the top of my head as we kept walking.

Walking past his brother to get outside was strange. Mike had a look on his face, like he knew everything already. Talk about a walk of shame.

Besides that embarrassment from leaving the shop with Chris as he boldly proclaimed his girlfriend was taking him out for breakfast, I surprisingly don't feel any shame about what happened last night.

I thought I would when Adrian and the rest of the town found out about us, but more than anything, I felt relief.

It was a strange feeling. Relief. I've been carrying so much shame and regret, the relief is completely foreign to me. I don't have that ache that races through my body, turning my limbs numb every time I think about my messy love life.

"My girlfriend is taking me to breakfast," Chris smiled widely, talking to himself.

My cheeks flamed, seeing how proud he was to call me that. He's playing up the girlfriend thing quite a bit, but I don't remember officially saying I would be his girlfriend. It was just implied.

I remember screaming my pussy was his several times, but that hardly counts as an agreement to be in a committed relationship.

...I'm not against the idea, though. Not anymore.

But I'm not the only Brewer that needs to be convinced.

"Hey, did my brother ever call or text you?"

Chris snorted. "No. Missy said that he left his phone at home."

"Huh. You would think he'd have gotten it by now." I know he was mad and acting crazy, but he's even more crazy when it comes to Missy, and not having a way to contact her would drive him insane.

"I'm not worried," Chris said, squeezing my shoulder. "I already quit. What's the bastard going to do?"

"Kick your ass," I scoffed.

"Yeah freaking right."

"Don't worry. The Brewer women will do their best to protect you."

"Woman," he tickled my sides, making me buck and laugh. "Why does everyone just assume I'll just roll over and take a beating from his punk ass?"

"Because," I giggled. "You're too nice compared to him."

"I'll show you nice," Chris growled, tickling my sides again.

I flailed and twisted away, but he followed my every step, all the way to the coffee shop doors. We were both laughing by then, and tears were streaming down my face.

"Get me my breakfast, woman," he smacked my ass as he opened the door, making me hop and stumble my way in. As the door's bell fastened above to alert the staff of incoming customers rang out, you could barely hear it over us. He reached out to steady me, both of us still trying to contain our laughter.

"Brittany Brewer and Chris Finley," Louisa, the older barista I used to work with, said from behind the counter with a huge grin on her face. She was hungry for gossip. I could tell by the look in her eyes. "So it's true. You two are together?"

"No, I just go around smacking everyone's butt and demanding breakfast in the morning," Chris teased her. "Come around the counter and I'll do it to you, too."

"I'm good, sweetheart. But thanks," she snickered. "You want your usual flat white, Britt? And a house brew for you?"

"And a couple muffins," I added.

"What kind? We've got lemon poppy seed and blueberry today."

"Ooh, both sound good," Chris looked at them through the display. "Let's get two of each. Are those Roseanne's cookies?"

"She dropped them off just half an hour ago."

"Throw in half a dozen of those, too."

"Jeez," I scowled at the growing pile of food. Louisa got out a paper bag and started stuffing it all in there. "Did you forget who's paying?"

He gave me a side eye, then slowly handed his card to Louisa with a cocky smirk. "You can just make me breakfast next time."

Louisa snickered, running his card and handing it back to him.

I sighed heavily, hiding my face in my hand to hide my embarrassment. As she went back to make our coffee, I smacked Chris with the back of my hand.

"Will you stop saying shit that's going to make people talk more than they already are?!" I hissed.

"Too late, honey," Louisa yelled above the sounds of the steamer. "You're the talk of the town."

"Great," I huffed, elbowing Chris.

He groaned, "Come on. Us being together is an excellent subject, I think. It's definitely not a bad thing."

"No, it's not," Louisa looked back at us. "We're all rooting for you two. Everyone's excited about the hot young couple kissing on Main Street."

"Good lord," I groaned, hiding my face again.

"Well, maybe we should give everyone something more to talk about. Come on, babe."

"Come on, where?!" I asked Chris as he grabbed my hand and started acting like he was going outside.

"I'm in the mood to make out."

"Get your hands off me," I jerked free, and he and Louisa laughed. "You're not funny! My brother-"

"Your brother ain't all that," Chris laughed, coming to settle his hands on my waist. I got butterflies from his gentle touch and the way his warmth seeped into my icy demeanor. His gaze was sizzling, making me want to squirm. I was suddenly feeling warm everywhere. His eyes were blazing with smoldering affection as he stared down at me. "Even if I were to get my ass kicked, it would all be worth it just to be with you."

Well, damn. Any lingering hesitation disappeared completely at that moment.

He brushed the hair behind my shoulder, then cupped my face along my jawline. His movements were so intentional, so tender that it made my heart hammer loudly against my chest.

He dipped his head, and I no longer cared who saw us. I leaned up, and right before his lips touched mine, the bell above the door rang out again.

I allowed my eyes to flicker to the side, seeing who it was just for a second, but I had no intention of stopping Chris. Not until I saw him.

My hand shot up, and pressed against Chris's chest, not pushing him away, but stopping him from coming closer as my feet fell flat back on the floor.

His brows knit in puzzlement, then he followed my stare.

"You gotta be fucking kidding me," he sneered, his arms tightening around me.

I was stiff in his arms, my body frozen from shock and dread.

Elias.

He was dressed in one of his usual jackets, but had jeans and a fitted black shirt underneath. He was still as handsome as the last time I saw him, even with dark circles under his eyes and stubble dotting on his face. Not having a clean shave actually made him more attractive somehow.

What stunned me more than anything was the gentle but pained look in his eyes. They were boring into me, disregarding Chris entirely.

"Hello Brittany."

Chris turned his body slightly, like he was trying to shield me from Elias.

"I thought I told you to fuck off back to where you came from?"

Elias ignored Chris and continued staring at me. If it wasn't for Chris, I think I would have broken down from the mess of emotions and guilt that came over me, seeing my professor again.

This is my hometown. My safe haven. How dare he come here right as I was starting to feel normal again? Right when I thought all the pain and guilt had been broken down and cleared away, he came to send a tidal wave of shame to drown me again.

"Brittany," he whispered, his voice so rough and raw.

Louisa was holding our two coffees behind the counter, that wide-eyed look on her face full of anticipation. It may have seemed like a simple enough greeting on Elias's part, but Chris's hostility towards him was clear as day. He looked ready to kick Elias's ass back out the door.

And I was the reason for it.

His rigid grip on me was all Louisa needed to know that I was the reason for the sudden tension between the two men. Soon, everyone would hear some version of what was about to happen in this coffee shop.

"I wanna go," I pulled on Chris's shirt, tearing my gaze away from Elias to stare pleadingly up at him. "Please."

Chris's hostile expression turned to one of pure concern as he looked back down at me. "Okay," he whispered, not letting me go as he moved to the counter to take our coffees and the small bag of pastries from Louisa's hands. He handed me my drink, then pushed me around Elias, muttering "asshole" as we skirted by him.

"I'd like the chance to speak to you," Elias reached out and put his hand on my arm.

I recoiled from his touch, leaning more on Chris, letting him be my shield as he pushed me forward, intentionally putting himself between Elias and me.

"I told you, if you want to tell her anything, it can go through me," Chris said venomously, opening the door for me to go through. "Get the fuck out of my town before I drag you out myself."

"Is that a threat?" Elias finally looked at Chris, that pained expression turning to one of disdain.

"It's a fucking promise, professor dickhead."

Elias stood up straighter, squaring his shoulders as Chris stood at his full height. It was a pissing contest if I had ever seen one.

"Come on," I pulled the hem of Chris's shirt, glancing over at Louisa. She was already on her phone texting someone about this, I'm sure. She kept looking up with that excited gleam on her face. "Let's just go."

Chris rested his hand on my back, but looked back one last time at Elias. "Get out of my town, asshole. She's not interested."

"I'd rather hear that from her after I've had a chance to explain myself," Elias said coldly.

"There's nothing to explain. You're a selfish prick. Simple as that."

"Chris, please, just stop," I urged, stretching out his shirt as I continued to pull him out the door with me.

He looked down at me, and I don't know what he saw on my face, but it caused him to back down and finally follow me. They were saying way too much in way too public of a place. I just wanted to go hide from the shit storm that was about to start brewing. I didn't want anything else to be said to clue Louisa in on what was happening between the three of us. She's heard enough.

"I'm divorced!" Elias shouted out right as we were finally leaving. "I have been separated from my wife for a long time, Brittany. Since before you. I'm sorry I never told you, but all I wanted to do was protect you."

It took a few seconds for me to completely comprehend what Elias had just said, and by then, the door had already closed behind us. Staring back, I felt a mix of every sort of emotion I was capable of, but shame and horror are ultimately what I landed on. Louisa was staring wide-eyed and open-mouthed at Elias, and there was no mistaking what she had just heard.

There wouldn't be wild rumors floating around about me. It would now most likely be the truth, which feels even dirtier than whatever Louisa could have assumed. By nightfall, everyone would know that Brittany Brewer was the town whore.

Chapter Fifteen

"Well, your brother's not here," Chris said as he pulled his truck onto my street. "That's good, I guess. Still haven't heard from him. Have you?"

I didn't answer. I silently stared out the window, zoned out on the houses moving by.

"I'm taking that as a no," Chris continued on, filling the silence with needless talking.

He's been talking nonstop since we left his brother's shop. I haven't said a word. Not after walking in to his brother and the other shop mechanic whispering loudly to one another.

Somehow, in the time it took us to hurry from the coffee shop back to there, they already knew what had happened. Mike even offered me an awkward apology, which I just nodded along to and then shut myself in Chris's front seat.

"Maybe he still doesn't have his phone," Chris kept yammering as he pulled into my driveway. "You don't have your car either. If you want, I can take you to go get it. It's not that- "

I didn't wait for him to finish. I opened and slid out of his truck, slamming the door behind me as I hurriedly walked to my door.

"Brittany, wait!"

Right as I was turning the stubborn key, he caught up to me. His truck wasn't even off. It was parked with its engine roaring loudly. Loud enough for some of my neighbors to peek out their windows.

"Shit," I stammered.

Shame was washing over me again. Chris had his hand on my arm, and it felt like a precautionary measure. If I pulled away from him, he would grab me, and we'd make another scene for the public today. Louisa and every other gossip hungry hen in this small freaking town would hear about it before I even closed my door.

"Are you mad at me? Did I mess up somehow?" Chris was rushing his words, looking frantic. "That dickhead was the one that-"

"Chris!" I snapped, seeing another curtain across the street flutter open and closed. "I'm not talking to you out here. Get inside or go home."

He stared down at me for a second, then reached around me to take my key from the doorknob. He skillfully locked it on the first try, then ran off with them to his truck as I waited on the porch. I was covering my face with my hands, trying to hide my agitation from the watchful eyes I could feel from my neighbors' windows.

His truck shut off, and when I heard his heavy boots on the steps leading up to my porch, I stepped back so he could unlock my door again. He put his hand on my back and urged me to go through first, probably worried I would turn tail and walk off if he didn't cut off my exit.

I thought about it. I thought about running to the woods or maybe to the park, but Chris's persistence and stubbornness wouldn't allow me that freedom. He'd likely catch me, throw me over his shoulder, and then we would be on the front page of the weekly town newsletter come Monday.

"Give me my keys." I stuck out my hand after he shut my door behind him.

"Nope. Not until you tell me what the hell I did to deserve this attitude you've suddenly got. I'm not the one you should be pissed at."

"I'm not pissed!" I lied.

"Bull shit," he huffed. "Try again."

"Jeez, Chris! Can you just leave it alone and let me be by myself right now?!"

"No! I'm confused as hell, so what the fuck did I do now?"

"What did you do?!" I hissed. "Chris! You couldn't keep your damn mouth shut. That is what you did."

He looked lost, his brows pulling down on his stressed face. "What the hell are you talking about?"

"YOU!" I stomped my foot in rage. "Why couldn't we just leave, Chris? Why?! Why did you have to turn around and have a fucking pissing match with him? Louisa heard everything. EVERYTHING!" I raged. "Now everyone in this damn town knows how much of a slut I was, sleeping with my married fucking professor in college. Everyone knows! Your brother, my neighbors.... EVERYONE!"

"That's not my fault! He said that shit. Not me!

He didn't deny my slut comment. Even though I said it, it still hurt thinking he probably thinks that way about me now, too.

"I can't fucking believe this," I muttered.

"Well, I can't either. How the hell did I do something wrong? I was defending you."

"You could have ignored him!"

He opened his mouth to say something else, then shut it again. He did that two more times until he said, "You froze first, Brittany. When he said he was divorced, you were the one that stopped. Not me. Yeah, I might have said too much shit in front of Louisa, but I wouldn't have said anything if I didn't feel fucking threatened at that moment. It wasn't my fucking fault."

"How the hell did you feel threatened?" I scoffed.

"BECAUSE YOU FROZE!" Chris yelled, making me startle back with the ferocity on his face. "You were listening to his bull shit! Of course, I felt fucking threatened! Who the hell wouldn't in my situation?!"

Did I freeze? I don't remember. I remember my heart going still and the ice in my veins, but I don't remember acting like I didn't want to get out of there. If I froze, it was only from shock. No other reason.

"Your insecurities are not a reason to start a fight like that," I whispered, my mind racing as I replayed everything I went down in that coffee shop repeatedly in my head.

"My insecurities?" Chris laughed humorlessly. "I don't think my insecurities are the problem here."

I glared at him. "What's that supposed to mean?"

"Exactly what it fucking sounds like." he tossed my keys to the ground and headed for the door. "You are so damn concerned over what everyone else is thinking. Did you ever stop to consider what the fuck is going through my mind right now? How the fuck I feel with the piece of shit chasing your ass all the way here? Did you consider me for even a second?"

He was breathing deeply, staring down at his boots while facing the door. I couldn't give him an answer, because I just realized that he was right. I wasn't considering him or his feelings. I was just worried about myself.

That realization brought another massive wave of shame and guilt over me, the largest one yet. I suddenly felt like I was drowning, unable to find my voice to deny his allegations.

"I'm guessing you still want to be alone right now. Right?"

I didn't answer him. I couldn't. My throat was still clogged with the strangling guilt as all the other ranging feelings shooting inside of me chilled me to my core.

He looked back and just shook his head.

"Fine. I'll give you what you want."

He opened the door and walked out, closing it softly behind him. I would have rather he slammed it shut, because maybe then it would have broken me out of my stupor sooner.

By the time my body and brain worked again, and I rushed to the door to tell him to come back, he was already in his truck, backing out of my driveway.

Was I unjust in my anger? He looked so betrayed. So hurt. There was so much truth to his words, I couldn't really blame him. Not anymore. No, he shouldn't have fed that fight with Elias, but ultimately, it was my fault that Elias was there at all.

Shit.

Elias was there. My professor, the one I had an affair with, was here in my town, and I'm sure everyone already knows those shameful details.

Everyone.

Mike knew so fast. That means Chris's mom likely already knows too.

How will Chris feel when his mother tells him she doesn't approve of him dating a harlot like me? Everyone knows Chris is a mama's boy, and she is the type of church-going lady that would never approve of a partner for her son that was involved in a scandal like mine.

"Damn it," I kicked a random empty beer bottle that was lying on the floor. It hadn't been there yesterday, but my mind was racing too much about other things to dwell on that for now.

I sat on the couch and dropped my face in my hands, feeling the burning behind my eyes as the dam broke.

How could a morning that started off so great turn into such a crapfest so fast?

Worse yet, how could I hurt the guy that had helped me feel happiness again because of my own transgressions?

"I am a slut," I muttered to myself, resting my head on the back of the couch and staring up at the ceiling. Tears were streaking down my eyes. I no longer had the will to hold them back. Soon, ugly sobs were tearing me apart, and I curled up into a ball, wishing the couch would just eat me alive to end all this bull shit drama I brought on myself.

I never felt so alone. So lost and broken.

Shit. Chris was trying so hard to make me feel better the entire way home, and I just shut him out.

I'm a slut and a bitch.

Right when I was about to fall into despair, grieving the loss of a man, I was just now beginning to realize how deep my feelings were for, my front door burst open.

The door banged loudly against the wall, making the floors shake. I opened my teary eyes to see Chris standing there, a determined look on his face.

"You're not getting rid of me that fucking easy," he growled, kicking the door shut with his boot and stomping his way towards me.

I sat up quickly, trying to wipe the mess of tears and snot off my face onto the backs of my hands. I was still struggling when he leaned over me, just a breath away. I was forced to drop my hands, so I tried just looking away instead. I didn't want him to see me like this, but he grabbed my face and forced my gaze.

"You're not a slut, Brittany. Not at all. You're just a pain in the ass. But you are my pain in the ass, and I'm not going anywhere."

"Let me go," I tried again in vain to turn my face away.

"Nope. This right here is mine."

"No, it's not! You don't want me!" I wailed, breaking down in front of him. "I'm fucked up, Chris! I'm not worth all this crap you have to go through! When the rumors reach your family, your mom-"

"My mom has little to nothing to do with us," Chris scoffed. "The rest of my family and the town, too. Quit thinking about everyone else and just think about me." His eyes were intense, staring into mine. "Do you, Brittany Brewer, without thinking too much about reasons or bullshit, like me? Don't complicate it. Do you like me?"

I hesitated for only a second, then nodded my head in his hands. I couldn't lie while he was looking at me like he was.

Chris's lips quirked slightly in the corners, obviously happy with the answer, and then he asked his next question. "Do you want to be with me?"

"Chris," I tried again to jerk my face away. "This isn't the time for-"

"Do you want to be with me?" he asked more forcefully, not letting me look away.

"Yes!" I confessed. "Yes, I want to be with you!" I cried. "I... I just don't want to be hurt again."

He rested his head on mine, breathing a sigh of relief. "Then, case closed. I will shoulder all the fucking pain in this world for you, Brittany. All of it. All I want in return is you."

My breath caught in my throat with a painful sob, and then his lips were on mine.

I could taste the saltiness from my tears. The bitterness of the coffee he drank. I could taste the sweetness of relief that he came back, and he was holding me together, as I felt like I was about to crumble apart.

I lost myself in the passion of our lips. I clung to his body, like I was the one now, fearing that he would run away. I was breaking apart in a whole new way. It hurt, but there was relief in this pain. Like picking away at a nasty scab so a wound could finally heal cleanly.

By the time the kiss began to ebb into feather-soft pecks and just being in each other's presence, I was lying underneath him on the couch. He had me pinned in place, and it was the only place I wanted to be.

"I thought you were gone," I whispered brokenly. "I thought... I thought we were..."

"I told you I'm a masochist," he scoffed lightly. "I wouldn't give up my pain in the ass for nothing. I just lost my temper for a second. That's all."

"Me too," I confessed. Even though I wish he hadn't said that crap back at Elias in the coffee shop, I know deep down it wasn't his fault.

"Is that an apology?" He lifted an eyebrow, looking smug, but his touch was tender as he softly wiped away some tears still dampening my cheeks.

"Nope," I almost laughed. "Just a confession."

"Hmm. So, you'll confess to being a pain in the ass, but won't apologize for it?"

"Not a chance."

"That's my girl," he laughed softly, his chest vibrating against mine. "You're going to need that fighting spirit right now."

"What? Why?"

"Because." he turned his head to look at the front door. "I just heard a truck pull up, and it sounded awfully familiar. Just wanted to make sure you still had some fight in you to protect me."

"Shit," I pushed against his chest until he got up and let me hurry to look out the window. I pressed my lips together, panicking inside my head when I saw who it was.

"It's not my brother," I told him. "But I'd still sneak out the back if I was you."

"Why?" He came up behind me, looking over my shoulder. Then he groaned. "Well, fuck."

It was my dad, and he definitely did not look happy coming up my porch steps.

Chapter Sixteen

Elias

"Damn it to hell," I snarled, throwing my phone on my passenger seat. My calls still were not getting through.

I rested my head on the steering wheel, groaning in defeat. That conversation did not go as I expected it to.

The panic I felt, seeing Brittany so close and comfortable to another man, had me walking into that run-down coffee shop without a set plan to act upon. I knew already, but seeing them just had me reacting and not thinking everything through.

Blurting out all those things I said while panic rushed through me was not wise. I realized that after they left, and the woman behind the counter called someone on her phone to relay the entire situation in a bout of gossip, all while I was still standing dumbfounded in the center of the shop.

I was heading to the only coffee shop in this awful town for my morning brew, since the brand of coffee at the hotel was the generic, cheap kind. After the lack of sleep, I needed an espresso or two. I never thought I would find Brittany in the store, pressed up against another man.

Fury still prickled my skin, creating a dirty, irritating itch all over me. Anger traveled through me, targeted at my ex-wife for causing Brittany to leave me to run into the arms of another man in the first place.

"I hate this blasted town," I groaned, hitting my head one more time on the wheel before looking up at the busy main street. The town was fully awake now. The businesses were all opening up. A small bank branch was setting out a sign with an ad for checking accounts. A family-owned hardware store was arranging a tool display in the window. Even that mechanic I was forced to visit yesterday had its garage doors open, and a car pulled into the first slot.

I don't know what I expected, really, but when Brittany spoke so fondly of her hometown, I didn't picture a dumpy town like this. I thought it would be more charming, with historic buildings and a village feel. This place was a step away from being impoverished in my book. How can a town only have one coffee place, with a single barista that looked like she would smell of cigarettes and hair spray?

I let my mind wander as I stared at the people loitering on the sidewalks. A man, big and burly, was getting out of a truck parked outside a bakery. Maybe they would have coffee too.

Focused on the bakery as I daydreamed of rich, dark caffeine and a fiery blonde, I noticed the writing on the side of the truck.

Perking up, I squinted as I read it over again, making sure I didn't just hallucinate that name.

BREWER CONTRACTING

What are the odds? In this small town, I guess they would be fairly decent. I looked up the company out of curiosity as sleep evaded me last night and discovered it was actually thriving for being in an area like this. The website listed a woman as the owner. A Melissa Brewer, who I summed up to be Brittany's sister-in-law after more digging. Missy was what Brittany always called her, and it must be a nickname.

I stared at the truck for a while longer, debating going in and asking the man questions. He didn't look like the type of guy that would give information about the owner of his company's sister-in-law to strangers, but I didn't have many other options. Not while Brittany had me blocked.

Then, before I could decide, the man came storming back out. His face was nothing but rage, which made my decision even easier. I didn't want to anger him further. That was for sure.

"Hmm," I watched as he started up the unnecessarily loud vehicle.

I don't know why the sudden urge came over me to follow him, but it did. I started my car too, then crept up behind him as he u-turned and drove away.

***

Brittany

Dad sat on a folding chair that Chris found in the kitchen, staring at Chris and me with a wary expression.

"So, this is official?" He pointed between us. "You two are together now?"

I bit my lip, nervous to respond, but Chris sure wasn't.

"Yes, sir!" He tossed an arm around my shoulders. "Your little girl is my girl now."

"Chris," I hissed, trying to shrug his arm off me. He wouldn't let me. He wouldn't even put an inch of space between us. I didn't know if he was using me as a shield or just being his normal, persistent self.

"Strong words coming from a kid that sneaked around instead of flat out dating her like a man before."

"Hey," Chris's brows knitted together. "That's not what happened."

"It's not?" Dad huffed. "Why'd it take another man to come into town for you to-"

"Dad," I stopped him. He wasn't being fair to Chris right now. "I was the one that wanted to keep, um... Keep us a secret. It wasn't Chris's decision. It was mine."

"Then what's changed now?" Dad crossed his arms over his chest, leaning back and giving us that look. The dad look that made me fidget in my seat.

"He... well.... He broke me down, I guess."

"He broke you down? Do you even like him, Brittany?"

Just the thought of admitting I might actually like Chris to my dad made me blush. "Yes," I whispered sheepishly.

"What?" Dad cupped his hand around his ear. "I can't hear you."

"YES!" I exploded, then glared at my dad for pushing me. "Yes, I like him! Are you going to be a jerk like Adrian now, too?"

Chris chuckled softly under his breath, rubbing my back soothingly, and I actually relaxed a little, even though I was still glaring at my dad.

Dad kept his stoic, grumpy face for a few more seconds before a smile broke free, and he actually laughed. "Nope. I just wanted to make sure."

"Make sure what?" Chris asked, still rubbing my back.

"Nothing," my dad continued to chuckle, gently shaking his head. "Nothing at all."

Chris looked like he wanted to push for a genuine answer, but I had a different question I wanted answered.

"What were you so pissy about when you got here?" Dad looked like he had steam blowing from his ears, telling Chris and I in a serious voice that we needed to talk.

"Oh. That," dad sighed. "Roseanne told me something. Seems that Loud-mouthed Louisa called to tell her something that happened in the coffee shop this morning."

My heart suddenly hammered inside my chest, shame filtering in again.

Chris laughed nervously. "What? They run out of light roast?"

"Huh," Dad huffed gruffly. He then stared at me in that way that made me feel like a little girl, squirming under her dad's disapproving gaze. "Want to tell me about this professor, young lady? Professor Dickhead, was it?"

Chris snorted, coughing to cover his laughter.

"Not really," I answered honestly.

"Well, I think you should." Dad didn't look amused. "Look. I was all for letting you put your big girl britches on and sorting your own love life out, but this thing with your professor sounds more serious."

"It's over," I grumbled, picking nonexistent lint from my pants. "I ended it the second I found out he was married. There's nothing to tell."

"So, he was married when... when you were.... together?"

Dad left the question hanging in the air with a pained look on his face.

"I don't know," I answered honestly. "His wife called me and said to leave her husband alone, so I did. I broke things off then and there."

"When was that?"

I pressed my lips together, reluctant to say the answer out loud. "Christmas," I finally admitted.

He kept quiet as she stared for another few seconds, then asked, "Is that why you left school early?"

"Maybe." I looked away, not enjoying being interrogated. "I wanted to come home. Is that so bad?"

"Not bad," dad sighed. "I'm just worried, Brittany. That professor made a scene, and people talk. You haven't graduated yet. What if this affects you getting your diploma?"

"How will it affect anything when it's over?"

"I don't know, baby girl, but I think we need to talk to a lawyer or something. Just in case."

"Really?" That seemed a little extreme to me.

"Better safe than sorry," he said, already pulling out his phone, most likely to text his attorney friend that helped Adrian adopt Hailey.

Chris stayed quiet as Dad and I talked more about the timeline of my relationship with Elias. I tried to keep details vague, and dad didn't ask for the gritty stuff, just classes I had with Elias and the dates our relationship started. It didn't make it any less uncomfortable or make me feel any less shame saying any of it with Chris sitting beside me.

Eventually, he sat back and just stared out the window with his arm on the back of my chair. I kept glancing at him, worried I was upsetting him again. He must have felt my eyes on him, because he looked back and grinned, easing my anxiety with that genuine smile.

We had a long night and a stressful morning. Maybe he is just exhausted.

Dad got a call as he was typing and looked irritated suddenly. "I'll be right back," he groaned, getting up and stepping outside before answering.

"I wonder who that was," I murmured, hearing my dad call whoever was on the other side of the line an asshole through the screen door.

"Maybe Professor Dickhead got his number," Chris grumbled.

My eyebrows pulled up with worry, and I glanced at him through my lashes. "I'm sorry," I whispered.

He smiled again, running his knuckles up and down my back. "I'm sorry too." His mouth quirked up in the corner, giving off more of a smirk than a sincere smile. "I'm sorry that I didn't make you fall for me soon. Then none of this shit would have happened."

I huffed, rolling my eyes back. "You were too scared of my brother."

"Bull shit. I just respected your brother." He lifted his chin. "I respected that right hook of his a little, too."

"See," I laughed softly.

He brushed the hair from my shoulder, then ran his fingers through the messy blonde strands. "I really wish I had noticed how amazing you are sooner, Brittany. Not just in bed," he smirked, "but just everything about you. Once I noticed that spark in your eyes at that bar all those months ago, I haven't been able to get you off my mind since. Every combative, feisty thing about you had me hooked more and more. I sure as hell wish I had seen that spark sooner."

My face heated from his words, and his touch on my shoulder and neck burned deliciously. It had me pressing my thighs together the more he touched me. I think he could tell by the smug look in his eyes. It was annoying, but made me heat up more.

"I'm still fucking here," Dad walked back in, taking his chair again. "And I heard that little bed comment, you bastard."

"Oops," Chris didn't sound sorry at all. "My bad."

"Little shit," dad ran a hand down his face. "Oh, boy. What a fucking morning. I need a nap already."

"I'm sorry, dad," I said apologetically.

"It's not because of you. I had to get up at the butt crack of dawn. You know Adrian slept on your couch last night? Poor Missy. Landon locked himself in the bathroom, and she had to call me to get him free since that punk didn't have his phone."

I thought something was off in my house when I got here.

"Adrian spent the night here?!"

"Yep. Got too drunk to drive home by the looks of it," dad waved at the beer bottles on the ground. "He is paying for it now."

Dad had that look on his face, like he had a secret he was just itching to tell.

"Paying for it, how?"

"Well," he huffed. "He's going on a hunt right now, and by that phone call just now, I'd say he's not going to find what he's looking for soon."

Chapter Seventeen

Missy

"Look! Look!" Hailey said excitedly, pointing at the night sky.

Shooting stars were passing by overhead. I laughed, pointing up at the sky for Landon, so he would look away from his s'more for two seconds. He was on his third and final one.

Four folding chairs were set up right outside the camper door. Rick helped me tow it out here this morning, after first helping me drill through and then change the locks on the kids' bathroom door.

Landon decided he was a big boy and could poop by himself and then screamed bloody murder when he couldn't get the door open to ask for help to wipe. My thick-headed husband never came home, so I had no choice but to call Rick before the sun even came up.

That poor man. He and Roseanne kept Mike and Izzy's kids' last night, so he probably didn't get much sleep. Then I had to call him bright and early because his son was acting like an idiot and his grandson was equally stubborn as his father.

Thankfully, Rick had extra door knobs without complicated locks to switch out the bathroom one with. He went ahead and switched all the bathroom knobs so it wouldn't happen again while listening to my replay of what happened with his son last night.

To say he was upset would be an understatement. Rick looked livid as could be as he hooked the camper up to his truck. He originally was going to pick Adrian up and force him to stay in the camper at his house for a while, but I had a better idea. An idea to get Adrian out of Brittany's and Chris's hair for at least a day.

"Mom, can I get the binoculars?"

Hailey had a big book of constellations on her lap that Britt had given her on her birthday. It went with a telescope we had given her. I think this is the first time she has actually used it. She usually just uses an app on her phone, but we don't have cell reception out here.

The night was clear and perfect for star viewing. I didn't think to bring her telescope when we left, but the binoculars are strong enough to work for now.

"Sure, baby. Do you know where they're at?"

"Yep. Aunt Britt put them in the chair."

She meant the storage seat underneath the kitchenette bench. It's where we hide everything we don't want Landon getting into.

Landon was licking the last of the sticky marshmallow off his fingers. I knew he was about to ask for more. He had that look in his eyes. It's the same look Adrian gets. Like father, like son. Neither are ever full, stubborn as all get out, and think they can boss me around to get what they want.

"Mama! More!"

I sighed, trying not to laugh. "No more, baby."

"All gone?" He puffed out his cheek, deciding if this was worth a temper tantrum.

"All gone, but if you wait until bedtime, mama will make popcorn and we can watch a movie."

His bottom lip jutted out and shoulders slumped forward. "Okay. We can watch mouse mouse?"

'Mouse mouse' were Tom and Jerry. Adrian got him watching that show not too long ago, and it's now Landon's favorite.

"Sure. I love mouse mouse."

"Mouse mouse is funny," Landon offered me a toothy grin. The tantrum has been avoided. For now.

"Mama. My dada is not here?" Landon looked back toward the trail we drove in on.

"Not yet," I sighed.

He nodded, sighing too. He was just copying me, but it was cute to see him act exasperated.

I thought about walking out towards the road a few times this afternoon to get reception to call Adrian, but I resisted. When Quinton took his first nap this morning, Landon and I walked down the trail a bit while Hailey sat with the baby. I called Rick and he said Adrian was looking for me. Furiously looking for me. If he didn't find me soon, Rick might come out to check on us.

I thought he would have figured it out by now. There are only so many places you can hide a camper in this town.

This was mine and Adrian's spot. He took me here on our first date. We ate smash burgers in the back of his truck and then made love under the stars. This might be where we conceived Landon. It's a strong possibility.

I know I texted him we could hide from him for days, but I was ready for him to find us. I miss the jerk.

"Mama! Quinton woke up!" Hailey yelled.

She came out of the camper two seconds later with Quinton in her arms, walking carefully down the camper steps.

"Baby hungry?" Landon asked as I took the baby and got ready to feed him.

"Your brother hasn't had his dinner yet," I told him, positioning Quinton to latch on after covering my chest.

"Come on, Landon. Help me find stars." Hailey held her hand out to her brother. He took her hand and followed behind her eagerly, skipping every few steps.

This has been a good day for the kids. We run on electronics so much that they needed a day to detox from the screens. Hailey is stuck to hers more than she should be, talking to her friends and playing her games.

Landon wants to be just like his big sister, so seeing Hailey playing instead of using the TV to distract her brother has been nice. I wish Adrian could have been out here with us today, too. The kids really would have had fun. Adrian was the funnest dad.

I was starting to feel a little dejected, missing my husband more and more by the second, when I heard tires pulling up on the dirt trail. I looked over just as headlights illuminated the entire field, making me almost go blind.

I recognized that truck. I spent a lot of time picking it out last Christmas.

"Daddy!" Hailey cheered. Her cheers were quickly followed by Landon's, both of them throwing their hands up in the air, running towards the slowing truck.

"About freaking time," I sighed, stuck in my chair as Quinton was still greedily feeding.

Adrian, my dear, temperamental, hot-headed husband, got out of his truck and slammed the door so hard I thought it might break. I cringed at the sound.

"Daddy! You found us!" Hailey wrapped her arms around his waist.

"Dada! You found us!" Landon latched onto his leg.

Adrian's furious eyes didn't move off me as he muttered, "Found you."

There was a threat in his tone. A threat aimed at me. Oh, this was going to be fun. I just was missing him before he showed up, but now I'm back to wanting to stick my foot up his tailpipe.

"Dada. We find stars, and... and we eat mish-mows. Mama said we can watch mouse mouse when we go night night!" Landon started spilling his entire day to his father.

Hailey picked up on his bad mood and was looking at me worriedly, falling back a little bit. Adrian looked wild. I didn't blame her.

He was in the clothes I had packed for him, and I considered making my first words to him a question about the postpartum diaper I had packed. I was curious if he was wearing it.

Instead, I just smiled brightly and said, "Hi."

His lip curled, and I could almost see the steam coming from his ears.

"We have leftover hot dogs and apple slices in the camper. Are you hungry?" I asked sweetly.

He didn't answer. His eyes swept down to my chest, seeing Quinton eating. I was suddenly thankful our youngest woke up when he did. If he was still asleep in the camper, I'm sure Adrian would have told Hailey to watch her brother while he dragged me off somewhere to start a fight.

"Dad!" Landon yelled, hitting his leg harder. "Dada! We watch mouse mouse and eat popcorn?"

Adrian flinched, but his jaw just tightened. He didn't say a word. He didn't even look away from me.

Hailey stealthily came up beside him and grabbed Landon's hand. "Come on, Landon. I'll make you another s'more and we can find the stars again."

Landon was instantly distracted by the promise of more sweets.

"Thank you, Hailey," I smiled at her as they passed by.

She nodded, then looked back nervously at her dad one last time before going into the camper and shutting the door behind her. She would still be able to hear everything since the windows were open, but Landon would be contained for now, at least.

With the big kids gone, I couldn't stop myself from asking, "How's the diaper?"

Adrian turned red, opening and closing his mouth several times before pacing away. He was holding the back of his neck, his arms flexed and he paced to cool himself down. I sat there patiently, waiting, letting him get it out of his system. I knew he was trying not to yell at me in front of the kids. At least he learned that during his time away.

When he was no longer red in the face, he stormed back towards me, quickly closing the distance. He leaned over me, quickly holding my face between his hands, and then kissed me senseless. I didn't resist. I missed him, too.

His kiss was desperate. Hungry. I could taste all his frustration, all his anger and worry. The tension in his body was evidence of how stressed and anxious he had been all day. He doesn't do well without me. I know that, but I also wasn't going to let him off easy for what happened last night.

He would not let me off easily for today. If we didn't have a baby between us, he would already be towing me off to really let out his frustration.

"You piss me off. You know that, right?" he gritted out, his teeth clenched as he rested his forehead on mine.

"You want to go there?" I laughed dryly. "Do you not remember last night?"

He groaned, standing back up. "That's fucking different."

"Fucking different how?" I raised an eyebrow.

"I didn't lock you out of our house!"

I laughed, grinning ear to ear. I now knew he listened and didn't try going back to the house. I half expected him to, but it's obvious he didn't.

"Who locked you out?"

"You!" he huffed.

"Hmm," I tilted my head. "I don't remember locking you out of the house."

"You said you did!"

"When?" I tilted my head the other way.

"Are you fucking serious, Missy?! In your damn texts!"

I pursed my lips, shaking my head. "I don't believe I said that. I think what I said was that my very helpful, amazing, sweet and available father-in-law changed the locks. I never said which ones."

Adrian looked down at me like I was stupid. "What does that mean?"

"That means, sweetie, that when our son decided to lock himself in the bathroom this morning, I had no way of getting him out. The lock was stuck. You left your phone in your little tantrum, so I had to call your dad, waking him up before the sun was even in the sky. Rick had to drill the lock, and then he changed all the bathroom locks in the house, so next time you decide to run off without your phone, leaving me alone with three babies, I wouldn't panic if it happened again."

Adrian's mouth dropped, all anger gone as guilt clouded his face. He placed his hand over his mouth, looking down at Quinton squirming on my chest before staring up at the camper, then back at me.

He finally got it. The wheels were turning in his head as he added up all the ways he had messed up last night and then today. I bet he was even adding in his little fit he threw when he got here, telling me I pissed him off.

What I did may have been a little shitty. Leaving in the camper to hide from him for the day with our three kids and not telling him where we were was petty. But it doesn't compare to how he left me. That without adding in the way he treated Chris and his sister.

"Shit," he groaned, throwing his head back. "Fuck, I'm an asshole."

"No arguments here," I scoffed.

As I was switching Quinton from one boob to the other, Adrian watched, his eyes filled with so much regret. I didn't need to say anything more. I knew he was going to be kicking his own butt now that he knew the truth about the locks.

But just one more little comment wouldn't hurt...

"I almost had to look up another handyman. That could have been fun. Last time I called a handyman over to fix something wrong in my bathroom, I ended up pregnant."

"Missy," Adrian said my name like a warning.

"Yes?" I stared up at him innocently.

He sighed and dropped down to his knees, resting his arms and chin on my lap. "If I grovel, will you stop?"

"Stop what?" I blinked in surprise.

"Stop being mad at me? Stop making me feel like I got a fucking knife in the heart you keep wanting to twist every few seconds?"

"Sounds violent," I laughed softly.

Adrian stared up at me with eyes like his son when he's scared of getting in trouble, making it impossible to stay mad at him.

I grabbed his chin and pulled him up to me, so our faces were just an inch apart. "Go put my babies to bed while I finish up getting this one fed, then we can finish this discussion in the back of the truck."

His eyes lit up, and a slow grin turned up his cheeks. "Yes, ma'am."

I pecked his lips, then sat back, ready to relax and listen to Adrian deal with Landon's sugar crash. That would be punishment enough.

As he stood, he stretched his arms up in the air. His shirt rose, revealing his entire midriff and a plastic hem poking out of the top of his pants. I quickly covered my mouth to hide my laughs.

He made a show of stretching some more, staring down at me with a smirk. "One way or another, these things are coming off in that truck, so be ready."

Then he strutted towards the camper, leaving me with the mental image of my husband in a diaper.

Chapter Eighteen

Brittany

"So, you're back home now?"

"Yep! Adrian is backing the camper into the garage right now," Missy said cheerfully, sounding so much happier than I expected her to be. "Hailey and I might stop by before picking the dog up from your dad's. Thanks for coming to check on Pickles for the last few days."

"No problem. I'm happy to help."

"See you soon!" Missy said, before hanging up.

Missy and Adrian camped out for the rest of the weekend, and just got back tonight, Sunday night. I have to hand it to my sister-in-law. She knows how to handle my brother better than anyone. He hasn't called me once, only sent me a short text two days ago.

Adrian:| I'm sorry I yelled. Tell that asshole if he hurts you, he's dead.

It was almost an apology and made me laugh when I got it. Chris, not so much. He scoffed, then when we went to feed Missy's cat, he kept threatening to scrub the cat's teeth and ass with my brother's toothbrush.

I probably shouldn't have brought Chris with me to do that chore, but he's been clingy since the ordeal with Elias happened. He's barely been away from me. My dad took me with him alone for a few hours right after the incident, so we could talk and visit his lawyer, and then Chris had to leave for a little while to get necessities for himself. I wouldn't let him share my toothbrush, no matter how adamant he was that it was the same as kissing. It still grosses me out to think about my toothbrush in anyone else's mouth.

When he went to his house to get clothes, he was gone for maybe twenty minutes and brought back an entire duffel bag full of his stuff. Lifting my eyebrow, I asked him if he was moving in. "You offering?" Chris replied with a crooked smile, so I dropped it before he actually did it. He has a way of breaking down my defenses and logic, and I didn't want to give in to something that premature.

He was worried. I get that. With Elias showing up like he did, causing that scene in the coffeehouse, I knew it was just a matter of time before he showed up again somewhere in town. I had already gotten a few emails asking to speak, so I knew he hadn't left yet.

Tomorrow is Monday. The long weekend will be over, and I know the university has classes. He will lose his chance at tenure if he doesn't finish out the term and leaves it to his PA. He will have to go back.

I'm hoping that means Chris will feel comfortable enough to go back home, or at least go back to work. If not for my brother, then for his brother at the mechanic shop. I have been so overwhelmed with

Chris twenty-four-seven that I haven't had much time to think about what to do about my ex-professor.

Dad took me to his lawyer friend, and we decided to put a retainer down just in case something bad happened. I hadn't considered the possibilities of repercussions if our relationship got out. Not serious ones, anyway. I thought the worst that could happen would be that I'd be looked down on, or maybe the class I took with him would be invalid, and I would just have to take it again.

The lawyer pointed out other scenarios in which I wouldn't be given my diploma, and some others where I might have to pay back my financial aid. Even the scholarships I had could be revoked, and I would be left without a degree and in huge debt. I honestly thought Elias had the most to lose from our affair, but I could lose just as much, if not more.

I probably need to talk to Elias and get this all taken care of, so this shameful chapter of my life could be closed for good before it gets that bad. His wife obviously found out about me. It wouldn't be that much of a stretch to think the school could find out about the relationship we had, too. It wouldn't matter that it was long over now.

I had so much to think about. So much to sort out and consider. It was just impossible to do any of that with Chris here.

As much as I needed to think on my own, I just didn't have the heart to tell him that bluntly yet. He was growing on me. More and more by the second. Even the persistence and clinginess I used to find annoying, I was getting butterflies for now.

"Babe! I need a plunger!"

Nevermind.

"That's disgusting!" I yelled as I passed the guest bathroom to head into the master.

Adrian had just hooked the plumbing up in the master bath last week, so it's the bathroom I've mainly been using. Once the floor is laid in my bedroom tomorrow, I can start setting up this place to feel more like a home.

Having Chris here with me was making the house feel more homey. He's been randomly fixing stuff that I would usually have to wait for my brother to get to, like the electrical work in the kitchen for the fridge, and installing the rods in the closets so I can unpack clothes.

The living room looks very lived in right now. It looks like some cheap set for a porno. There are blankets and pillows spread out on the ground from us crashing here on the floor while watching a movie last night.

"Ha," I sighed. "Guess I need to get cleaned up for company."

"Company?" Chris walked in, buckling his belt. "What company? You expecting someone?"

My eyes involuntarily roamed to his exposed torso, his jeans hanging a little low, so his happy trail showed to the top of his boxers. He still hadn't put on a shirt today. I wasn't complaining before, but Adrian will have a cow if Missy sees him like that.

"Missy and Hailey might stop by, so go get on a shirt."

Chris looked worried for a split second. "Uh, just Missy and Hailey?"

I smirked. "I'm not sure. She didn't say."

"Huh," he scratched the back of his head. "So, your brother....."

I had to press my lips together to stifle my laugh. "I think you're safe. Missy wouldn't bring Adrian here yet. She knows you're here."

Chris instantly relaxed. "Yeah? Cool. That's cool. I mean, not that it wouldn't be if he came to. I just, you know, didn't want to have to lay your brother out in front of you or anything."

"Uh, huh? Sure," I laughed. "Go get your shirt, then help me get our mess cleaned up."

Chris helped put the bedding back on the bed and threw away all the beer bottles and pizza boxes from the last few days. I tried to hurry and wash all the tupperware I had stolen from Missy's with leftovers we helped ourselves to. She had leftover pulled pork and also some kind of taco bake that was to die for. Even Chris said so.

Adrian likes his leftovers from Missy, so I know she will need the containers back. He might bitch about the food being gone, but he was gone for days, so he can kiss my ass if he wants to complain. He shouldn't have thrown a fit like a brat if he didn't want me to take his leftover food.

As I was finishing up drying the dishes, and Chris was in the bathroom, probably cleaning his mess from earlier, because I could smell bleach wafting down the hall when the doorbell rang.

"Shit!" Chris muttered.

I laughed under my breath, then yelled out, "Keep scrubbing!" as I made my way to the door.

They got here faster than I thought they would. I expected Missy to take at least an hour trying to slip out without Adrian and the boys. It's dinnertime, and the boys get irritable when they're hungry. All of them.

I didn't even check as I pulled open the door, swinging it in with an expectant smile.

That smile dropped quickly when my eyes met the person on the other side.

It wasn't Missy. It wasn't Adrian or my dad, or anyone else I would have expected. It wasn't even Louisa, who would be a lot more welcome to my home than the person standing before me.

"Elias," I whispered, my blood running cold.

His lips pulled up into his easy, familiar grin. "Hello, Brittany. I hope I am not disturbing you. May I come in?"

***

Chris

"Good lord, what did I eat?" I groaned, scrubbing the huge stain I had left behind.

Eating nothing but pizza, leftovers and beer for days was not a good diet for healthy digestion. That was for damn sure. Thank fuck Brittany is cool about shit like this. She wasn't squeamish at all like other girls would be.

Damn, I'm falling for her more and more every day. By next week, I expect us to be shitting with the doors wide open, hiding nothing from one another. That's how committed love should be, right?

"Hey, babe. How about salads for dinner tonight?" I said as I came out of the bathroom feeling accomplished, and surprisingly, a little hungry. "Or maybe subs. Something with a vegetable on it. I can't push out any more of these monster-"

My words stopped as I stepped out into the living room and saw Brittany standing at the door with the Dickhead on the other side of the screen with flowers in his hand, the two of them just staring at each other. Brittany looked panicked, but that asshole looked a little too happy.

"What the fuck. Are you fucking stalking us now? How the hell did you find her house, you piece of shit?" I stomped over to the door, pulling my stunned girlfriend behind me.

Professor Dickhead reluctantly pulled his focus away from my girl and onto me, his smile becoming forced.

"Hello to you too."

"You fucker." I clenched my teeth. "I thought I told you-"

"To take my snooty ass back to Eugene?" He interrupted me, coldly. "Yes, I received your message. Forgive me for not trusting that Brittany was, in fact, taken care of. Considering your circumstances and the chatter around town, I was finding it hard to leave the woman I love, my sunshine, to someone like you."

Brittany scoffed softly behind me. "You never loved me, Elias, or you wouldn't have put me in the situation that you did."

His eyebrows pulled down. "What situation would that be? I tried to protect you."

"You put my future in jeopardy!" Brittany raised her voice. "Forget the fact you are married-"

"Was married," the dickhead corrected her.

"MARRIED!" Brittany emphasized. "You can't just show up in my hometown. At my fucking home! If the school finds out-"

"They won't." Elias took a step forward, almost pressing against the screen. "That's not even an issue."

"It wouldn't be if you fucked off like I told you to do," I snapped. "Why don't you play the airplane game and take off, you prick."

"Brittany," the dick completely ignored me. "I know you. I know that this town, this," he gave me a snooty glance, "gentleman, is not what you want or need. You deserve so much more than what this town can give you. So much more than this country bumpkin can give you."

He took a heavy breath, his eyes boring past me to my girl. My girl, who had been completely silent for the last few seconds, did not deny anything this asshole had to say.

"I'm fully divorced now, Brittany," he continued on. "I was never with her while we were together. We were separated, just anticipating the inevitable divorce before we ever became involved." He placed his hand on the screen. It was like I wasn't even there. "I love you. I've been in love with you since you first set my gloomy life ablaze with your sunshine and wit. If you could give me another chance, I can do it right this time. I can show you how much you mean to me and give you the world."

Silence. Brittany still didn't say a word, and I felt this burning ache of worry in my chest.

The asshole slowly stooped down, setting the flowers on the porch before standing back up, never moving his gaze off her.

"I have to go back for now, but I hope to hear from you soon. Please," his voice shook slightly, "come back to me. At least give me a chance to start fresh."

Another long silence stretched between the three of us. Between the two of them. It felt like they had both forgotten I was there. He was staring at her so intensely, and she was pressing her lips together to the point where they turned white, and moisture was glistening in her eyes.

"I'll be waiting to hear from you," he said, pressing his hand to the screen one last time before turning and walking back to his out-of-place car.

I just stood there, dumbfounded, beside Brittany as he got in his car and drove away.

Chapter Nineteen

Brittany

"I'll be waiting to hear from you."

I didn't know how to react. I didn't know what to do or say as Elias carried on about knowing me or whatever. I was worried about saying anything and dragging this bull shit conversation out any longer. I argued back, but that just seemed to stir him up more. I decided to shut up and wait him out instead.

My neighbor across the street, an older woman that I think just waited in her front window for something interesting to happen, was already peeking out her curtains. I'm sure more rumors are going to spread around town now. Kicking Elias off my porch would make things worse. If I just stood there and let him say his peace before he took off, I thought that would make the rumors more vague.

I do need to talk to Elias. But not about the bullshit he was spewing. If I lose my degree because of him, I might very well recruit my brother to deal with him the Adrian way, and we can use the retainer fee to deal with the aftermath.

My degree was all that was on my mind. I worked hard to finish school. I would be crushed if all my hard work was ruined because of my stupid mistake with my professor.

Why can't he just leave me alone?

"Are you shitting me right now?" Chris mumbled.

I looked up, coming out of my worrisome thoughts. His eyes were shadowed in anger, which took me back for a moment. They weren't directed in the direction that Elias just drove off in, like my worried eyes had been. They were glaring down at me.

"You can't be fucking serious."

"What?" I furrowed my brows in confusion. Why did he look so pissed off at me?

"You're actually considering reaching out to that bastard now, aren't you?"

My mouth hung open for a second before I recovered. "What the hell are you talking about?"

"You," Chris practically growled. "You just stood there. Nothing to say?"

"What the hell did you want me to say? Did you want me to invite him in for a beer?"

"No, but a clear 'fuck off and never come back' would have been nice."

I pinched the bridge of my nose. "You said that clear enough for both of us. I just wanted him to leave."

"That's why you listened to his crap instead of telling him to leave?"

Now I was getting angry. "Did you want me to knee him in the crotch and choke him out or something?"

"Yes!" Chris stressed. "Fuck, Brittany. You didn't say shit. You were listening to the guy like you were hanging on to his every word."

"I just waited for him to finish talking and leave."

"Could have said it," Chris muttered, pushing past me.

I followed him, confused by his sudden outburst of anger. I did nothing to invoke this. I was just as pissed, but my anger was directed at Elias showing up at my house the way he did. How did he even know where I lived?

Now I'm getting irritated at Chris too for getting huffy about shit that wasn't my fault.

"Did you give your address?" Chris asked as he started moving around the bedroom, stuffing all his clothes in his bag. Was he packing to leave?

"Did I give Elias my address? Are you serious?"

"Elias?" Chris scoffed. "Back to first names and not Professor Dickhead anymore?"

"You're the one being a dickhead right now. What has gotten into you?"

Chris stopped, looking exasperated as he put one of his hands on his hip, the other moving warily down his stressed face.

He looked lost for a second, then sighed and finally met my eyes. "Are we dating right now, Brittany?"

His question confused me. Didn't we already establish that we were? Did he think I would just spend the past few days locked in my house playing house with him if we weren't dating?

Maybe he did. It's not like we hadn't slept together before this anyway. I didn't know if he wanted reassurance, or if he was trying to make some hypothetical point in asking.

"Huh. Guess not." Chris looked pissed again, and I realized I hadn't answered him yet, even though it had been a few seconds. I was too taken aback by his entire demeanor. I thought it was a hypothetical question, anyway. Huh. Guess not.

"Chris," I groaned, feeling like I was just taken by a whirlwind of craziness and raging emotions that came out of nowhere. "You're really pissing me off."

He scoffed, shaking his head. "Same here. Let me just get out of your hair, so you can talk to him like you want. You already gave him your address, it seems. Guess the asshole is unblocked again?"

I knit my brows together. "I haven't said shit to him. But apparently you have."

Elias mentioned something about Chris messaging him. I had no idea. How or when Chris could have done that was the real question. I've had Elias blocked, and I doubt they just magically exchanged numbers somehow.

Chris turned his face to the side, but not before I saw the defiant guilt flash in his eyes. "So what if I did? Fuck him. Fuck him and his snobby ass."

"Chris," I let my face fall into my hand. Did he provoke Elias? Is that why he showed up here?

"Brittany," Chris mocked my tone, still shoving his stuff around in his bag.

And how the hell did Elias find out where I lived? My head is pulsing, trying to stir up some logical possibility as to how he found my address. This place was never listed in my school documents. Only my dad's address was. Did he go to my dad's house? My dad and Roseanne would tell him anything about me. That can't be where he got my address.

This is a small freaking town. Maybe Louisa told him where to find me. Anyone could have. Maybe that isn't the right thing to get hung up on right now.

I sighed heavily, dropping myself on the bed as wariness and stress pressed in on me like a ton of bricks. Chris was staring at me, looking more sad and tired than angry now. It was like all the anger just subsided from both of us, leaving us in this awkward state of silence and reflection. I was scrutinizing every single second of what had just happened, trying to make sense of it all.

"Hello!" I heard my sister-in-law's voice coming from the front room, followed by the soft slamming of the screen door. "Who left the flowers?"

"Shit," Chris scratched his head, grabbing his bag and walking past me out the bedroom door.

I hung my head a little, despair making my chest tight. Why was he leaving? Did Elias showing up make this all just too much for him? Did he just decide to give up? After all that persistence, was he done with me now?

"Chris!" Missy sounded excited, but then in a less enthusiastic voice she added, "Everything okay?"

"Go ask her," Chris muttered coldly. I could picture his expression, even though I couldn't see him.

"Mr. Chris? Are you leaving?" Hailey asked.

I got up, ready to fight if he was cold to my niece.

"Yeah, squirt," Chris sighed, sounding less hostile and just tired now. "I got to head out. Sorry."

His expression when I walked out matched his tone. He looked back at me, his eyes tightening slightly in the corners before he turned to the door.

Hailey looked at him like she suspected he had done something, then ran off to her room in my house, saying something like she was going to make sure Chris didn't mess with her stuff. Missy stood staring at the door, the flowers Elias left on my front porch in her hands.

"What happened here?" Missy asked, placing the flowers in the kitchen sink before turning to my fridge.

She must be planning a big grocery haul. She was assessing the meager contents, frowning at the beer bottles and pizza box. She kept side eyeing me. I knew she was trying to hide her concern, waiting for me to open up.

"What do you mean?" I played stupid.

"You know what I mean," she gave me one of her perfected mom looks. "Chris didn't look too happy when he left."

I huffed, rolling my eyes. "That's an understatement." I felt her gaze and tried not to look up and meet it. Eventually, I cracked. "Elias came here," I mumbled.

"Elias?!" Missy gasped loudly. "As in...."

I nodded, "Yeah. Professor Dickhead."

Missy's face was contorted in confusion, looking back at the flower, then at me. "You told him where you live?"

I huffed, shaking my head in disbelief. "No. Not at all. I have no idea how he found my house."

"Wow," Missy looked around, like she was assessing my entire house, just like she had just assessed my fridge. She then looked at me. "That's creepy, Brittany. Like, really scary. What if he comes back?"

I didn't think about that.

I wanted Chris to leave just long enough, so I could think, but now I desperately didn't want to be alone in this house. My heart clenched painfully in my chest, picturing the way he had just left.

Was Chris coming back?

***

Chris

"Shit," I hit my steering wheel, regretting leaving about ten seconds after I pulled out of Brittany's driveway.

I was pissed at the moment, but now I'm scared about what my outburst will mean for us in the long run.

I don't know why I got so mad. Maybe it was my own insecurities. Brittany was so hung up on that asshole for so long that it took her forever to take me seriously. Right when I got her serious enough to consider being with me, he shows up on her doorstep, spewing shit about being better for her than I am.

"It's bullshit," I grumbled, looking around me for a good spot to turn around.

I've been wanting to turn around for a while now. I keep getting this itch to go back to her, but then the heaviness of that slice between us after exploding comes back to mind, and I'm not sure about what to do.

Why can't she call me? Text me? Something! Why can't that stubborn woman tell me to come back? She was silent while that asshole was talking bull crap. She's being silent with me now, too.

She said she was just waiting for him to leave. Was she waiting for me to leave, too? Did she ever actually ask me to stay with her, or did I just decide that on my own?

Does it fucking matter? I finally had her. Why am I letting myself get worked up and sabotage everything like this? I should have stayed there and just fought with her until everything was settled. I shouldn't have given up like I did.

That's not me. Why did I leave?

I know why. My own insecurities are why I let everything get to me like I did. Fear of losing her. Fear that she would choose him and not me.

"Fuck that," I sneered. Like I would ever let that happen.

I kept driving until I got home, pulling my truck into my mom's driveway. Since I left, I might as well switch my laundry out and pack new clothes. I can go back smelling and looking good, then show her why I'm really the right man for her. No, I might not have a fancy degree or drive an overpriced foreign car that is too low to the ground to be considered comfortable. I am great with my hands though, and I know I can give her what she needs.

Brittany doesn't need the frills Professor Dickhead can give her. She needs what I need. Someone that makes her feel comfortable being herself, who she can fart and burp in front of. Someone that can keep up with her drinking and swearing. Someone who likes her flippant personality and who matches her stubbornness.

She needs me, and I need her. I'm not backing down. Just regrouping.

"I'm home," I yelled out as I walked in, bag over my shoulder.

"In here!" Mom yelled from the kitchen.

There was something about her tone that made me wary as I got near. Her expression as I walked into the kitchen told me she wasn't happy.

"What's going on?" I asked.

She waved her hand at the empty chair across from her. "Have a seat. We need to talk."

Chapter Twenty

Seated across from my mom, I could almost feel her tension. She was wringing her hands in front of her, almost like she was trying not to wring my neck.

"Your vein in your forehead is about to pop." I pointed to my forehead, indicating the vein in question.

Mom's eyes narrowed further. I expected her to laugh or even yell. She was deadly quiet, like she was still working out what exactly it was she wanted to say.

That scared me. It scared me a lot.

"Mom, whatever it is, just spit it out. I gotta get back to Brittany's-"

"Don't say that harlot's name in this house," mom cut off my words, gritting her teeth. "You're not going anywhere, Christopher Daniel Finley. I forbid it."

"Forbid what?" I asked in disbelief. Was mom serious right now? "You're forbidding me from what? Seeing my girlfriend?"

"Don't call her that!" She slammed her hand on the table. "Don't you ever call that dirty, home wrecking girl that!"

"Dirty home wreck-" I could even finish the word. "Who the hell are you talking about, woman?! This is Brittany Brewer." Brittany has always been one of the few girls in this town that's avoided the scarlet letter from my mom and her church-going group of friends. At least she was.

Mom scoffed loudly, throwing her entire body into it. "I know who she is. No better than her mother, that girl."

I was stunned for a second. No one ever mentioned Adrian and Brittany's mother. Not anymore.

"You're out of your damn mind," I muttered under my breath, still not believing this entire conversation.

"No, I'm not. You are, Christopher. That girl broke up a marriage, and now you're playing house with her." She shook her head. "You're the one out of your mind."

"I'm not listening to this." I stood up abruptly from the table, my chair scraping loudly against the linoleum.

"Sit your butt back down! I'm not done-"

"You are done," I snapped. "You don't even know what you're talking about. Brittany did nothing wrong here. You're assuming shit because of fucked up rumors."

"Don't you curse at me, Christopher Daniel!"

"Don't make me cuss at you!" I exploded, "Fuck, mom! You're trying to ruin the best thing that has ever happened to me and I won't let you! I mean, shit." I took off my hat and ran my hand through my messy hair. "I love her, mom," I stressed. "She's the endgame for me. Now that she's mine, I'm not letting her go for anyone. Even you."

Before she could argue more, I picked my bag back up and headed back for the door. Fuck clean clothes.

Mom muttered something as I walked out. It sounded a lot like "Over my dead body," but I didn't care to ask her to repeat it.

I meant what I said. Mom would not ruin this for me. No one was.

***

Brittany

"That's complete crap," Izzy huffed. "He didn't tell you to protect you? What does that mean?"

"It means he's an asshole. And a coward. He could have told her, and chose not to. Any man that claims to be protecting you by lying and hiding facts that could hurt you, isn't in fact protecting you. They're protecting themselves from your informed decision." Missy looked vicious, even with my nephew hanging off her boob. She was pissed when she found out what had happened.

I was sitting in Dad and Roseanne's living room, my stepsister and sister-in-law with me, as Dad and Adrian installed cameras and a security system in my house.

Dad and my brother were mad, but Missy's anger rivaled both of theirs. I think because of her own trauma, since she dealt with a whacked out stalker before. She related Elias to the fucktard that tried to kill her all those years ago.

Missy demanded I come stay with them until a restraining order could be put in place, along with several other things. She started pacing the house, checking all the locks and the windows, making sure there wasn't any way to get in.

For once, Adrian was the one that had to calm her down. The more I told her about what happened, and about what happened at the coffee shop, the more emotional she became. Her reserved anger turned into hysterically angry tears before I even finished talking.

Hailey called Adrian, and he showed up soon after. Then dad minutes after him. Dad promised Missy I wouldn't be alone for a second and that's when Adrian suggested a security system.

My brother also threw a few jabs at Chris, abandoning me in my time of need, but dad shut him down real quick. I didn't want to talk about Chris with Adrian, and Dad, thankfully, didn't ask where Chris went. Dad was too focused on securing my house.

Now I'm at dad's for the foreseeable future. Adrian looked a little too smug about Missy's suggestion to stay with them, so Dad stepped up and said he would put me until we figured something else out.

Stupid Chris. If he hadn't left like he did, I could just have stayed home. I didn't think he would leave me that easily.

My heart still felt heavy thinking about it. His expression when he left was enough to keep me from reaching out to him. I don't even fully understand why he got so mad. All because I didn't say more to Elias? What more could I have fucking said?

"Mama! Tan-Tan eat cookies!" Landon came running in the living room, telling on Ethan, Isabelle's kid. His little chubby cheeks were puffing out in a pout. Missy told him no when he had asked for one.

"Ethan Lewis Finley!" Izzy yelled.

"I only had one!" Ethan yelled back. "Grandma said-"

"After dinner is what I said! Grandma is not your mom. Put it back!"

"I want," Landon demanded, on the verge of a full-blown tantrum.

Izzy smiled apologetically at Missy.

Missy just sighed. "One cookie," she relented. "Ethan, give him one, then put the rest up until your grandma gets back, please."

"Okay!" Ethan yelled back, sounding pleased with himself. Probably because he didn't get in trouble.

"Those kids. No wonder they like coming over here so much," Izzy laughed with Missy. "They get filled with sugar and are never told no. Your dad is worse than my mom," Izzy looked at me.

"Aren't all grandparents like that?" My dad's parents passed away when I was in middle and high school, but I remember they were like that too. They spoiled me and Adrian a lot.

"You would be surprised," Izzy shook her head. "Josie and Ethan hate going to Mike's mom's house. That woman is too much, even for the kids."

I furrowed my brows. "What do you mean?"

Izzy sighed, leaning back in her seat like she was exhausted just thinking about Mrs. Finley. "She's just... a lot. Very cynical and overbearing. The kids don't like being corrected on every little thing they do, and I get tired of her advice about parenting really quickly."

"Scarlet's that bad?" Missy looked concerned, eyeing me from the corner of her eye. "I have only met her a few times, but she was always nice."

"Oh, she's nice when people are watching. She plays the perfect Christian woman well if she's out and about, but dealing with her at home is a different story. I love the woman. Since she gave birth to the man child I married, but it's hard to like her all the time, if that makes sense."

I knew what she meant. It wasn't much of a secret that Chris's mom was cynical and overbearing.

Missy was biting her look, looking at me oddly. She was probably concerned since I was dating Chris. At least, I thought I was. I have no idea what's running through that jerk's mind now.

Izzy stared between Missy and me, and then her expression turned into one of understanding, her mouth dropping open. "Oh, Brittany. I'm sure you have nothing to worry about. You and Chris just started dating. You two are older than Mike and I were, too. Chris is practically moved out now. As soon as that apartment above the shop is finished, I'm sure you won't be seeing much of her."

I shrugged, acting unconcerned. "I'm not worried."

"Yes, you are." Missy stared down at my hands, then back up at me. "You've been wringing the heck out of the throw pillow since we brought her up."

I frowned, tossing the pillow at her, aiming at her free arm, so I didn't hit the baby. "Fine. I'm worried. You've heard the bullshit rumors going around about me."

"Yeah, but they're exactly that. Bullshit." Missy tossed the pillow back at my face. "Anyone that knows you will know that."

I huffed on a laugh. "That woman doesn't care about the actual truth. She's going to run with the rumors. Won't she?" I looked at Izzy.

Izzy looked apologetic, but nodded softly. "She usually does."

I looked pointedly at Missy, who just sighed and shook her head. "Okay, but what can the woman do? Like Izzy said, Chris is moving out. I think the bigger issue right now is your stalker. We can deal with your boyfriend's mom later."

Missy was right, but it still bugged me. Scarlet Finley was not as big of a concern as Elias, but somehow, it felt like she still was. With the rumor mill running, and Chris leaving the way he did, I don't even want to imagine what's going through that woman's mind right now.

***

Chris

Flowers, check. Salads and a rotisserie chicken from the grocery store, check. Twelve pack of "I'm sorry" beer, check.

After a quick trip to the grocery store, and a side trip to the only store in town that sold clothes, so I could pick up a pack of underwear and t-shirts, I was finally on my way back to Brittany's.

I thought she would have called me at least once, but she hadn't. I was trying not to let that bother me. She was never the first to call me. Why would this be different? She probably needed to cool down and sort her thoughts out, too.

I'd give her my peace offerings, spend some time making up with her, then we could pass out naked in the living room watching DVDs like we had been doing. Easy. We'll be back to how we were before closing our eyes tonight, and can put all the bullshit from the day behind us.

I still can't believe all the crap my mom tried to feed me today. Mom called me once or twice after I left, leaving a nasty message about me making a huge mistake on her last attempt to call me, but she stopped after that.

I had hoped my mom would have given my girlfriend the benefit of the doubt. Guess not. She'll come around in time, I'm sure, but I'm not dealing with her shit talking right now. I'll set her straight later, when I actually want to talk to her again. Hearing mom say all that bullshit just made me want to get out of there and get to Brittany faster.

Pulling up outside of Brittany's house, I was surprised to see Rick and Adrian on ladders outside, both mounting cameras. One was pointed towards the street and the other Adrian was working on was pointed towards the detached garage.

"What's going on here?" I asked Rick as I walked up the walkway.

Rick looked me up and down, then went back to feeding a cable through a hole drilled through the wall. "What does it look like?"

"Looks like you're installing cameras."

"We got a genius here," he scoffed.

I stood awkwardly, bags and flowers in my hands, wondering if it would be okay to just walk past him into the house. The way I left Brittany earlier wasn't my proudest moment, but I wasn't sure if Rick knew about that.

"Um, need any help?" I asked awkwardly.

His eyes shifted down at me for a split second. "Nope. I think I got this."

"Huh," I sensed he didn't want to be disturbed at the moment, so I decided to just leave him alone. "I'll, uh, head in then," I moved around his ladder.

"Why?" Rick muttered. "My daughter's not in there."

I stopped with my hand on the handle. "Where is she?"

He shrugged his shoulders. "Not sure. Where have you been?"

I lifted my bags. "Getting clothes," I tried to smile, but I was sensing more and more that I might be the reason Rick was angry right now.

"Getting clothes, huh?" Rick wiped his hand on his bandanna before shoving it back in his pocket, then climbed down the ladder. "Did you decide to go get clothes and flowers before or after that asshole showed up at my daughter's house?"

Crap. I didn't want to answer him, knowing I was going to just piss him off further. "Missy was here," I ended up saying instead.

"Missy," Rick snorted. "She's about as scary as a bag of kittens. If that asshole came back, a lot of good she'd have done."

So that's why he's so pissed. "I was coming right back," I argued.

"I've been here for almost two hours, boy. Nice try. Now, Brittany isn't here, and she won't be back for a while, so I suggest you head out, too."

"Where is she?"

He shrugged. "Somewhere safe."

I was about to ask where that could be, feeling pissy myself now, but then Adrian walked around the house.

"What the hell are you doing here?"

My lips twisted into a scowl. If I didn't have my hands full, I would have flipped him the bird.

"Brittany's not here, asshole," Adrian added bitterly.

"I gathered," I muttered. "Where is she?" I asked Rick again.

"None of your fucking business," Adrian snapped.

"Hey!" Rick barked at his son. "Go do the back door. I got this taken care of. I don't need your help."

Adrian grumbled, but obeyed. He muttered "bitch" under his breath, but at least he wasn't throwing punches my way while my hands were full. That would be embarrassing, considering Brittany and everyone else already think the dude could kick my ass.

"The lot of you are going to do me in. I swear," Rick sighed, running his hands down his scruffy beard. "My daughter is at my house, where she will remain until we get a restraining order in place. That professor showing up here uninvited left a bad taste in all our mouths. All except yours, it seems."

"That's not true." It bothered me, but I let my insecurities get the best of me and left. "I told that dickwad to fuck off several times."

"Good for you," Rick moved to the bench, picking up another camera still in its packaging.

Good for me? I don't know why I'm standing here arguing with this old man. I needed to talk to Brittany.

I started walking back to my truck, then Rick yelled out, "No sleepovers at my place, boy! If that's where you're heading, you don't need those clothes!"

Fucking hell. Could this day get any fucking worse?

Chapter Twenty-One

"I don't know if I want you to see my aunt right now," Hailey safe-guarded the front door of her grandpa's house, using the other miniature people to form a barrier between me and the door across the stairs. "You touched my TV."

I got here five minutes ago, and before I was even out of my truck, Hailey ran to the front door and blocked me from going in. I thought she was on my side, but I guess her loyalty only goes so far.

"How do you know I was the one that touched your TV?" I sighed, gripping the flowers tightly. "Your aunt could have been the one to touch it."

"Nice try," Hailey popped her hip, putting her hand on it with so much attitude, she almost reminded me of Brittany. I smiled, despite the little girl's hostility. "Aunt Britt doesn't play Fortnite. You messed up my stats."

"Ah, come on," I groaned. "I had to practice somehow, right?"

"Oh, that's bad, Uncle Chris," Ethan clicked his tongue, shaking his head. "You suck at Fortnite."

Sighing, I scratched my head with my fingers, still gripping my flowers and the bags from my earlier purchases. They were getting heavy, and my hands were hurting.

Landon was looking at the bags in my hands expectantly, and I was Josie's favorite uncle. The two little ones would be easy to move. I thought about tossing the chicken to see if they would run for it, but I don't think Missy or Izzy would like me treating their toddlers like dogs. Hailey was my real obstacle right now.

"What do you want?" I asked point-blank. She wanted something. I could see it in her greedy little eyes.

She lifted her chin. "V-bucks."

"What the hell are those?"

Ethan sighed, exchanging a glance with Hailey. "Mama said Uncle Chris wasn't the brightest. I'm sorry."

"It's not your fault." Hailey's eyes narrowed at me. "I figured he wasn't, since he made Aunt Britt cry."

My heart sank. "She cried?"

Hailey shrugged her shoulders. "Give me V-bucks, and I'll tell you."

"Hey," I grumbled, waving the flowers at her like a weapon. They were all wilted and falling apart now. "You're not being very nice." I tamed down what I really wanted to tell the eight-year-old. "Little hustlers. How about I give you...." I checked my bags to avoid the one with the beer. "A deli chicken and salad if you let me pass?"

"Chick-um," Landon perked up. Hailey had to grab his chubby hand as he took a step forward. "My chick-um?"

"Sure," I smirked. "Just get your sissy to move her tail out of the way."

"Sissy move." Landon looked up angrily at Hailey. Hailey just wrinkled her nose at him, sticking out her tongue.

"What's in the other bags?" Ethan asked.

Josie was already on it, pulling at the plastic to see inside. She looked so disappointed to see the beer and underwear that I offered her the broken flowers to placate her.

"Underwear," I admitted to my nephew. "Want that too?"

"Eeeew!" all the kids said together.

"Ew?!" I shook my head. "Every single one of you fart rockets wears underwear!"

The curtains fluttered in the window beside the door right then. Probably because the kids were loud in their disgust of undergarments. Little brats.

Missy scowled at me from the other side of the window, then the door finally swung open.

"What are you doing here?" She asked, all huffy and puffy.

"Hello to you too," I scoffed.

"Fow-ers," Josie showed Missy the broken bouquet in her hands.

"My Chick-um!" Landon yelled, pulling his hand out of his sister's hold.

Missy pretended to admire the flowers Josie was showing her, but she noticed how messed up they were looking now. Her smile was forced.

"Pretty," she lied, then looked at me. "I've got a bone to pick with you, buddy."

I groaned, staring up at the sky. "Well, get in line. There's a long one forming."

"Because you made Brittany cry!" Missy hissed in a loud whisper.

So she really cried because of me? I hated but loved hearing that at the same time. She never called, so I thought she just didn't care.

"I did not cry," I heard Brittany's exasperated voice from inside the house. My heart quickened, and I straightened up, trying not to look so pathetic.

"You were crying on the inside!" Missy yelled behind her.

"The only one crying was you, crazy."

Brittany came up from behind Missy, opening the door the rest of the way, so she could see out. The dog ran past their legs out to the front yard, making the kids squeal and laugh.

They wouldn't part the sea for me, but a dog? Yeah. No problem.

While jumping out of the way of the dog and kids, the bag with the chicken in it broke free from my fingers, the plastic handle snapping from the sudden jerk. It dropped, and that stupid puppy stopped, nose up in the air. It circled around and snatched the fallen chicken rolling free from the broken plastic container, then darted for the open yard, dodging kids as it ran.

"My chick-um!" Landon screamed furiously.

"No!" Missy yelled, "There are bones in that! Stop, Hunter! Stop! Bad dog!"

"Shit," I muttered, putting the rest of my bags on the porch. Brittany was pressing her lips together, trying not to laugh as I raced off to help Missy rangle the dog.

The kids were running amok in the chaos. I almost wiped out twice, taking a kid with me as a casualty. Eventually, I managed to tackle the fucking puppy, tattered chicken and all, right into a muddy tire burnout pit.

The chorus of cheers from the kids and Missy's clapping did little to appease my annoyance. It wasn't until I heard Brittany's mystery laughter from the porch that I saw the humor in this situation. Brittany and Isabelle were holding each other in tears.

Good. If I ever make her cry, this is the way to make her do it. I'll wrestle a hundred puppies high on chicken fumes in mud pits if it makes her laugh like that.

"Bad dog!" Missy waved her finger in the puppy's face, then wrestled what was left of the chicken out of its mouth. "No chicken for bad dogs."

"No chicken for anyone," I groaned, struggling to hold the squirming puppy. "You owe me $10, you stupid mutt."

Missy giggled before ordering the kids to pick up all the chicken pieces around the yard. She then looked down at me.

"I guess you can come in now," she eyed the mud all over me and the dog with laughter in her eyes, "after you're done washing you and the dog with the hose."

"Are you serious?" I huffed. "I thought you were nicer than this."

"Oh, I'm the nicest person you'll ever meet. Until you give me a reason not to be." She raised her eyebrows.

"I didn't do anything! I thought you were on my side?!"

"I'm on Britt's side," she said matter-of-factly. "And after you left, Britt made a face I hadn't seen in months."

I swallowed down the lump in my throat and asked, "What kind of face was that?"

Missy looked back at the porch, at Isabelle and Brittany, still snorting and chortling to one another. Missy's expression softened, and I could see the adoration for her sister-in-law in her eyes.

"The kind of face that brings out the mean in me. Made me want to protect her all over again." She crouched down, getting level with me and the dog, then said in a low, serious tone, "Don't make me regret rooting for you, Chris Finley. It's not Adrian you need to worry about if you break his sister's heart. It's me."

I got it then. I got why everyone was so pissed at me, even though I felt like I didn't do much to deserve their wrath. Their fierce love for her far outweighed any feelings they felt towards me. I knew the Brewers were protective of their own family. I just was never at the brunt end of their protectiveness before.

Brittany was loved. I couldn't fault any of them for the way they loved her. Hell. I understood that feeling all too well.

A silent understanding passed between me and Missy, and I nodded, agreeing to her terms.

"Where's the hose?" I hoisted the muddy dog up in my arms, earning a sloppy lick on the face before he started squirming again.

Missy laughed, pointing to the back of the house. "Out back. I'll send out soap and towels to help."

Out back, I found the hose and an overturned children's pool leaning against the siding nearby. I awkwardly turned it over with my foot, then set the oversized puppy in the grass beside it before trying to wrangle him and the hose at the same time. I had to get the mutt rinsed before putting him in the pool, or we would just be swimming in muddy water instead of getting clean.

It took lots of cursing and wrestling, but I finally got both me and the dog rinsed from most of the mud and into the plastic pool without him getting free.

Then I heard the back door open.

"Your dog's a real pain in the ass," I sneered without looking up, thinking it would be Missy.

"Thanks," a sweeter, sexier female voice responded.

I almost let the giant turd of a dog go when I looked back and saw Brittany instead of Missy on the back porch. She had towels and a big bottle of dish soap in her hands.

"Damn it," I growled as I fell face first in the water, barely catching the mutt as he twisted out of my hold.

Brittany's full body laughter did that thing again. All my irritation turned into pride at hearing her laugh.

"Need some help?"

I was soaked head to toe, wading in the muddy filth. I had scratches and puppy bites all over my arms and legs. "As much as I'd love to wrestle around with you in this mud, I don't think it's a good idea to vet dipshit here, more excited than he already is."

"Hmm," she bit her bottom lip, eyeing me with a teasing smirk. "You make it look so fun, though."

Fuck. That look in her eyes was going to make washing this giant bucking fleabag so much harder. Hard, harder.

"I tell you what. After I'm done washing him, I'll muddy you up, and you can be next."

Her blue eyes lit up. "Is that a promise?"

"If you want it to be!"

She looked hopeful, then shook her head. "Maybe some other time. Four little sets of eyes are watching us right now, and Dad's on his way back with my brother."

I scoffed, wanting to muddy her up and wash up right here in the open of her dad's backyard all the more after what happened earlier at her house.

Then I thought about what Missy said, and that cooled me down quite a bit.

"Hand me that soap?" I nudged my chin at her hands.

Instead of handing it to me, she set the towels down on the steps and rolled up her sleeves, helping wash the mutt as I held him still. With her doing the washing and me doing the holding, it went a lot smoother. He was clean in minutes.

I couldn't say the same for myself.

"That's my good boy." Britt grabbed his collar and led him to the stairs. He shook violently, sending water flying everywhere, so Britt was covered now too. She just laughed and squealed before grabbing a towel and drying him off as best she could.

"Hailey! Come get your dog!" she yelled, leading the puppy up the stairs, then pushing him inside while handing the rest of the towels to Hailey.

Hailey gave me a look before the door shut. I probably looked like an idiot, sitting soaking wet in the dirty pool, but I was too busy staring at Brittany to move.

"You need help there?" Britt raised an eyebrow.

I shrugged. "I'm waiting for you to wash me, too."

She laughed, shaking her head, but walked down the steps with the last clean towel, offering it to me.

"How about an actual shower inside?"

As she handed her towel to me, I grabbed her arm instead and yanked her into the pool with me. She fell on top of me with a high-pitched scream. I caught her laughing at her surprised, pissy expression.

"What the hell?!" she sputtered, pushing her wet hair out of her face.

"Oops," I laughed heartily. "My hand slipped."

"Your hand slipped?!" she yelled, then squealed again as I rolled with her beneath me.

She was submerged from her neck down as I looked over at her. She sounded pissed, but she was smiling, a playful glint lighting her eyes.

"Slipped again," I muttered, then made a show of slipping and pressing all of my weight into her.

That fire lit in her eyes, and I knew I had to stop, or we'd be giving four sets of little eyes a show that could put me on everyone's shit list all over again.

Grabbing her tightly, I rolled us over again, so this time she was on top. She was in control, but made no moves to get off from straddling me.

"Now I need a shower, too."

My cocky grin could not be contained. "Good. I'm your good boy, too. Wash me."

"Are you my good boy?" She challenged, raising an eyebrow.

No. I was her insecure boy who fled earlier at the doubts creeping into my mind.

"Maybe just your boy," I admitted somberly. She looked confused for a second until I elaborated. "I acted like a jealous brat earlier instead of like the man you needed me to be. I'm sorry."

Understanding softened her face, and she nodded, looking a little guilty herself.

"I get it. I got a lot of baggage. If I were you, I would have run away too."

It hurt to hear her say such things about herself.

"No, baby. No. Don't mistake my insecurities as your own baggage." I brought my hand to her worried face, smoothing some of the frown lines near her perfect lips. "You're too good for me. I always knew that, but somehow deluded myself into thinking I was a big shot for finally getting the Brittany Brewer to agree to go out with me. I was humbled today. That was all. You have no baggage. When I look at you, all I see is perfect, and that scares me sometimes."

"I'm far from perfect." she looked down shyly.

I scoffed, wishing she could see her the way I see her. Just for a second.

"There isn't a single thing about you I would change."

She looked up at me through her lashes. "Nothing?"

I adamantly shook my head. "Nothing."

I like my girl when she's feisty and back-talking. When she's strong and confident, ready to tell me off when she's pissed, and ready to knock a mother fucker out when there's a need.

This shy, meek demeanor isn't what I want her to be when she's with me. I should have manned up today and stayed instead of running off like a little boy when something happened I didn't like. Maybe she wouldn't be making this kind of face now.

"I'm sorry I acted like a boy today," I brought her face closer to mine. "From now on, I'll try to be the man you need me to be."

A slow, shy grin lit up her beautiful face. "That was cringy as fuck, Mr. Man."

I threw my head back and laughed at her jab. "That's my girl," I soared, loving the return of my feisty Britt.

I didn't care if eyes were watching us from inside. I needed to at least kiss her right now.

As I was leaning in, ready to at least claim her lips, the back door flew open.

"Get your crusty lips off my sister!"

"You ass! I said to leave them alone," Missy appeared behind her husband, reaching up to grab Adrian's ear and pull him back inside. "Sorry!" She yelled at us over Adrian's cursing protests. "Continue with your smutty mud bath!"

As the door slammed closed, and we heard the loud tones of Missy and Adrian fighting, Brittany and I just stared at each other before bursting into laughter.

"Lord, he's never going to change." Brittany rested her head on my shoulder as her body continued to shake with laughter.

"Yeah," I chuckled, rubbing her back. "I guess not."

To be honest, I don't want him to change. I don't want anybody in this family to change their protective affection for the girl who only shows her vulnerability to those she loves.

Chapter Twenty-Two

"Stay out of my room," Hailey glared at me as Brittany and I stood together at her father's front door, wishing everyone bye.

"That's awfully stingy of you." I rubbed my chin.

"I don't care." Hailey crossed her arms sternly over her chest. "You're making me look like a noob."

"Like a boob?!"

Brittany hit me sharply with the back of her hand. "Quit picking on a child."

"I'm not! She called herself a boob!"

"Noob!" Hailey stomped her foot as my nephew laughed at me. "You're like an old man."

"What a boomer." Ethan elbowed Hailey and the two of them giggled like little gremlins.

“Quit picking on your uncle,” Roseanne rested her hands on Ethan’s shoulders. She smiled at me as sweetly as one of her sugar cookies. “Thanks for staying for dinner. You’re welcome anytime, Chris.”

“Don’t tell him that, mom,” Izzy smirked at me. “He’ll eat you out of house and home.”

“Will not,” I argued before kissing Roseanne’s cheek. “Dinner was great. Thanks again.”

Dinner was anything but great, with multiple people glaring at me the whole time, but the food was good, and Roseanne’s always nice, so my complaints don’t lie with her.

“Are you sure you’re going to be alright?” Missy asked Brittany in a low voice that was full of concern. “I really think you should stay here with your dad.”

“Me too,” Adrian huffed gruffly, sending me another murderous look. “Better yet, just move your stubborn ass back in with us.”

Brittany looked at me from the corner of her eyes, amusement playing all over her features. I had already promised her dad up and down a million times over that I wouldn’t leave her alone in her house again. I’m not making the same mistake twice. I should have known better with all the trauma this family has about crazy stalkers.

“I think my stubborn ass will be fine.” Brittany rolled her eyes. “You guys are making a big deal out of nothing.”

“It’s not nothing,” Missy huffed. “Maybe I should just stay with you, too.”

“NO!” Adrian and Brittany said at the same time. Obviously, for different reasons.

I slid my arm around Brittany’s shoulders, pulling her close to me, despite the angry glare from her brother. “I’ll be by her side all night. Well into the morning.”

"You mother fucking-"

Missy slapped Adrian's chest, then sent a pointed look at the kids not two feet away, watching everyone with open ears and wide eyes.

"Watch your mouth. There are kids listening."

Hailey looked annoyed, but Ethan looked excited. The kid liked the idea of me potentially getting into a fight; it seems. Since my brother showed up for dinner with Roseanne and instigated a lot of Adrian's malice towards me, Ethan has been on the edge of his seat waiting for the first fist to fly.

Landon was mimicking his dad, saddled up on Missy's other side with a scrunched-up chubby face. He was trying to look pissed, and almost passed the mark. But I knew if I produced food of any kind, I could win him over.

"Un-koo Kiss be bad?" Josie pulled on my pant leg.

"Yeah, he's bad," Hailey mumbled. "He ruined my Fortnite stats."

"Holy heck," I pulled my wallet out of my back pocket. "How much are these freaking 'g-bucks' you want? How much will it take for you to forgive me for my sucky playing?"

Hailey eyed my wallet greedily. "It's V-bucks, Mr. Chris, and I think a hundred will do."

"Hailey," Missy said in disapproval.

"Fine." Hailey rolled her eyes. "Fifty."

"How about you forgive him and I won't ground you from your video games for being disrespectful to an adult?" Missy gave Hailey that look that made me want to get in line and obey.

"Mom! He is the one that went in my room and-"

"You are the one that asked him to play with you first. Drop it," Missy said sternly.

Hailey crossed her arms and marched off, looking ten ways to pissed and not budging from her attitude. She walked right into the kitchen where Rick and Mike were doing dishes, then I heard Rick ask her what was wrong.

It was time to leave, before the old man got all huffy and puffy with me again.

"Okay, well. Thanks again for dinner," I told Roseanne, giving her one last hug. "See you later." I hugged my sister-in-law, who looked like she was enjoying the banter at my expense way too much. I ruffled Ethan's and Josie's hair, avoiding Landon's since he looked like he would bite me. "Missy, see you soon. Adrian," I looked him square in the eyes, trying not to match his petty level of hostility. "I'll see you eventually," I muttered as I pushed Brittany out the door.

"Tomorrow!" Adrian yelled after us. "Be at work!"

"I quit!" I hissed under my breath as Brittany laughed at me.

"Two week notices are a thing, motherfucker!"

"Adrian!" Missy slapped his chest again.

Brittany was laughing her pretty little head off by the time I got her in my truck and went around to get in on the other side.

I stopped and just stared at her, feeling exhausted and exasperated. "Was that funny to you?"

She slipped down into her seat, head back and laughing freely. This is a completely different Brittany than the girl I first saw when I showed up there. She was herself, laughing uncontrollably at my expense. Fuck, she was beautiful.

I couldn't stop myself. I reached over the truck to grab her beaming face. Her fit of giggles just stopped as I brought my mouth down on hers.

"You're irresistible when you smile," I husked as I pulled away, staring into her beaming eyes like they were beacons to her soul.

"Fuck that," she bit down on her bottom lip with a mischievous gleam. "I'm irresistible all the time."

A deep, airy laugh escaped me. Lord, this girl was already my everything. I hope she realized that.

"Remember that when we get back to your house, because I'm not going to be able to hold myself back from your irresistible self."

"That almost sounds like a threat, Chris Finley."

"Oh, it's a solid promise, Brittany Brewer." The future Mrs. Finley, I wanted to add. I barely held myself back from saying that out loud.

The entire drive home was filled with the same level of teasing and banter. Brittany's bra even managed to find its way off and flung into my face right before we stopped at the only stoplight on the way to her house.

Fuck me. I almost parked the truck right there and took her for anyone to see. Wouldn't be the first time we put on a show for the gossip-hungry hens of this small town.

I managed to keep it in my pants until we got to her house, but the second my truck was in park, it was game on. She knew it too.

Brittany hurried out of the truck at the same time I flung myself out of the driver's door. Both doors slammed shut simultaneously as she sprinted for her front door and raced to catch up to her. The door was barely open as I caught hold of her waist and flung her over my shoulder as she squealed and laughed.

I made sure to flip the newly installed cameras off before shutting the door behind me. Heaven knows her asshole brother was watching right now. Two weeks notice my ass. I made a promise to their father to stay with Brittany. That's what I plan on doing. I'm going to stay diligently by her side from now until however long needed. Forever, if that's the case. Shit, I'm sure I could get some sort of job at the school when she starts working. Room helper Chris, professional kid wrangler. I can do it. For her, I would do anything.

Right now, I have all kinds of things in mind I want to do for her. All things involving less clothing and more teasing until one or both of us explodes.

"Fuck," I moaned, staring at her ass in my face. I bit down on it, earning me a punch in the back.

"No biting, you jerk!" she yelled and laughed, raining her fists down on my lower back.

"Fuck that," I growled, then bit down harder than before.

Brittany screamed, thrashing over my shoulder. I laughed darkly as I tossed her to the bed.

"Pants off. Now," I commanded, pulling my borrowed shirt off over my head.

"No! You're just going to bite me some more."

"Damn right I am," I huffed, kicking off my pants and grabbing the waist of hers to pull them off myself.

"Let me bite you, then. See how you like it."

I laughed at her threat. "Go ahead, darling. I like a little pain."

"We'll see about that," she sneered, hooking her legs around my waist and yanking me down on her half-naked body.

She locked her arms around my neck, holding me against her as she sank her teeth into my chin. I didn't expect it, hissing loudly as I bucked myself right against her moistening, warm center.

"You asked for it," I groaned, hooking my arms under her legs and opening her up for me.

With no preparation, I pushed into her. Her teeth loosened on my chin as a fierce groan escaped her. My woman arched her back, pushing into me as I rocked back and stretched her again.

"Fuck," she hissed. "Go faster."

I smirked, chuckling darkly to myself. "I'm good like this."

I slowly eased out of her, all the way to my tip so it was just kissing her opening, then slipped into her tight wetness again, moving at a snail's pace as she thrashed beneath me. My hands tightened under her knees, preventing her from taking what she wanted from me.

"I swear, Chris, if you don't move your ass-"

"What?" I laughed dryly, leaving lingering kisses along her jaw. "You gonna bite me again?"

"No," her eyes flashed with fury as I slowly rotated my hips, stretching her without sending her over the edge like she wanted. "Last chance, Finley," she closed her eyes, absorbing the torturously slow fiction between us.

"I'm so scared," I whispered in her ear, unable to hide my amusement. I was torturing myself too, but this was worth it.

"Fine," she huffed. Then her hands moved to my chest. I didn't know what she was going for until it was too late. She grabbed my nipples and twisted, making me buck away from her.

"Shit!" I looked down and rubbed my reddening chest.

"That's what you get," she sounded very pleased with herself.

I was still inside of her, but just barely. She kicked me away, so I fell on my ass on the ground, yelling like a banshee the whole way down.

Her giggles barely took the sting away from my sore ass and nipples. She climbed off the bed, taking advantage of my distress to mount me. She rocked her body on top of mine, her head hanging back as her eyes closed. I forgot all about the pain in my ass and chest as she rode me like the freak she was.

Grabbing her waist, I was about to pick her up and get us back on the bed, not wanting a carpet burn from her rug, but then she stopped and reached for my nipples again.

"Lay the fuck down and take it, Finley. I won't warn you again."

"Yes ma'am," I decided a carpet burn was worth it. This was almost too good to be real. I felt like I was suddenly living out one of my greatest fantasies. Brittany commanded her pleasure, riding me like a fucking porn star as I laid helpless to just watch. I was ready to bust a nut already.

Her grinding as she built the right kind of friction was fascinating to watch. Her eyes were clouded with euphoria. It was like she was high on my dick. I grabbed her hips and rocked her body, so her insides squeezed my dick just right. I could tell it was doing it for her too when she moaned even louder and her head fell back.

Her perfect tits were bouncing with every thrust. I felt like I had died and gone to heaven. Her hard nipples were taunting me. I had to taste them.

As my tongue and teeth teased her chest, her legs shook. "Fuck. Suck them harder, Chris," she demanded.

I groaned, doing as commanded. My hands were squeezing her ass and hips so hard as I slammed up into her, I knew she would have bruises. She was going to have marks all over her body, just from me. Her chest, her ass, her perfect skin. It would all be marked by the passion of this moment.

That caused me to suck, squeeze and slam into her even harder, making her scream. I wanted to imprint myself on her fucking soul, so no one else could ever affect her like this ever again.

"Cum on this dick like you own it, baby," I hissed, feeling my own ending coming.

"I do own it." Brittany grabbed the back of my hair and yanked it backward. "Say it," she seethed.

"You own it," I hissed with angry passion. "And I own this."

I slammed her down on me as I thrust up violently. She gasped as her body convulsed into endless spasms. She caught her breath and screamed an attempt at my name. Or maybe she was saying she was cumming. It was too hard to tell.

I took advantage of her spasms to get her on her back, hammering into her. Her convulsions didn't stop until long after I emptied myself into her. She was still writhing beneath me as I eased out of her.

"Mhmm," she spasmed one last time while biting her lip.

I laughed breathlessly, just watching her. "Feel good?"

"No," she lied, pulling me down to rest my weight on her. Her eyes sparkled as she gave me one of her devious grins. "You're going to have to try again."

Chapter Twenty-Three

Brittany

"I've never been on a family dinner date before," Chris mused, driving us to the diner to meet my family.

"You haven't?" I raised an eyebrow at him.

He gave me a confused glance, and then his face changed to apologetic when he realized what I was talking about.

I laughed lightly under my breath, enjoying his discomfort.

This was going to be the first time Chris was around all of my family since the incident at dad's house last weekend. Adrian still saw him occasionally at my house, but after Missy told him to leave Chris alone, or she would go for round two of hide-and-seek again, my brother had been less aggressive and just grumpy when they meet.

After the tension of that day died down, and the threat of Elias seemed to lessen, our relationship felt like it had slipped into a steady pace. The newness of it all is still there, but there is a comfort in the calm moment where we just exist in the same space at times that I have come to like. Every night we eat at my house and watch TV until our clothes end up coming off, or we fall asleep. Usually it's both of those things in that order.

Chris has been staying with me again. I thought that was because of Elias, but I think he's avoiding his mom, too. She will call him repeatedly at random times, but he never answers and just looks annoyed afterward. When I ask, he tells me not to worry about it. His mom was "just tripping" over something.

I can't help but to think that I'm the cause of her "just tripping" behavior. Izzy mentioned in a text once that I should avoid Scarlet for the time being. When I went with Chris to his brother's shop a few days ago, Mike mentioned something similar. Mike also said we were the talk of the church or something like that before Chris elbowed him and told him to shut up.

After the incident in the coffee shop, and the rumors spreading around, I knew I would be the talk of every social event in this town for some time, but I can't even imagine what Chris's mom might be saying.

"Peggy is your aunt, right?" I asked absentmindedly, staring out the window.

Chris gave me the side-eye, then said, "Yeah. You know she is. Why do you ask?"

I shrugged, trying to look passive. "I just wonder if your aunt disapproves of us like your mom does."

Chris sighed, then reached over to rest his hand on the back of my headrest. The fake leather protested in his grip.

"How do you know my mom doesn't like you?"

I looked at him like he was stupid, raising an eyebrow and said, "Educated guess."

"Fucking Mike. I told him to keep his mouth shut."

Chris had that same expression he always got when his mom started calling and texting him. It just confirmed to me that I was the problem.

With a heavy sigh, I went back to staring out the window. There was a noticeable tension in the truck now, and it didn't take long for Chris to break it.

"Damn it," he groaned. "I'm sorry, Britt. Mom's just...." He twisted his lips like he couldn't find the right words.

He was cute when he was distressed like this. It made me relax a little, seeing how much he was stressing over his mom.

I leaned towards him, resting my head on his shoulder. "I know. Izzy told me enough, so I know."

It's no secret Scarlet Finley is overly-righteous and outspoken about her beliefs. After the rumors spread, I didn't really expect her to like me.

"Please don't let it get to you, babe," Chris hugged my shoulder. "She didn't care for Isabelle much when my brother first got with her." He narrowed his eyes and added in a deep grumble, "He sure was better at keeping his fucking mouth shut about her opinions, then."

I bit back a laugh, because that same talkative spirit in Scarlet was passed down to her sons. At least they can hold themselves together to protect the feelings of the woman they care about. I liked it.

"So Peggy?" I lifted a brow, staring up at him.

His face softened, and he shook his head. "Nah. Peggy loves your family. You're her most loyal customers. Add that to the fact that she doesn't go to church either."

"So your mom doesn't like that I don't go to church?"

Chris pressed his lips together, like he realized he had said too much. That just made me laugh.

"You're a funny one, Chris Finley," I poked the corner of his cheek. "I don't remember you sneaking off to warm a pew last Sunday."

His eyes brightened, and a crooked grin lifted his face. "I was too busy warming your bed."

"I think that night we slept on the floor," I giggled. "Ah, maybe that's why your mom doesn't like me. I'm corrupting you."

"Every night," Chris's hand wandered to my butt, giving it a good squeeze.

I rested my head on Chris's shoulder the rest of the drive, just enjoying the silence as my thoughts of his mom kept running through my head. I don't envy him. I grew up without a mom for most of my life, but my dad and brother were so supportive and overprotective that I didn't feel a mother's absence much. Then Missy came. She was like the collective mother-figure for us all.

Scarlet doesn't seem like the supportive mother figure from what I've heard from Izzy. Over assertive and judgmental are better terms for her. I guess I shouldn't let it get to me that the woman doesn't like me. I just wish she hadn't been causing Chris so much trouble in the process of hating me.

We got to the diner, and I saw my dad's and Adrian's trucks in the lot, along with dozens of other cars. I took a deep breath, knowing I would see half of the town here tonight. There weren't many other places to eat, and this was the local hang-out before the bar picked up.

When Chris and I walked into the place hand-in-hand, a noticeable silence rested in the diner, many familiar faces turning to openly stare.

"Aunt Britt!" Hailey waved from a long table in the back. It was two six-tops pushed together. "Aunt Britt! Mr. Chris! Over here!"

"Hey squirt!" Chris put on a smile, then led us both to where my family was sitting. I tried not to hang my head as people continued to look our way.

"Right here." Hailey patted the chair next to her excitedly. Chris tried to sit there, but Hailey put her hands in the way to block in, frowning in deep offense. "Not you. This is for Aunt Britt."

People around laughed softly at Hailey's possessive display, which caused the awkwardness in the diner to dissipate. People started picking back up with their conversations again. That made me feel a little more relaxed.

There were always rumors floating around this town, but I had never been the center of them before. It was an uncomfortable feeling.

"I know! I know!" Chris grabbed the back of the seat, pulling the chair out. "I was just getting it for her. Chill out."

"No, you weren't," I mumbled with a laugh.

"Hush and sit," Chris winked at me, pecking my lips before I took the seat.

"Can you not?" Adrian groaned, looking disgusted. "I don't want to lose my appetite."

Chris sat beside me, then pulled my chair closer to his, despite my niece's protests. He kept his eyes locked with my brothers as he grabbed my chin and placed the sloppiest, wettest, most exaggerated kiss on the corner of my lips, almost disgusting me. I laughed as I pushed against his chest.

"You're making me lose my appetite," dad growled.

I barely held back my laughter as I wiped the spit from my mouth, and Chris looked sheepishly at my dad.

"My bad."

Landon was looking at us like he was confused, then looked up at Missy and Adrian.

"Aunt Bitt is like mama?"

Missy looked at him with confusion. "Like mama? What do you mean, baby?"

Landon pointed at Chris, then at Adrian before saying, "Daddy eats mama too."

Missy's face turned red as she rolled her eyes and elbowed my now smug-looking brother.

"That's different," Adrian grunted out.

Roseanne looked at my dad with a coy smile and asked, "Is it different when you do it, too?"

Dad was the one to turn red now. He quickly picked up his menu and hissed at his new wife behind it, "Stop it, you."

Roseanne chuckled and patted his cheek. That cleared the rest of the tension at the table.

Peggy came by herself to take our orders, and just like Chris said, she was as friendly as ever. She was all smiles and even winked at me after writing down my order of chicken and fries. She called Chris "trouble" and teased him a little about his sloppy way of kissing, telling him he must have learned that from the dogs his mom usually fosters. The slower mutts with behavioral issues.

"See," Chris whispered in my ear after Peggy walked off to get our drinks.

He was right. Peggy was her normal self, and everyone else in the diner seemed to be acting normal now, too.

Missy and Roseanne started talking about a new pie recipe, or maybe it was a crust recipe. Something about cooking that I didn't care to pay much attention to. Missy did all the cooking in our family and Roseanne now did all the baking. When they weren't feeding me, I could handle the basics or order out. I wasn't interested in cooking or new recipes.

I was interested in my newest nephew. I grabbed him from Missy just moments after Peggy walked away. Quinton was wide awake and staring up at me in that sweet way babies do. I knew it was a matter of time before he wanted his mom again, so I soaked up all the content, cute, best-babyish happiness I could before that time came.

Hailey, despite not wanting to sit by Chris, sure had a lot of questions for him over the course of dinner. I felt like I was in their way as Hailey drilled him about her game.

"Did you play it?"

"Nope," Chris shot back.

"Did you open it?"

Nope."

"Did you turn it on?"

"Wouldn't you like to know?" Chris smirked.

"Mr. Chris," Hailey pinched her fingers in front of her face and pulled them down while taking a deep breath, like she was trying to calm herself. "If you messed up my game again, so help me-"

"He didn't touch your game, kid," I cut her off. I snuggled my nose against my baby nephews. "No. No, he didn't."

"You look awfully good with a baby in your arms, darlin'," Chris strummed his fingers down my back.

"The fuck she does," my brother growled.

"Adrian!" Missy smacked him.

"Daddy beep!" Landon said proudly, then laughed when Adrian sent him a thumbs up before going back to his Chris-exclusive scowl.

My brother looked pissed, but my dad suddenly looked horrified.

"You okay there?" Roseanne patted his cheek.

He snapped his mouth shut, frowning deeply. "I don't think I am."

Roseanne and Missy chuckled.

"Why aren't you okay?" Missy asked.

Dad looked at me, then at Chris, and his frown deepened. "She's too young to have kids."

I rolled my eyes, deciding to step back from the conversation and let Chris deal with the fallout of what his off-handed comment started.

"Really?" Missy raised her left eyebrow, leaning back in her chair. "She's older than I was when I had Landon."

Dad coughed uncomfortably, "Well.... They just started dating and...."

Missy's eyebrows raised to her hairline as he tilted her head in an "and?" manner shut him up on that train of thought. My brother put a baby in Missy before the two of them were even really dating. He was just her handyman persistently trying to occupy all her time, not yet putting a ring, or even a label on it.

"See. We're already ahead of the game," Chris stupidly commented.

I sighed, seeing the anger rising in both my brother and my dad.

"I'm on birth control, guys. Chill. No babies here." I snuggled Quinton's nose, making him giggle. "None but you, my perfect little angel. You're the only baby I need."

"You mean those sugar pills I've been feeding you?" Chris laughed, rubbing my back.

I stared at him. "If my brother kicks your ass after dinner, it's all on you."

"Psh," Chris waved his hand in the air, but looked a little nervous when a threatening smile lifted Adrian's face.

When our food got there, everyone hushed about babies and started moaning over their meals. Dang Missy and her burgers.... She was cute, dancing in her seat with excitement as the fried onions and cheese dripped over the sides of the bun. She looked like she was ready to orgasm with every bite. My freaking brother looked ready to help guide her there.

"Keep it in your pants, Missy," Chris muttered, stealing one of my fries to dip into his chili.

"I can't help it! It's so good!" She said with her mouth half full.

"Yeah it is," Adrian muttered. "You missed a spot, baby. Here," he scooped some of the drippy cheese off the side of the burger with his finger and guided it to her mouth.

"Gross, guys," I acted like I was gagging. "Your children are present."

"We're used to it," Hailey sighed, shaking her head and nibbling on her chicken tenders.

"Someone might end up with another baby soon," Roseanne laughed, glancing up at Rick.

"There will be no more babies for a while," Missy said before taking another bite.

"We'll see about that," my brother murmured under his breath, still watching Missy.

My phone started buzzing on the table, and I normally wouldn't check it, but I was desperate to look away from my brother who was eye-fucking Missy right in front of me while I was trying to eat, holding the last baby that one of those looks caused.

I lifted my phone absentmindedly, not expecting to find anything interesting with the email notification, but upon further examination, alarm bells started to go off in my head. I clicked on the banner and when it opened to the full message, I truly felt like I might get sick.

Holy fuck. What the hell was this?

Chapter Twenty-Four

Dear Miss Brittany Brewer,

In our records, we see that you have applied for the completion of your degree and to participate in the Spring Graduation in May.

Unfortunately, we have recently been alerted to a serious matter requiring further investigation before a decision on the acceptance of the completion of your degree in Elementary Education can be made.

An anonymous tip was submitted to the ethics committee that a relationship of an inappropriate nature may have occurred between you and Professor Elias Miles. According to our university's Standard of Conduct, Section D, Policy 4900, a relationship of an intimate nature between a member of university staff and a student is strictly prohibited.

If these allegations prove to be true, it would result in the classes you have taken under Professor Elias Miles' guidance being void. This would cause your course guide to become incomplete.

Along with an incomplete course requirement inhibiting your ability to graduate this spring, dismissal from our university may also be a possibility at the conclusion of the investigation.

If you would like to submit a formal statement to be reviewed alongside other evidence submitted to the ethics committee.....

The rest of the email blurred as tears of rage filled my eyes.

How? How was this happening?

"Baby?" Chris rubbed my knee, then dragged my chair closer to his when he saw I was tearing up. "Brittany?" He grabbed my face between his large hands. "What's wrong? What happened?"

He looked down at my phone, but I turned it over quickly, out of shame. Quinton fussed in my arms. I pushed the baby towards Chris, then hurriedly got up from the table, feeling like I was about to lose it.

This was my fucking degree. My fucking future. How the hell did this happen?

"Brittany?!" Chris yelled after me, but he was stuck with the baby.

My brother yelled after me too, but I had a one-track mind right now. I didn't want to face them until I had more answers.

Ignoring the stares of the other people at the diner, I pushed out the door in a huff. With blurry, rage-filled eyes, I clicked through my contacts on my phone until I got to Professor Dickhead, then unblocked him. If this was some twisted ploy to get me to talk to him, it took it too fucking far.

"Brittany," Elias answered on the second ring.

His tone was anxious, but that didn't stop me from laying into him.

"What the hell did you do?!" I screamed into the receiver.

"Brittany, I-"

"What the fuck did you fucking do?! My degree?! You're fucking with my degree now?!"

"Brittany, it wasn't-"

"Did you think this would get me to fucking talk to you? You fuck up my life and somehow that will magically make me want to become your dirty mistress again?!"

"BRITTANY!" Elias yelled back, his tone more firm, more dire than I had ever heard it before.

I panted, catching my breath. I had gotten so worked up that I felt like I was sweating. Tears were falling down my cheeks, making my hair stick to my face.

"How could you," I whispered, the fight in me turning into helpless dread. "How could you do it?"

Elias took a deep breath, sounding frustrated like I was the one that caused this. "It wasn't me," he said in a flat tone. "I am guessing from the nature of your call, and just the general fact you are even talking to me, that the school informed you of the investigation now underway. I'm sorry, Brittany, but it wasn't me."

"What do you mean, it wasn't fucking you?" Who the hell else could have said anything to the school? No one at university knew about Elias and me. "Was it your wife?"

He let out a low sound of displeasure. "Ex-wife, and no. She had nothing to do with this anonymous report. No. The report came from outside of the school. Outside of the community. My ex's father would not allow his daughter to tarnish my reputation like this." He paused for a long time before adding, "And I would never resort to such a despicable tactic to gain your attention, Brittany. I am highly offended you would even think that to be a possibility."

Thinking more rationally, I realized Elias wouldn't do something like that. I feel guilty despite everything for jumping to that conclusion. After all the effort he made us go through to keep our relationship a secret, I knew it was way too out of character for him to ruin my life, since it would effectively ruin his career, too.

"Then who?" I whispered. "Who else fucking knows, Elias? Who?"

He was quiet again, making me nervous about what his answer would be.

"I'm dealing with it, Brittany. I'm sorry they even reached out to you, because I have been trying to clean this mess before you got entangled too. Because it was a single report from an arbitrary source, the accusation should be easily swept under the rug. Please, just hang on for a bit and let me deal with it."

An arbitrary source? How arbitrary?

"Who?" I asked again.

"Brittany, I-"

"You know, don't you? Who reported it, Elias?"

"I don't think you should-"

"WHO?!" I demanded.

There was a heavy sigh on the other end, and I knew at that moment I wouldn't like whatever he said. I felt like it would be as more damaging than the email I had just received, but I still had to know.

"A Scarlet Finley."

My stomach dropped. I felt like I would be sick.

Elias continued one, "She called the admissions office, who put her through to the dean a few days ago. I'm sorry, Brittany. I tried to call you when I heard they were launching an investigation, but I was unable to get a call to go through, and calling from one of the school's landlines seemed like it would be incriminating, since I have been firmly denying everything. I thought I could make this all go away, and you would never be involved. I'm sorry, Brittany. I truly am."

Chris's mom was the one that reported me? Why? Did she hate the idea of me being with her son so much that she was willing to ruin my future to separate us?

I didn't know what to say. What to do.

"Brittany?" Elias sounded concerned. "Are you there?"

Right then, Chris walked out of the diner, staring at me with knit brows. My heart was hammering in my chest, and I wasn't sure what to do.

"Brittany?!" Elias yelled in my ear.

Chris's eyes tightened, and I knew he heard.

"I have to go," I muttered, then clicked the phone off.

Chris was staring at me in disbelief. There was accusation in his eyes.

I can't even imagine how I looked at that moment. So many thoughts were running through my head, and none of them were good. His mother was the one that put my future in jeopardy. If Elias couldn't fix this by lying his ass off, I didn't know what I would do.

Do I need to move? Do I have to go back to school? Can I go back to school with something like this on my records?

What the hell should I do now? How do I recover from this? How....

How do I face Chris and tell him what his mother has done?

"Having a friendly chat out here, I see?" Chris said as he took a step forward, grabbing the phone from my hands.

He checked the call log, and I let him, knowing it wouldn't matter.

He saw Elias's number at the top, then cursed under his breath. "Fuck, Brittany. What the hell? What's going on?"

I snatched my phone back, fighting back the heat building behind my eyes. I opened the email back up, then handed my phone back to Chris.

His eyes ran through the words, his brows knitting more. "Shit, Brittany," he rubbed his jaw. "That... that sucks."

I looked up at the sky, willing myself not to cry. He was reading the email repeatedly, muttering curses under his breath each time.

"Shit. What are you going to do? I can't believe that asshole reported you."

"He didn't," I whispered, still staring up at the sky.

"Bullshit," he scoffed. "He really said he didn't? Are you sure this shit is even real? What if he made this whole thing up to get you to call him? Is this a real email address? Like, an official one from the school and not one he made himself?"

"It's real," I said in a low voice, trying not to let my voice shake. "It's a dot-E-D-U address. It's official."

"Holy shit, Brittany. What are you going to do?"

Chris took another step towards me, reaching like he was about to pull me into a hug. I involuntarily recoiled, taking a step back.

"Brittany?" Chris sounded confused, but I still hadn't looked at him directly. "Brittany, what's wrong?"

I looked down at the ground. My heart felt like it was ready to beat right out of my chest.

"Do you want to know who reported me?"

"What?" Chris stepped closer, his shoes invading my shadow on the ground.

I took a heavy breath, feeling it shuddering in my chest. Then, I raised my gaze to him, "Do you have any idea who it was that reported me? Elias said it wasn't him, but knew who called in. Take a guess who."

"Brittany," Chris rubbed his hands up the sides of my arms. "Baby, you're scaring me."

"Take a guess," I insisted. "Just off the top of your head. Who do you think might hate me enough to report me to my school for sleeping with my fucking professor?!" My voice rose slightly with every word. "Take a guess!"

"What the hell? I don't know. Are you sure it wasn't the dickhead?"

I laughed humorlessly as I shook my head. "Go ask your mom who reported me, Chris. Ask her."

Chris's mouth dropped, his eyes going wide. Then his jaw snapped shut, and his eyes grew cold. "That's not funny, Brittany. She wouldn't."

"She obviously did," I said flatly.

Chris shook his head. "No. No, she wouldn't do that. Did he tell you that? He's obviously lying, Brittany. There's no way-"

"He knew her name," I interrupted him. "Elias knew your mother's name. How else would he know that?"

"Google search?" Chris shrugged. "There is no way."

"A Google search for your mom? Are you delusional?" I shook my head. "He said Scarlet Finley. You google your mother's name and see what pops up, because I know she won't. She sure as heck isn't going to be listed as your mom. Your mom doesn't even have social media in her own name because she's scared the government is going to follow her. He said clear as fucking day, Scarlet Finley." I shook my head, fighting the burn in my eyes.

"She wouldn't," he said again, but this time sounding a little less sure. "He had to hear her name somewhere else. Like at the bar or the shop. He was in town for days, Brittany. Are you just going to trust him blindly?"

"Well, this is an easy puzzle to solve." I lifted my chin. "Ask your mom."

"What?"

I felt a cold resolve come over me. Like the calm before the storm. "You don't have to trust me, and I don't have to trust Elias. Ask your mom. Go home right now and ask her."

I moved past him, heading back to the diner door. People were watching us through the window, but they hurriedly turned around in the seats as I looked up at the windows.

"Where are you going?" His tone sounded a little panicked.

"To talk to my dad," I muttered. "I'm going to need his lawyer, after all."

Chapter Twenty-Five

"Fortunately, because this is strictly hearsay and there has been no concrete proof of an intimate relationship between you and Professor Elias Miles, I think the fight for your diploma will be an easy one."

I sighed, sitting back in my chair at the lawyer's office, out of relief.

"The bigger issue might be with your employment. I have already put precautions into place, including the statement I took from you last week, but because this allegation is coming from a member of our community, I can not assure you there won't be prejudices in place when you do begin your role as a teacher." My lawyer sighed loudly, shaking his head while looking at a document on his desk. He then slid it over to me. "I do not suggest this lightly, but I do think it would be in your overall best interest if you were to deal with Mrs. Finley. The legal way. A defamation lawsuit would be the fastest way to ensure your degree and employment remain secure."

I scanned over the paper, not really reading the words. My mind was too busy thinking about what suing my boyfriend's mother would do for our relationship.

I just didn't understand why she would go this far.

"But is it defamation?" I asked meekly. "I... I did have an.... an intimate relationship with him. My professor, I mean."

Mr. Jones gave me a sympathetic look. "But did you barter sexual favors for better grades, Miss Brewer?"

I timidly shook my head.

Mr. Jones nodded, smiled tightly, then said, "You gained nothing from your relationship with this professor, from my understanding, and the basis of Mrs. Finley's claims to your school were that you traded the acts to advance your grades. She even claimed that there are more than likely other faculty or staff you performed such acts for in order to maintain your GPA and acquire scholarships. This, at the root of it all, is defamation. And it all stemmed from malicious intent. She was retaliating because you began a relationship with her son. I think a defamation suit would be more than admissible in your case."

But what would that do to Chris?

My gut twisted every time I thought about it.

It's been three days since I last saw him. After yelling outside the diner, I left with my dad and haven't been back home since. He argued with me for a minute more, asking for me to talk it out some more. He was adamant that it had to be some mistake.

I couldn't. I didn't want to say anything I couldn't take back, and that was his mother. His fucking mother.

My dad and I spent the weekend getting all the information my lawyer needed about the case the school was building against me. Saturday morning, for the brief window of time when the admin office was open, I had the school send me all the evidence they had. I had to throw the 'I got a lawyer' card around a bit, but I was able to see what exactly was said to the dean.

Now here I am, talking to my lawyer about suing the woman responsible.

What's killing me more than anything is the fact that he hasn't called me since I left him standing outside in the parking lot. He stared after my dad's truck with this devastated look in his eyes, but never called me. Not once.

No visit to my dad's place. No reaching out to see if I was okay.

Nothing.

To be fair, I haven't reached out to him either. Even when I saw him dropping in on my house through the security cam. I had my phone gripped tightly in my hand, waiting for him to reach out and ask where I was, but that call never came. He walked in and then walked back out five minutes later with his bag in his hand.

He never even looked up. Usually, he would flip off the camera or show his ass. Something to irritate my brother or my dad. He never looked up. I never even saw his eyes. They were downcast the entire time.

"Miss Brewer?" Mr. Jones said my name softly. "I know it's not an easy choice, so why don't you take the rest of the day to think about it? We can circle back to the issue in the morning after our conference call with your dean."

I smiled tightly. "Sounds good. Thank you for all your help."

He patted my hand on the desk, lying over the papers. "This too shall pass. Handle it one day at a time, and you will have your degree in no time."

The pressure behind my eyes was making them burn. I nodded stiffly to keep the moisture from pushing forth.

With the papers in my hands, I solemnly walked out to my car, debating what to do.

***

Chris

"Get up," Mike grunted, kicking the side of the bed.

I groaned, wiping the spit from my mouth. Looking around the room, my chest felt empty when I realized where I was.

My dream was so fucking wonderful. Brittany was in my arms, teasing me about being a shit shot on that fucking video game Hailey was always talking about. We were laughing and happy, but that was so fucking far from the reality of our relationship now.

I was back at the apartment over my brother's garage. I had been there for days, avoiding Brittany and everything else out of shame.

She did it. My damn mom was the one who called Brittany's school. How was I supposed to face her now?

***

Three days ago...

Brittany was wrong. She had to be. I knew my mom wasn't our biggest supporter, but she would never stoop that fucking low.

I was sure of it. I bet Professor Dickhead orchestrated this entire thing to get Brittany to talk to him. It worked, didn't it? Brittany ran right out of that diner and called him right away.

I kept telling myself that, but it didn't make my stomach stop twisting into knots.

My truck skidded over the gravel of my mom's driveway as I put it into park before the tires even stopped turning. The forest was dark, but mom had her lights on, lighting the way up to the front door. Two dogs were barking from the kennels around the back side of the house. Mom must have volunteered to foster strays again.

"SHUT UP!" I sneered, my anxiety not able to take much more chaos.

All I did was make the dog bark louder, irritating me more. "Fuck," I hissed. Fumbling with the door.

I was about to fish my key out of my pocket, since the door was actually locked, but then mom came and opened it. She looked surprised to see me as her door swung in, and then, seeing my anger, a frown settled on her face.

"You come to your senses and decide to come home?"

I didn't say anything, my mind reeling as I tried to get my thoughts in order. My mom didn't need a response to carry on.

"You and that Brewer harlot get into a fight? I warned you. I warned you about girls like her. No decency. What happened? Did you catch her with another man already? I told you. I told you she would-"

"Did you do it?" I cut her off, asking through clenched teeth.

Mom stopped short. Her eyes went wide for a second, then she looked around like she was searching for an explanation of what I was talking about. "Did I do what?"

"Mom," my voice was low and cold. "I'm only going to ask you this once. Did you do it? Did you call Brittany's school?"

The expression of understanding and the sudden stubborn set of her jaw told me all I needed to know.

"Well," she huffed. "You didn't leave me with much choice, did you?"

My fist went flying, slamming into the wood siding. Hearing that Brittany was right, that that dickhead was right about my mother, had the last tethers of restraint snapping inside of me.

"Chris!" Mom yelled, gaping in shock. "What do you think you are doing?!"

"What do you think you're doing, mom!?" I screamed. I paced back, barely holding myself from getting in her face. I tossed my hat to the dirt, then pulled at my hair. "FUCK!" All my rage exploded out of me, echoing in the night sky.

"Me?! All I did was warn that school about one of their students. Who knows how many professors that girl had corrupted? They had a right to know."

What the fuck was I hearing? "Are you fucking kidding me?! You have no idea what the hell you're talking about!"

"I know enough." She lifted her chin. "You didn't want to see reason, so I had to do something."

"You're fucking insane," I scoffed in disbelief. "You're sick. How could you?! How could you do that to her?" My voice started out low, but then exploded. "HOW?!"

Mom jumped back, placing her hand over her chest. "I already told you. If she's innocent, then there's nothing to worry about for her, is there? Now, quit yelling and get in the house. I'm sure you haven't had decent food in a while. I can fix you up some-"

I walked away, walking back to my truck. You can't reason with her level of insanity, and I didn't want to snap to the point of hurting my mother. No matter how badly she's hurting me.

"Hey! I'm talking to you! Christopher Daniel Finley!"

Without another word, I started my truck. The tires spun out before getting traction to tear out of her driveway.

My mom really did it. Professor Dickhead wasn't the one responsible for this one. It was my own mother.

***

Three days. It's been three fucking days and I haven't gotten out of this pit of guilt and shame to reach out and apologize to Brittany. I haven't even gotten out of this bed, out of this apartment much, except to get my things from Brittany's.

When she wasn't home, it was a relief. I wasn't ready to face her, but I had nothing at my apartment. I sure as hell wasn't seeing my mom again. Not after she wrecked my entire life. I had no choice but to get my clothes from Brittany's. When I walked into an empty house, I felt empty too. As much as I wanted to see her beautiful face, I was relieved, but only for one reason....

The break-up is coming. I could feel it. Why would she want to be with me now?

All the effort, all the time, all the heart and soul I put into breaking down those walls of hers, and all of it goes to shit because my own fucking mother sabotaged me. I was hiding, unwilling to face the ending that was sure to come.

"Get your ass out of this bed." Mike kicked the mattress again.

I groaned, then rolled over, not wanting to deal with life today. I wanted to go back to my dream. Sleep was the only way I could see Brittany without fear of her leaving me.

"I'm serious, man." Mike yanked the blanket from my legs, then groaned. "Ew. Fuck, dude. When was the last time you showered?"

"Shut up," I mumbled, my face pressed against the mattress.

"Seriously, man. This is pathetic. You need to get your ass out of bed and fix this shit. Not hide from it. What would Brittany think if she saw you like this?"

I couldn't help but to laugh dryly. "What does it matter? She's going to dump me the second she sees me, anyway. Smelling good won't stop that."

"It might," he started walking around the room, surveying the mess. "What happened to that persistent dude that didn't give up without a fight? You seriously going to just waste away like this?"

I turned my face against the mattress to follow his movements as he picked up my bag and started searching through it. He pulled out a pair of boxers and a cleanish shirt. All my jeans were on the floor, so when he gave up with the bag, he started picking those up one at a time, sniffing them, probably to find the cleanest ones.

"She's going to leave me," I mumbled. "She's really going to leave me."

Mike sighed. "How do you know? Have you even talked to her yet?"

I scoffed. "Would you stay with someone whose mother fucked up your life?"

Mike groaned, "Come on. Mom did it. Not you. You're giving up before even trying."

"I'm hiding," I whispered. "She can't break up with me if she can't see me."

"Oh, she can. All you're doing is making it easier for her. Get your ass up and get in the shower."

I closed my eyes, looking away. I didn't want to get in that shower. The memories of having Brittany in there were enough to choke me. That was the real reason I couldn't clean myself up. That shower was where I finally convinced her to go out with me. Ironically, I feel like if I get in there and clean myself up to face her, it will all end.

Mike was moving around the room. The sound of clothes shuffling around and being shoved in my bag was easy to identify. Why he was cleaning up this pigsty, I didn't know. What was the point?

The room was a reflection of its owner. I fucking wreck.

"So," Mike mumbled, making the bed dip as he sat beside me. "I talked to Roseanne today.

My eyes opened, and I turned my head to stare at him. I didn't ask, but he still smiled and started giving me the details I craved.

"Seems Brittany might still get her degree. Her lawyer handled the school like they had planned from the start."

A small spark of relief lit inside my chest. "Good," I mumbled. "She worked hard to graduate."

Mike nodded. "Yep, she did. Roseanne said that the worst-case scenario now would be that those classes she took under that asshole might be invalid. Even if the allegations get tossed, which they fucking should, they may decide to make her retake those classes under another professor, just to be sure there was no nepotism or whatever."

I sat up as a new kind of fear raced through me. "So, she would have to go back?"

Mike shrugged. "That would be a question for her."

Shit. If she left this town again, I had a feeling she would never come back. Not after this. Brittany was always bigger and better than this small town. Everyone knew it. She only came back because she loved her family.

But her family could afford to visit her wherever she lived. After this kind of scandal got out, all revolving around her, she wouldn't want to face the rumors again.

Brittany carried shame heavier than anyone I ever knew. I had to break through so many of her insecurities to get to her. I saw the effect that bastard had on Brittany when he showed up at the coffee shop.

If she left, she'd never come back. I was sure about that.

"Can't she just go to a college here?"

Mike shrugged. "Again, that isn't something I can answer. But do you really think she'd trade a prestigious university for a certificate at a community college? I don't even think that's possible."

Shit.

"Fuck," I grumbled, pushing myself out of bed.

Mike smirked, handing me the pile of clothes he compiled for me. I ripped them out of his hands and headed straight for the bathroom.

"Oh, yeah," he called out as I closed the door. "You're going to have a visitor soon."

"Who?" I looked around the door. Hope budded in my chest.

Mike shrugged. "Someone that will care if you stink. Wash your ass and be fast about it. He'll be here soon."

He?

That hope that just budded died out as I thought about which he it could be.

Chapter Twenty-Six

Brittany

"Aunt Britt!" Hailey ran to hug me when I let myself into their house.

Adrian's truck was parked outside, which had me ready to turn around and head back to dad's. I couldn't stomach another day of being there, with dad hovering over me asking if I wanted this or that every other second.

After what the lawyer told me, I wanted to talk to someone, and Missy was the only one I knew would listen and understand.

"Hey." Missy poked her head from around the corner of the kitchen. She looked me up and down in that way she does when she knows something was wrong, but didn't ask. Instead, she said, "I didn't expect you. I was about to toss some nuggets in the oven for the kids. Want some?"

I smiled sadly. Such a simple fucking question, and an easy decision to make. "I'd love some."

"Dino nuggets! Coming right up."

"What about my leftovers?!" Adrian hollered from the fridge. "You said there were two containers!"

Missy pointed the end of her wooden spoon at him. "If you wake up that baby, you're taking him to work with you. I don't care if you have to hang drywall or build a freaking mausoleum, you're doing it with him strapped to you."

Adrian glared at the spoon, then at her. "Dad was over here earlier."

Missy pursed her lips, averting her gaze. "Only to drop off the iPad. Hailey left it at his house."

I took a seat at the bar, watching as Adrian pressed up, chest to chest, with Missy. He gazed down at her with a hard expression. "Did he take my leftovers?"

Missy lifted her chin, not backing down. "You didn't need both of them."

"Damn it," Adrian smacked his hand down on the counter. "I told you, those were-"

His rant was cut off by the fierce screaming of their baby. I chuckled under my breath as Missy proceeded to beat Adrian with the spoon, yelling at him to get him back to sleep or pack a bag to take him. Adrian yelped and conceded quickly, knowing he just dug his own grave.

"That man," Missy shook her head. "God did not grant me enough patience to deal with him today. I swear, I'm going to lose it for real."

She went to the coffeemaker to flip the switch. Getting two mugs from the cabinet, she started preparing one for me without even asking. She knew. She always does.

"So," Missy said, pouring creamer into one of the mugs, "How did it go with Mr. Jones? Did he hear back from the school?"

I tapped my finger on the counter, glancing at the monitor to see if Adrian was in Quinton's room. Quinton was still screaming. When I saw Adrian there, I knew he wouldn't be able to hear anything we talked about.

"It went as expected. Well, except..."

I glanced one last time to be sure Adrian was still busy with the screaming baby and then looked back to see Hailey had gone out back with Landon to play with the dog. Only the cat remained in the living room, lounging in the middle of the ottoman.

I leaned forward, then said in a low voice, "He wants to sue Scarlet."

Missy's eyes went wide. "Wow. Really?" She pursed her lips, tilting her head as she thought about it. "It makes sense."

"You think so?"

"Yeah," Missy scoffed. "She didn't just tell your school you had a relationship with a professor. She said a lot of not true things. Unless you have more you're not telling me."

I rolled my eyes. "Yeah. I was sleeping with all my professors. Every single one of them. Even the women."

"What?!" Adrian snapped, coming up from behind me. I hadn't even noticed Quinton had stopped crying.

All three of us looked at the monitor when Adrian yelled, holding our breath as Quinton stirred in his sleep before going still again. We all exhaled in relief at the same time.

"What were you saying?" Adrian hissed quietly.

"Nothing," Missy and I muttered at the same time.

Adrian narrowed his eyes at me, then at Missy. "What's going on?"

I rolled my eyes, and Missy put on a sulky grin, distracted him the best way she knew how.

"Good job, baby. You got him back to sleep." she pulled on the hem of his shirt, pressing up against him.

"Uh, uh. None of that. What were you two talking about?"

"What?" Missy blinked innocently up at him. "You don't want me to reward you for your effort?"

His lips twitched, and his eyes glanced down at her chest before he sighed and pushed her away.

"I'm not stupid. That timer for the chicken goes off in ten minutes. Not enough time, so I know what you're up to. Just tell me."

Adrian looked at me for an answer.

I sighed, then decided to just tell him. He would find out anyway.

"Mr. Jones wants me to sue Chris's mom."

He scoffed loudly. "Good! Do it! Why wouldn't you? The bitch is ruining your life."

"Adrian," Missy slapped his chest.

"What? She is."

I shook my head. "It's not that easy."

"Sure it is," Adrian shrugged. "The woman will think twice next time she tries opening her mouth if someone finally holds her accountable."

"Adrian," Missy pulled on the hem of his shirt again. "Seriously, just stop."

"What? I'm not lying. She's a fucking bit-"

"It's not Scarlet," Missy cut him off.

A look passed between them, and then his eyes went wide as he threw back his head. He finally got it.

"Ahh," Adrian nodded. "Well, what does Chris say about this?"

Missy slapped his chest again as I sank down on the stool.

"What?! Why can't I ask that?!"

I rested my chin on my fist against the counter. "I haven't talked to Chris."

Adrian's eyes went wide. "Really? I figured he'd want an update the second you got out of Mr. Jones' office."

I shrugged. "He didn't know I went there. I haven't talked to him since Friday."

His eyes narrowed, his jaw tensing. Maybe I shouldn't have told him that.

"Babe, can you get the kids for lunch?" Missy tapped his chest. "Help them wash up and stuff."

They exchanged another one of those looks before he sighed and nodded his head. He patted my shoulder as he passed by.

"I'm sorry." Missy smiled gently at me after Adrian closed the sliding door. "I didn't tell him anything you haven't already told him. He didn't know. He probably thought Chris would, you know, be Chris and not leave you alone, even if you were at Rick's."

"I know," I murmured. "I'm not mad. It's just a suckfest all around. Chris hasn't talked to me, and if I do end up suing his mom, he probably never will again."

"He'll call," Missy reassured me. "He's probably just embarrassed."

"Or he's listening to his mom." I let the invasive thought slip through.

Missy silently poured our coffee. After setting mine in front of me, she asked, "If you don't sue her, what happens?"

I stared down at the warm brown liquid. "I don't know, but I know I wouldn't be able to work here. The school isn't going to hire me if I have a past that includes a student teacher relationship. Mr. Jones thinks this needs to be put to rest legally, so the school has no ground to pull my contract out from under me."

Missy took a long drink from her cup, then asked the next important question. "If you can't work at the school, what will you do?"

I thought about that the entire drive over. I ran every scenario through my head, wandering which would end with the best result. Which I would be able to live most with.

There was already a solution to all of this settling in the back of my mind, creeping more and more forwards the longer I fought over what to do.

"I'd have to leave," I whispered. "I… I would probably change my major to something more administrative, then move far enough away that the gossip from this small town and my previous college didn't affect me. If I can't be a teacher, what else is there for me here?"

"You mean you wouldn't want to work at the coffeehouse with mouthy Louisa?" Missy teased.

"Definitely not," I snorted. "Man, I'm done with all these mouthy, righteous busybodies with nothing better to do than talk trash on anyone and everyone. Scarlet never would have known about Elias if not for the rumor mill. I hate it. I wish I didn't have to worry about rumors every time I left the house. No matter what happens with the school and Scarlet, I don't see that ever ending." I took a drink of my coffee, wishing it was something stronger. "I hate it here."

Missy reached across the counter, rubbing her hand over mine. "It sounds to me like you already made up your mind."

I stilled, but she squeezed my hand in hers tighter. I felt her warmth seeping into me. It made me want to cry.

"But what about Chris?" I said in a small voice.

"What about Chris?" She shook her head. "If you guys still aren't talking, and neither of you are making a first move, it doesn't sound like you have much more to consider."

I gnawed on my bottom lip. "But... But I don't know what to say to him."

She shrugged. "He obviously doesn't either. Still, one of you has to break the silence first."

I knew she was right, but I just couldn't be the first to reach out to him. Not when his mom was the root problem. I'd either start crying or cursing him and his mom to hell the second he answered.

"I feel like there's a wall between us I just can't get over," I whispered roughly. "I don't know how to break through it, and it just feels bigger and bigger every hour that goes by."

"Do you feel like you are making the wall bigger, or that he is?"

I shrugged. "Probably me. I'm just scared of getting more hurt. I... I don't want to hurt him, either. I keep thinking that this is my fault. If I hadn't gotten involved with Elias, this never would have happened. She wouldn't have found anything to report to my school."

"Nope." Missy shook her head. "Don't you dare start that crap. She is a nasty bitch and would have just found another way to be one. You are not going to shoulder her nastiness, too."

I scoffed lightly, hearing Missy use the term she slapped my brother for earlier. "Maybe, but Chris would still be dealing with a girlfriend his mom hates. How do I overcome that?" My eyes began to burn, filling with the heartache I'd been holding in for three days. "I... I thought he loved me, and I loved him. I thought... I thought that this could be..."

"Oh, Britt," Missy came around the counter and hugged me. "You don't build up walls with those you love. You put you first, Brittany. Don't make yourself miserable for love. That's not what love is."

***

Chris

Fuck.

When my brother said there was a guy here to see me, I was hoping it would be Rick. Actually, before he specified the gender, I was hoping it would be the woman I'd been too chicken shit to face for the last few days. I craved Brittany. I wanted to see her, even if she was pissed at me and I feared facing the end of... of us.

I sure as shit didn't want to be sitting here awkwardly in the mess of a living space above my brother's garage with her brother.

Adrian sat in the dusty old chair with a deep scowl on his ugly mug. The vein in his neck was already pulsing. He hadn't said a word to me yet, but that scared me more.

I mean, I wasn't scared or nothing. I could hold my own if I had to. I was fairly sure I could anyway....

But that look on Adrian's face was beyond his normal irritation. This was the Adrian from high school that would explode on a dude for doing little more than checking out his little sister, or talking shit about his lack of a mother. This was the side of him no one had seen since he met Missy.

Well, maybe except Missy's ex, but that bastard deserved the homicidal side of Adrian. Even the cops that arrested Adrian for it agreed with Adrian's reasons. I know my mom did something unforgivable, but he wouldn't try killing me because of it. Would he?

Mike was standing awkwardly against the far wall near the stair, reluctant to leave. He knew that look Adrian was giving me. He might have thought this was amusing half an hour ago, but one look at Adrian's pissy expression wiped that snickering grin right off his face.

The bell for a customer rang from downstairs. He shot us a nervous glance, and I begged with my eyes for him to ignore it. Pretend he was out to lunch or some shit. That wasn't that hard, was it?

"Um, I'll be right back," he muttered before heading downstairs.

Shit.

"Um, I should go see if he needs my help," I said cautiously, not meeting Adrian's stare.

"Sit your ass back down," Adrian sneered coldly.

My body went stiff. Crap. I was going to die.

"Um, nice… nice weather today, huh? I was, uh, thinking about, uh, getting the truck washed. Chances are the second I do, it will rain, though. That's how it goes, doesn't it?" I stammered nervously. "I'm out of soap and shit, anyway. I can just get the truck washed before running to the store."

Adrian said nothing. He just continued to stare back at me with those violent eyes.

"I'd offer you a drink, but, you know, I gotta go to the store. This place isn't exactly up for visitors yet, anyway. I meant, I've never really had anyone. Well, besides your sist-"

I caught myself, but not before Adrian raised an eyebrow and his jaw tightened.

Fuck.

"It's a little hot in here," I murmured, running my fingers under the collar of my shirt. "It's hot in here, right? I can turn the ac up and-"

"Shut your trap, asshole," Adrian leaned forward, resting his elbows on his knees. "Just shut up."

"Well, you're not saying anything and I just-"

Adrian cracked his paint-stained knuckles, each pop making my throat tighten more until I could no longer speak.

"You have no fucking idea how hard I'm trying not to kill you right now," he said in a low whisper. "No fucking idea."

I scoffed, but it was forced. Even to my ears, I sounded pathetic. "Y-you wouldn't k-kill me."

"Not yet," he muttered. "I promised Missy I wouldn't. Not yet. I'll hold back because my sister needs you."

My blood thawed, and my soul lifted for a second hearing those words. "Brittany needs me?"

His lip curled threateningly. "The fucking nerve of this prick," he said under his breath.

I rode on that high from hearing Brittany still needs me. "She needs me. Where is she? Your dad's or her house? I can-"

"You're not going anywhere near my sister, asshole," Adrian stopped me.

"But... You said-"

"I said she needs you. Not that she wants to see you."

My chest fell in defeat. "She... She doesn't want to see me." I scoffed quietly. "I guess I wouldn't either."

Adrian sat back, some of his malice slipping from his expression. "Why are you acting like that when you were the one that ghosted her for days?"

"I didn't ghost her," I mumbled quietly.

"You didn't? Because the shit I overheard from Missy says otherwise."

"What did Brittany tell Missy?" I unconsciously moved to the edge of my seat, desperate to hear more.

"That you have a little dick and a big mouth."

I scowled deeply. "Only one of those is even close to being true."

He smirked. "You're right. She said nothing about your mouth."

"So she was talking about my dick with your wife?"

Adrian's expression went full hostile again. "Watch it, asshole."

"No, you watch it." I snapped, the tension finally breaking through me. "You came here, Adrian. If you're just here to make me feel more like shit, just fucking go. You can't make me feel any worse than I already do."

I stood up as the adrenaline rush and the anxiety gave me the urge to pace. Yank out my hair. Yell or scream until my voice goes out. Adrian sat watching as I let myself come apart.

"My mother. My mother made that call. Mine! If Brittany loses her degree, I'll never be able to face her again. That's if she even lets me. I'll always be the reason she couldn't graduate. Not that dickhead professor, but me. Mom did it because of me. I can't ever see Brittany again..."

My thoughts turned dark. Lonely. I felt like there was something heavy pressing against my chest.

"I love her. I fucking love her. I love her so much I don't know what to do. I don't know how to fix this for her."

As I kept pacing, yanking on my hair and tearing my hands down my face roughly until the pain sated the edge of my frantic state, Adrian watched me with stoic features. My ears were buzzing. My heart was racing. Every anxious thought, every worry, every scenario of my life with Brittney no longer in it made me feel like I was drowning.

"There is something you can do," Adrian cut in the middle of my despair. "That's why I came. We've been talking to her lawyer, and there's a solution to all of this that she's not wanting to do because of you."

"What's that?" I heartbeat quickened, like I already knew the answer.

Adrian looked uncomfortable suddenly. It was like he was suddenly the one who was anxious. He was picking at a piece of fuzz on the arm of the chair, twirling it between his fingers.

"What?" I asked again when he didn't answer right away. "What doesn't she want to do?"

Adrian sighed, running his palms over the tops of his jeans. "She needs to sue your mom, Chris."

I froze, the air going cold in my lungs.

"Excuse me?"

"Look." Adrian stood up and walked closer. "Your mom said some pretty messed up shit when she called the school. She didn't just accuse Brittany of having a relationship with her professor. She told the freaking dean she was sleeping with everyone to keep scholarships and raise her grades. That's why this shit blew out of proportion in the first place."

A chill ran up my spine. "Mom.... my mom said that?"

"I can show you the official report if you want. It's vicious. She was trying to ruin Brittany's life."

I felt sick.

Adrian continued on, "If we don't fight this at the source, Brittany might still be able to get her degree since there is no evidence of anything, and because we have a lawyer fighting for her, but that won't help her here."

"What do you mean?" I asked hesitantly.

Adrian gave me a look like it was obvious. Like I was missing the issue. "Do you really think the school here will hire her if she has a history of having student-teacher relationships? Do you really think all your mom's righteous hag friends will keep their mouth shut about her after she officially graduates until we deal with your mom? If Brittany doesn't do this...."

Adrian pressed his lips together, hesitating again.

My nerves were going haywire. "What?!" I shouted. "If she doesn't sue her, then what?!"

Adrian took off his hat, rubbing through his hat hair, looking exhausted. "Brittany was already looking at other options, Chris. She was asking Missy about San Francisco after getting out of the lawyers this morning. If she doesn't listen to the lawyer and sue your mom, she might have to change career paths and move, so the shit your mom started doesn't follow her the rest of her life. Do you want that, because I sure as shit don't want my kids growing up without their aunt? I don't want my little sister alone in some crazy big city, where who knows what else will prey on her next."

My mouth went dry. Before, I was freaking out thinking about Brittany going back to school. Because I knew she would never come back if she left this town again.

My fears were coming true. Only this was worse. Her only option to stay was to go after my mom. That was what Adrian was telling me.

"What do you want me to do?" I asked, my voice low and heavy.

Adrian pressed her lips into a tight line, his eyes intense as they drilled into me. "I want you to convince her to do what the lawyer says. I want you to tell her to sue your mom."

So, I either had to hurt my mom or lose the woman I love.

"She wasn't going to tell you," Adrian whispered in a rough, deep rumble. "Dad told me to stay out of this, but... but we're... we're friends. Even if I want to punch your fucking face in and lock my sister away from you, you're still my friend. I couldn't sit back and not say anything." His face twisted sourly. "Even if Missy's going to give me blue balls later for opening my fucking mouth."

I got it now. Adrian making a fuss about Brittany moving to the Bay Area wasn't that big of a deal to them. She's been in college for years.

They can afford to visit her all the time. Shit, they would probably buy her an apartment and themselves a vacation house without batting an eye.

If Brittany moved, the only one who would really lose her would be me.

***

Brittany

"Are you sure you're going to be okay going back to your house alone?" Missy asked, helping to pack the last of my clothes into my suitcase.

I was holding the baby after being told to stay out of the way. Apparently, I pack the wrong way. Shoving clothes into a bag and calling it good to drive them ten minutes across town was unacceptable.

"The cameras work, so you'll know if anyone shows up at my house. I doubt Elias will show up again."

She frowned deeply, folding one of my fucking thongs into a little triangle like a freak. "Maybe I should stay over," she muttered under her breath.

"Nope." I shook my head. "Not a chance. I need solitude so I can think."

Everyone has an option of what I should do. Everyone. Dad has been hovering. Roseanne has been giving me those pitying looks. Adrian has been a grumpier asshole than what was normal for him when he heard anything about me having a sex life...

Missy would be the only one I could stomach right now, but she comes with three needy kids. I love all of them, but I am feeling more and more trapped by the day.

And with this big decision that needs to be made, I want a chance to think. I want quiet and no one else around to tell me what to do. Even Hailey has been asking too many questions. I just want to be alone to weigh everything out and try to choose the path that will leave me with the fewest regrets.

I think I've already decided. But.... But I want to be sure.

Deep down, I know the real reason I want to be alone, and the real reason I want to go back home was because I was hoping.... Hoping Chris might come see me if I'm back where we belong.

My stomach was in a knot of anxiety. I had given myself an ultimatum. Not even a fair one, but it was the only thing I could think to do to let fate, the universe, divine intervention, anything to make this choice for me and help me accept what that choice will be.

I was giving myself twenty-four hours, just one more day. If I don't hear from Chris or see him before I go in to speak with Mr. Jones in the morning, then I'm going to let that be the answer.

If he's going to choose to stand by his mom, I would not hold that against him. I would not be angry or vengeful. I wasn't going to reach out first and demand he choose me. If he loved his mom enough to overlook this, then I would too. I would not carry out the lawsuit. I would just leave.

I know what it's like to grow up without a mom. I know that deep, gut-wrenching feeling of betrayal and hate when you thought about the woman that should have chosen your happiness over their own. I know that pain, and even though I was no longer sure about where me and Chris stood, I was sure I cared for him enough to not want him to experience that. Ever.

Chris was always a bit of a mama's boy. I knew that and I also knew she didn't like me. I can't blame him for any of this. All I can do is leave quietly, and let us be a wild, drunken mistake like we were always meant to be.

But if he does come see me....

I don't know what I will do. I feel like my resolve is already set. I am preparing for the worst, getting mentally ready to face that when the time comes. That's why it's not entirely fair to Chris, because I'm not giving him a choice. I'm not going to be the one to reach out first.

When I wake up in the morning, it will be the end. I'm going to drive to Mr. Jones' office, tell him I don't want to ruin Scarlet's life, or make it more miserable than it already is, and I'll just start the preparations to restart somewhere new.

Missy did it once. She started over here, and look at what happened. She's married to my perverted, overprotective brother, has three kids, and exudes happiness even in the worst of times. I can do that too. I can go somewhere, start over fresh, then live a life that doesn't have to be weighed down by all the drama from my past.

I want that. I don't want to be stuck in all this drama and bull shit. I don't want everyone to know every detail of my life and use those details against me when they choose.

I love my family. I love them all so much it hurts.

Something Missy told me earlier has been playing on repeat over and over again in my head.

"You don't build up walls with those you love. You put you first, Brittany. Don't make yourself miserable for love. That's not what love is."

If I stay here, I don't ever see a time where I can not be miserable. I might be with the man I thought I could build a future with, but

I'd be miserable being in this town and near his mom. I don't think I could do it....

Missy helped me load my car, then waved to me as I backed out of my dad's driveway. She and the kids were going to stay until dad got home to explain to him everything that happened today. I didn't want to be talked out of going home, so she volunteered to speak on my behalf. I don't know what I'd do without her.

When I pulled up to my house, my disappointment stung in my chest when Chris's truck wasn't there. I knew he wasn't there. I don't know why I let myself get deluded into hoping as I drove.

The house felt empty. Really empty and cold.

Adrian had finished most of the work. The kitchen was finally finished, and so was the master bedroom. All that was left was outside work, and a few things he mentioned needed to be done to the garage.

It was a charming house. With furniture, I'm sure it would be amazing. I could see it now. A couch set with a better TV and an area rug in the living room. Pictures of family and other random decor on the walls. Missy would insist on me putting runners in the halls, since it would help suppress those creaks and groans in the flooring when someone was walking to the bathroom in the middle of the night.

If I was living here alone, I wouldn't have to worry about that.

I threw the luggage Missy neatly packed into the guest room, deciding to deal with it tomorrow. It was a minor problem putting up clothes, compared to some of the bigger ones I've been dealing with. It could wait. Everything will be dealt with tomorrow.

I walked around the house, not realizing I was searching for something until the disappointment constricted my chest again. None of Chris's belongings were there. Not one. Not even a pair of freaking boxers or a dirty sock. He took everything. All of it.

As I laid in bed, letting the loneliness sink in, I realized time was almost up. My phone was on, fully charged, lying next to my bed. It was completely silent, not having gone off once except a text from Missy telling me to call her tomorrow.

Tomorrow. Everything will be done tomorrow.

Chapter Twenty-Seven

Tomorrow came.

I sat up in bed wide awake, from before the sun began to rise in the sky until it was blaring through my sheer curtains. Everything inside me was numb.

Tomorrow came, but Chris never did.

No calls. No text. No barging in like he used to, overwhelming me with his persistence until I was putty in his hands. Nothing.

It was tomorrow, and I knew once I left this bed, that was the answer to everything. The countdown ended and I guess with it my relationship did too.

Was I this numb and empty when I found out about Elias? I remember being pissed, but I don't think it ever felt like this.

My body was completely still, clinging to the numbness, because I knew once the numbness faded away, the prickles of pain would grow until it became unbearable.

When my phone vibrated on my nightstand, that was the catalyst forcing me to move. My head snapped toward it, but when I saw my dad's name and face pop up on the screen and not his....

I broke.

I screamed. I cried. I threw every pillow, every blanket, from my bed in a fit of rage. I was fully vulnerable. My emotions had erupted in a volcano of violence and tears.

When there was nothing left to throw, nothing left to scream, when my body ached from the exertion of it all, I fell face-first into my mattress and just cried.

I cried and cried, tears and everything else soaking into my mattress and pressing back into my face. I let it all go until even tears wouldn't come out any more. Just broken sobs until my chest shook with exhausted hiccups.

What hurt more than anything, more than being the center of rumors, more than my career and schooling being threatened, more than having my shameful secrets exposed, was knowing I had never felt this broken or vulnerable over anyone else ever in my life. From the moment I left my dad's until I woke from my restless sleep, a deep part of me still had faith Chris would appear.

Then tomorrow came.

I couldn't even blame Chris. He wasn't aware of the choice I had to make. He had no idea I had placed him in my cowardly countdown, forcing chance to make my decision for me.

Now that the countdown was over, I had to face the choice that elected. The pain right now was incomparable, but I had to build my walls back up and move on with my plans. Once I left this bedroom, I had to accept this was the end.

It took me longer than I would have liked to close myself off again. Building back up that armor of protection was painfully draining.

Probably because it had been so painstakingly removed not long ago. Everything was fresh. It felt like rubbing salt on a wound.

When all the tears were dried, and I could speak without my voice breaking or shaking, I called my dad back, right at the moment I found the strength to get out of bed.

"Britt?" Dad sounded anxious as he answered.

"Hey dad," I said, my voice sounding stiff.

"Brittany," he sighed. "I was about to get ready to go over there. Are you okay, sweety? Mr. Jones said you never showed up for your meeting."

"Oh," I whispered, forgetting all about that part of today. "I accidentally overslept," I lied.

"That's a relief." Dad was quiet for a long time, then asked, "Are you going to head to the lawyer's office now then?"

"I don't think I need to," I said calmly. "Dad. I'm not doing it. I'm not going to take legal action against Scarlet."

Dad was quiet for a long time again, the silence heavy. His breathing was uneven, like he kept trying to say something but gave up before words came out. Eventually he asked, "What are you going to do then, Brittany? Jones told me what your options were. If you're not suing, then..."

The smallest crack in my newly constructed walls started to show, and I had to quickly swallow down my emotions to not cry as I said, "I'm going to leave."

***

Chris

"Better?" I asked my brother, turning in a circle so he could inspect my new outfit. The best Tractor Supply had to offer.

Mike leaned in and smelled me. "Way better. You don't smell like a steaming pile of shit with rotten onions sprinkled on top anymore."

"How fucking rude."

I looked at myself in the reflection of the glass window separating Mike's office from the garage. I look a little better today. After Adrian left yesterday, I wanted to go right to Brittany and beg her not to do anything stupid or rash. Mike stopped me to point out how absolutely disgusting I was.

Even with a shower, I still smelled just from putting on dirty clothes and forgetting deodorant. And my hair was a wild mess. I looked fucking sick from not eating or drinking much, and brushing my teeth wasn't really effective without toothpaste.

While running around town to get all the shit I needed to get clean, Mike and I also talked about what to do about our mom. Suing her was not really something I was excited about telling my girlfriend to do, but when I compared it to losing Brittany completely.....

Did that make me a bad person that I was okay with letting my mom fall into trouble to keep Brittany by my side? It's not like mom didn't have it coming after the shit she pulled.

But she was still my mother.

When I asked Mikey what he would do, he said he'd do whatever it took to keep Izzy by his side. He said he'd hold mom down and let Izzy shave her head if mom pulled that shit with her. Mom was way over the fucking line. Like, a mile over the line. Several miles. All the miles.

The whole mom thing had me conflicted a bit, but the thing I knew for sure was that I couldn't lose Brittany. I wasn't going to let her go. Hiding away as I grew mold in my pits and between my ass cheeks over the last few days was a mistake. I should have been with her from the start, clinging to her until she had no option but to forgive me for being the son of the woman that potentially fucked up her degree.

Better late than never. I was going to start now. She would never consider moving away by the time I was done.

"I'm heading out," I said, smoothing back my stray hair. Mike took away my dirty old hat.

"Don't forget these." Mike handed me the flowers he picked up at the grocery store this morning.

"Thanks," I waved.

"Good luck! Let me know if you need help holding mom down for her."

I snickered at my brother's attempt at being funny.

Jokes aside, I felt like I was sitting on a live wire the entire drive. I was anxious as could be, sweating through the old spice even with the AC blowing on full blast. I avoided Brittany way too fucking long. Just thinking about being in the same room with her had me hyperventilating behind the wheel.

Driving to Brittany's, it only dawned on me when I was almost there that she might still be at her dad's and not at her own home. She wasn't here when I got my stuff on Saturday. Maybe I should head to Rick's instead.

When I saw her car in the driveway, I was so relieved. She already came back home. Maybe this was a good sign. She was getting back to normal.

With a deep breath, I tried to steady my nerves before I got out of the truck. I grabbed the flowers, then headed up the walkway to the steps. Each step I took made tingles travel up my legs, and I deluded myself into thinking it was from the itchy wool socks I was forced to get at the feed store. They didn't have much of a selection. Static was a bitch.

When I finally reached the front door, I avoided looking at the camera as I steadied myself again. Adrian, that dick, was probably watching me right now. If I thought too much about that, it was just going to freak me out more.

With my hand raised, I was getting to knock when the door suddenly opened before I could.

There she was. Brittany. My heart was beating wildly seeing her beautiful face after days of just dreaming about it. But in my dreams, she didn't look so cold or so stiff.

"Britt," I breathed, her name slipping out like a plea.

Her eyes narrowed, making her look more severe than I had ever seen her before. What was even more severe was her tone as she asked, "What are you doing here, Chris?"

Sputtering, I tried to force myself to come up with an answer. This change in her disarmed me. She was reluctant before we turned official, but she never had this tone, this expression with me. Annoyance, yes, but never this icy, frigid harshness.

Awkwardly, I extended the flowers out to her. She turned her nose up, looking at them with disgust.

"No thanks. I'm heading out. Did you forget something when you came to get all your shit the other day?"

Was that it? Was she pissed I left?

"No, no. That's not-.... I.... I came to... to see you."

Brittany scoffed. "A little late, isn't it?"

"Wh-what?"

"Nothing," she sighed, looking away to close the door and lock it behind her. "I have somewhere I have to be."

"Brittany," I stepped in her way when she tried to walk around me. Fear was clenching my chest. "Are.... Are we okay?"

She laughed, and not the good kind. It was not the laugh I loved. It was frosty and angry.

"Seriously?"

"Yeah," I stammered. "Seriously."

The first flicker of emotion shimmered in her eyes as she bit her lip and looked away. She slowly started shaking her head, staring off into the distance.

"Why?" she whispered, her voice sounding on the verge of breaking. "Why did you wait until now?"

My eyes widened. "To... to come see you?"

"Yeah," she huffed. "To see me." She bit her lip again, shaking her head before meeting my dumbfounded stare. "No calls. No texts. Why wait until today of all days to show up?"

Her expression was so sad. Her eyes were pleading, like she was begging me to throw her some sort of lifeline.

"Brittany," my mind raced, trying to come up with an acceptable answer. "You... You could have called me."

I regretted it the second I said it. Those beautiful eyes of hers narrowed, and her walls went back up. All vulnerability left her expression. She was the stone cold woman who opened the door again.

"You're right," she scoffed. "My bad." She shouldered her bag, then said, "Well, no, Chris. We are not okay."

She walked around me, heading for her car. I would not give up yet.

"Is.... Is it because you're wanting to sue my mom?"

Her eyes rolled back as she let out a humorless laugh, never breaking her stride. "Of course you heard about that. Stupid fucking small town. That's why you came, isn't it? You don't want me to sue your mom."

"No, Brittany... I-"

"Don't worry," Brittany snickered, whipping around before opening her car door. "I'm not suing anyone. Your mom is safe."

"Wait. No, I-"

She got in and slammed her door shut before I could get a damn word in. The flowers dropped from my hands, crashing petals first onto the pavement as I watched her drive like a mad woman down the street.

What the hell just happened?

***

Brittany

My eyes were burning, but I fought back my tears as I drove off. I tried my hardest not to look back, but my eyes still wandered to the rearview mirror. Seeing the look on Chris's face ruined me.

Tears were blurring my vision. I only made it two blocks before I had to pull over to the side of the road and let myself come apart again.

My choice was made. I thought I was prepared to see it through. I was on my way to talk with Missy about my next steps, but when I opened my door and saw Chris, all that pain came back again. Keeping my walls up was the hardest thing I ever had to do.

But he only came for his mother. He heard about the lawsuit. Of course he did. This fucking small town doesn't let anything stay a secret for long.

It hurt thinking that the only reason he came was because of his mother. That should solidify my decision, but it only made me want to turn around and scream in his face. I wanted to tell him everything, lay everything out, and do what he has always done to me. I want to persistently force him to choose me.

But I can't. I know how hard life is without a mother. I also know that this town has nothing for me anymore. I can't do it. I can't take the rumor mill, the gossip, and the constant invasion of privacy. I can't do life in this small town where I grew up any longer. One rumor can ruin a person completely, and I just can't live with that anxiety again after this.

Chris Finley had deep roots in this place. He would soon join his brother at the garage, co-owning and not just as an employee. He would still attend church with his mama on Sundays. He'd get over me just as fast as he got over Missy, or any other girl. Eventually, he would start a family with a church-girl his mama approved of. He would drive her insane while smothering her with all the affection he had. They would have babies, settle into regular living like every other couple here. School, work, dinner, church, repeat.

That was the life I saw for Chris. That's where I envisioned him at his happiest. He had no future in this place with me, because my future in this town was ending.

I had to bottle everything up. I had to get past this pain, all this heartbreak, and stick to my choice, because it wasn't just for me. It was what was best for him.

I never should have let that man break down my walls. It just hurt us both in the end.

Chapter Twenty-Eight

Missy

"It's going to be okay." I brushed Brittany's hair from her face as I hugged her against my chest.

"It's not," Brittany shook her head. "It hurts."

"I know," I murmured, feeling her pain.

Brittany sounded okay on the phone just an hour ago when she told me she was coming over, but when she got here, she collapsed into my arms and started crying her eyes out without saying a word. I'd never seen her this upset.

I still wasn't sure what happened. She hadn't said anything other than it hurts, but I had a feeling it had to do with Chris. So did Adrian, who was currently pacing on the back porch, looking ten shades of pissed while talking on the phone. I thought he had called Chris, but he keeps saying "dad" so it's more than likely Rick.

"Auntie Bitt kay?" Landon asked, pressing into my other side so he could pat Brittany's head.

"She's a little sad," I told him.

Landon looked so concerned as he patted her head with more ferocity. "It kay kay, Aunt Bitt. All be-wer?"

Brittany shook her head, then scooped out a hand to pull Landon into our embrace. Her face was resting between his and my chest. Landon hugged her back with all his might.

Adrian came storming back in, slamming the sliding door so hard I was scared it would break. "Dad's on his way."

I nodded, imploring him with my eyes to calm down. He grit his teeth, taking off his hat and raking his hand through his hair.

"Daddy, are you going to go beat someone up?" Hailey asked sternly, with her arms crossed over her chest.

"No, he's not." I gave both of them a pointed look.

Hailey's eyes narrowed, then she looked at Adrian. "I'm coming too."

"Go get your bat," Adrian told her.

Hailey walked away with a determined look in her stern eyes.

"No. Adrian, no. We don't know what happened."

Adrian waved his hand dramatically at Brittany sobbing between me and Landon. "That's all I need to know, damn it. Someone made her cry. I'm just returning the favor."

"No one made me cry!" Brittany wailed, looking up just enough to glare at Adrian.

"Someone did!" Hailey stomped her foot. "Grandpa said it was ugly, Miss Scarlet being mean. I'll make her cry too."

"Hailey," I said her name in warning.

"What?! Dad can't hit her. He's a boy."

"You can't hit her either. Hitting someone doesn't fix the problem."

"Fixes some problems," Adrian's eyes flashed.

"Yeah, and I'm a little girl, so she can't hit me back!"

"No hit!" Landon yelled, hugging Brittany tighter. "Aunt Bitt said no."

"I said no," I growled at Adrian. "You're going to get our daughter arrested. Do you want that?"

"She's a minor," he grumbled. "Charges won't stick."

"Adrian!"

"We're joking!" Adrian snapped back.

"You may be joking," Hailey mumbled with a cross face. "I'm not." Adrian's bad habits are rubbing off on her. We're going to have a talk about that later.

"Mama," Landon was frowning at his dad and sister. "Daddy and sissy, no hit."

"No, baby," I smiled at him, then glared at Adrian. "Your daddy won't do it."

Adrian put his hands up. "I promise I wasn't going to hit Scarlet. Hailey said that. Not me."

"Then who were you going to get, dad?" Hailey looked expectantly at her father.

His eyes darkened and his lips thinned. "Not a woman," he eventually admitted.

Brittany raised her head from my chest to glare at her brother. "You leave Chris alone."

His stubborn air was back. Adrian lifted his chin, exposing his tense jaw. "No. I wanna know what the fucker did to make you like this."

"Beep!" Landon yelled at Adrian, putting his entire body into it.

"He didn't do anything!" Brittany admitted. Her eyes were rimmed in red, patchy skin, and her tears were all over her cheeks. "I did it! I was the fucker and broke things off!"

Adrian's eyes went wide. "Why? Did... Did he take his mom's side?"

Brittany shrugged while wiping her cheeks with the back of her hands. "I didn't give him a chance to take sides. I'm not making him choose between his mother and me."

"Why not?!" Adrian yelled. "He would fucking choose you!"

"Beep!" Landon got up and stood between his aunt and father. Landon had no idea what was going on. He just knew his favorite aunt was sad and wanted to protect her somehow. I have a feeling if he was a little older, he'd be running to get his t-ball bat to tag along with his sister and dad.

Lord help me.

"He shouldn't have to make that choice." Brittany looked away stubbornly. "It wouldn't matter if he did."

"Why wouldn't it matter?" Adrian picked our raging toddler up, moving him to the side so he could kneel in front of Brittany. "Why wouldn't it matter, Britt?"

She bit her lip as her eyes filled with new tears. They broke free as she met her brother's gaze.

"I'm not staying here, Adrian. I can't."

His eyes grew big. "Yes, you can. We sue the bitch and you stay. Easy as that."

"No," Brittany shook her head sadly. "A lawsuit will not change this town. Not for me."

I rubbed her back, knowing how much pain she has been in since coming home. Chris and his mother were just the half of it. It was the shame of finding out about her professor's marriage, then the constant fear of the rumor getting out. Then, when it did, the only thing pulling her through was Chris.

But then his mother, the queen of the gossip train, ruined her reputation completely. She would have a hard time staying because of that. The situation was too similar to Brittany's own mom's history in this town.

Adrian and Brittany don't talk about it, but I've heard from others about why their mom disappeared when they were both so young. Their mom couldn't escape the rumor mill either, and chose to abandon her family after her affair with another married man was discovered. She left Adrian and Brittany and moved away to start a new life. She wanted nothing to do with anything this town had to offer again, including her own children.

I get it. I also know why she's so closed off to someone like Chris's, who is so deeply ingrained in the foundation of our town. He broke her walls once, but after his disappearance at the peak of Brittany's crisis, I don't think he'll ever be able to break her walls down again.

Brittany might not fully grasp yet why she's struggling so deeply, but I can see it. She doesn't want to do to Chris what her mother did to her Rick.

I don't want my friend, my sister, to continue on in this much pain. I agree that leaving now is what's best. She needs to heal. She needs to go to a place where she can allow herself to grow vulnerable again. I can't see her ever doing that while living here, even with Chris.

The thing I found ironic in this entire situation was Adrian on his knees, telling his sister to talk to the man. Two weeks ago, Adrian wanted to put Chris on his knees after kicking his legs out from under him. It breaks my heart that Chris broke not only Brittany down, but Adrian too. And now everything has gone to crap because of one woman's arrogance.

"You're going to move?" Hailey asked with big doe eyes. "Like, back in the camper with us? Or are you going back to your big school?"

Brittany smiled sadly at my daughter. "No, baby. I'll probably be moving somewhere a little further away this time."

"Damn it, Britt. You don't have to do that," Adrian grabbed her hands.

She smiled sadly, tears shimmering in her eyes. "I want to."

Adrian's face clouded over, and I knew he was hurting. "Why?" He pleaded.

"I just can't do it anymore," Brittany whispered. "I'm not happy here. I'm not going to hurt someone else while faking it."

Adrian still seemed confused, but he didn't press. I think he could see what I did, that Brittany was beyond devastated and the more she talked about it, the more it was hurting her. She didn't need to say anything more for us to see that.

"Aunt Britt," Hailey sobbed with a shaking breath, then ran to Brittany's side to hug her fiercely. "You can't move."

"Auntie Bitt," Landon mirrored Hailey's actions from Brittany's other side.

My heart ached for all of them.

Rick came in a few minutes later, out of breath and frantic. Adrian probably put their dad into a panic with whatever was said in that call.

"Brittany!" Rick stopped short, seeing all of us surrounding Brittany on the couch. After taking a relieved breath, he said, "Shit. Adrian made it sound like you were dying."Seconds later, Quinton started screaming from his room and Rick looked at me guiltily. "Oops."

"It's okay," I smiled gently. "We'll go get him. You come sit with your daughter."

Adrian whined, "But I don't wanna get-"

"Shut it," I grabbed Adrian by the ear. "We need to have a talk, anyway."

Hailey looked up from Brittany's shoulder to call back to her dad, "Don't let her take my bat!"

As Adrian gave Hailey a thumbs up, I pushed him more hurriedly to our youngest's bedroom.

"You are seriously the worst influence there could possibly be sometimes," I hissed.

"I'm sure that's not true," he grunted.

His heart wasn't in the teasing. His flippant attitude could barely cover the grief I saw in his eyes. When we got in Quinton's room, I headed for his crib and flipped off the monitor before picking him up. His crying stopped before I even lifted him. Our baby just doesn't enjoy waking up alone.

"Always be my sweet little boy," I whispered as I kissed a tear from his cheek. "Don't let your daddy corrupt you with baseball bats and beeping words."

"Missy," Adrian grumbled in a low voice.

"Hmm?" I turned around and Adrian was on me. Before I could react, he pulled me close and buried his face in my neck. Quinton laughed with one of his cute little baby laughs, thinking it was one of his daddy's games, but I knew it wasn't. Adrian was hurting.

"I don't want her to leave," Adrian mumbled. He took a ragged breath, then groaned, "Fuck."

"I know. But she's not happy here. You know she won't ever be."

"But why not?"

I sighed, knowing I was going to have to spell it out for him. He was a man, and just didn't get it. I totally did. I left my hometown because I didn't want to live somewhere where I would be stuck in a lie of a life like my mother. Brittany was in a very similar situation.

"She's breaking chains, Adrian. She can't pretend to be happy here for the sake of us. You always told me that Brittany was too good for this town, and you were right. She can't do the gossip and invasive community any longer."

"This is her home," Adrian pulled me over to the glider, sitting in it, then pulling me and Quinton in his lap. He smiled weakly at Quinton, who was watching him intently. "The kids can't grow up without their aunt."

"She's not going to China. We'll still see her often. It's not going to be any different from when she was away at school."

Adrian was mindlessly tracing the seam on the foot of Quinton's onesie, deep in thought. Then he said, "I don't understand why she just ended it with Chris like that. Without telling him anything. He would have chosen her, Missy. He... He likes her. Likes-likes her. The way I like-liked you when we were dating."

"We dated?" I smirked, tilting my head.

He scoffed, acting offended. "I wooed the socks right off of you, Missy the Midget."

"That you did," I giggled. "The socks and everything else, and then I was pregnant, and we married in the blink of an eye."

"Psh," he huffed, looking a little smug about himself. "I had to trap you before someone else did."

"Someone else like Chris?" I raised an eyebrow.

"Like anyone," he growled, narrowing his eyes at me. "Are you trying to say something?"

I shrugged. "I think Brittany just assumes that Chris will move on quickly once she is gone. She isn't being stubborn just because she's a Brewer and that's what you guys do."

"What Brewers do?" Adrian raised an eyebrow.

I laughed, rubbing my nose against Quinton's while he giggled. "Brewers stubbornly make decisions for everyone. Don't they?"

Adrian sighed, taking off his hat and rubbing the top of his head. "I don't think Chris is moving on that easily, Missy. You didn't see him yesterday. He-"

"Wait," I snapped my head to stare down at my husband. "You saw Chris yesterday?"

He suddenly looked guilty. "Maybe."

"Adrian," I groaned.

"It's not what you think. I didn't go to fight him. I went to ask him for a favor."

"What kind of favor? To jump off a cliff?"

Adrian smirked. "No, but I'll try that next time."

"Not funny."

Adrian rolled his eyes. "I know. I promise I didn't hurt him or anything. I just wanted him to talk Brittany into doing the defamation lawsuit. I thought if he told her to, she would be more okay with doing it. I mean, I don't want her moving and he sure as hell doesn't either."

I closed my eyes and counted to ten, trying not to lose my cool at Adrian for stepping in when Brittany didn't ask for it.

"Missy," Adrian grabbed my face, forcing me to look at him. "Chris was a fucking wreck. Looked like shit. Smelled like shit. He was more broken than she was. I don't think he's getting over her anytime soon, baby. I think he really loves her."

I took a minute to process that, then said, "That's just going to strengthen Brittany's resolve. It's not going to change it."

"Why do you say that?"

I bit my lips, measuring my words in my head before speaking them out loud. "She doesn't want to hurt Chris the way your mother hurt your dad."

Adrian looked more confused, then angry. "What the hell. Brittany is nothing like our fucking mother. Brittany didn't-"

"Sleep with a married man?" I lifted my brows. "The rumors and gossip of which didn't ruin her reputation around town? It didn't hurt the relationship between the person she cares for and his family?"

Adrian had that stubborn set on his face as he muttered, "It's different."

"I know it is, and deep down, Brittany knows it too. But she also knows her limits, and she reached them. This isn't just about Chris or his mom. This isn't about the school and her career. It's about her trauma from her mom and her fears of turning out just like her. This is about this town, and Brittany needing to escape."

Adrian's deep scowl softened into sadness the longer he thought about everything I said. Then he sighed and rested his forehead on my shoulder.

"Fuck, I know you're right. She's more touchy than anyone about town gossip."

"And she's been the center of it for weeks," I reminded him.

Adrian groaned. "Shit. I'm taking that bat and going on a spree. Everyone who talked shit is getting their mailbox smashed in."

"No, you are not, and I would appreciate it if you stopped influencing our children with your violent tendencies."

"No promises." He looked up at me with an evil glint in his eyes. "At the very least, I'm egging Scarlet's car."

I rolled my eyes. "Do it without our daughter, please."

"No promises."

Before I could use violence on my frustrating husband, Rick knocked softly on the bedroom door and came into the room. "Hey guys. What do you have planned for the rest of the week?"

Adrian and I exchanged a look. Then I shook my head and shrugged. "Nothing besides helping Brittany. Why?"

He nodded, scratching his chin, then asked, "Um, I was at Jones's office when you called. Brittany needs to be up at her school on Friday."

***

Adrian

Missy and dad were with Brittany at the table, going over the details of her meeting with the ethics board on Friday. I was told to go away with the kids. Apparently, I talk too loud for Brittany's and Missy's liking today.

Brittany had to meet with a review board and prove she was innocent of everything. There was no telling how it would go, and dad was trying to convince Brittany to just file a defamation claim against Scarlet for now just so it was on record. She could lift it after, but Mr. Jones thinks it would be best to have it there for now.

I know Missy wants me to stay out of this. They all do, but I just can't sit back and let my sister have everything taken from her. She needs at least one win, and so does that shit-smelling jerk.

"Dad, Landon is eating mud pies," Hailey whined, pointing at Landon sitting in the middle of a mud puddle with dirt on his face.

"Stop him for me. I gotta make a call."

Chapter Twenty-Nine

Brittany

"There's no snow," Hailey pouted as we walked to the dean's office.

Dad chuckled and patted her head. "That's what happens when the weather warms up. We don't have snow at home either."

"She was hoping there would still be some here," Missy explained to my dad. "It hangs on longer here than at home. She remembers from visiting Brit."

Dad nodded. "Ah. Well, you'll have to wait till next winter."

Hailey crossed her arms over her chest. "I wanted to build a snowman while we waited."

My dad, Missy, and after a very stubborn argument, Hailey came with me to attend my meeting with the dean and ethics committee.

They're not allowed inside with me. Only my lawyer, who is already here and waiting in the conference room.

"You can go back with your dad if you're worried about being bored." Missy raised her brow.

Hailey huffed. "I'm not bored. I don't want to go back to the boys." She firmly grabbed my hand. "I wanna stay with aunt Brit."

"This is as far as you can go." I tried to smile warmly, but my nerves made it difficult. "I'll be right back out when it's over."

Hailey pursed her lips like she was going to argue, but then Missy grabbed her shoulders.

"Hey, there's a pond over there. Let's see if we can find an open bench."

Hailey hung her shoulders. "Fine. But I'm not going far."

Missy laughed softly. "You're as overprotective as your dad."

Hailey raised her chin proudly, like having my brother's protective streak was a badge of honor. "If you need me to get my bat, just let me know."

I chuckled softly. "You got it."

Missy came forward to grab my hands. "We'll be waiting." Her eyes were steady, telling me she had my back, no matter the outcome.

"Thanks," I whispered, squeezing her hands back.

She took Hailey's hands, and the two walked towards the pond. Hailey's disgruntled expression lasted until she saw the fish swimming about, then she skipped ahead excitedly, distracted in an instant. I wish something as simple as fish could help turn my mood.

"You gonna be alright in there by yourself?" Dad asked calmly.

"I'm not by myself. Mr. Jones is there waiting."

Dad frowned. "You know what I mean."

I knew. My lawyer and I wouldn't be in this meeting alone. Elias... No. Professor Miles would be there too. This was a final meeting between all parties to lay this matter to rest once and for all.

"I'll be fine. I don't think either of us are stupid enough to say anything we shouldn't."

Dad held my stare, probably assessing if I was really okay. To be honest, I wasn't, but it wasn't because of this. My head was a mess for a million other reasons, none of them waiting in that meeting room waiting to decide my fate at this school. The guilty party was two hundred and fifty miles away, stuck in that small town I would never be a part of again.

"Okay," dad pulled me in, hugging me tightly. "Good luck, kid."

"Thanks, dad."

With a kiss on my head, dad left to join my sister-in-law and niece. With all their backs to me, I let my forced smile drop and my true feelings show.

This meeting didn't truly matter. Not anymore. After this was done, I was leaving everything behind no matter what the committee decided, then starting again somewhere new.

Then I would be alone. Again.

I let my melancholy show as I walked alone through the halls to the room where the fate of my school career would be decided. I had planned on pulling myself together, hiding behind my wall of fake smiles and false bravery, but before I could surface that wall again, someone I didn't expect caught sight of me from down the hall.

Elias.

There was an expectant look on his face that had me turning around, looking for an escape.

"Miss Brewer!" Elias called out to me, hurrying to catch up before I could get far. When I didn't stop walking, he just yelled louder. "MISS BREWER!"

"Seriously?!" I seethed. My eyes were wide as I glanced around the vacant halls, thankful this part of the building was usually empty. "What the hell, dude?"

"Dude?" Elias raised his eyebrow as he closed the distance between us.

"Yeah. Dude. Or would you prefer I call you Professor Dickhead again? What the hell are you thinking, yelling like that?"

"You wouldn't stop." Elias gave me an innocent stare.

"Gee. I wonder why."

He sighed, looking around to emphasize the lack of people. "No one is here, Brittany."

"No, but that doesn't matter." I lowered my voice to add, "We shouldn't be seen together."

Elias chuckled lightly, like my concern was a joke. "There's nothing to worry about anymore."

"Bullshit, there's not. You're not the one losing your degree."

He was smiling, but his eyes looked sad. "You won't be losing your degree, Brittany. You won't be losing anything. I can assure you."

My eyes narrowed suspiciously. "How can you assure that?"

His smile went crooked. "Because I handled this, just like I told you I would."

He reached for my hand, and I didn't resist. Not while I was trying to figure out what he meant by 'he fixed this'.

Elias stared down at my fingers, rubbing his thumb against my nails. If he had done that a year ago, I would have gotten butterflies in my stomach. Now I felt nothing. Just confusion on what he would say next.

With a hesitant smile, he stared up at me through his lashes. "I quit. I resigned from my position at this school."

"What?" My eyes went wide. "You quit? Why would you do that? Did they force you to step down?"

"No," he chuckled softly. "Not at all. Although I wish it had been something as climatic as that. It would have made for a far better story. Young, handsome, bachelor professor sacrificed his career in order to save his former student." He chuckled softly to himself, staring down at my hand in his. "I simply called in a favor and had everything resolved cleanly. Then I made the choice myself to step down and take a position in Chicago come next fall."

My stunned silence was enough to make him laugh. There was a shy hesitance to his expression that did not help me as I tried to make sense of what he had just said.

"Why?" was the only question I could form. After so much struggle, the only thing I could ask was one paltry word.

His smile was tender. He slowly brought my hands to his lips, kissing each one individually. "I did it for you."

For me? Why? There was nothing between us anymore. There hadn't been for months. I just couldn't understand any of his reasons for going so far as to quit. Not if he was saying it was for me.

"I know I lied to you," he said in a shameful tone. "I'm deeply sorry for that. I don't think I will ever be able to express how regretful I am of the man I tried to be before you left me. Yes, I was a married man. But I had been separated for a very, very long time. Our marriage had a time limit, and I was trying to hold you at arm's length to avoid complications that would prolong my inevitable divorce. Instead, you got hurt."

Elias grimaced as I tore my hands from his at the reminder of what he had done to me. What had led to us being in this position right now?

"That doesn't tell me why." My voice was firm. I didn't want any more excuses or bullshit.

His eyes softened, and his brows angled down in the corners, giving me a dumbfounded look. "You're my sunshine, Brittany." He said it as if I was missing something so obvious. "How else can I show you how serious I am about wanting you back?"

Tensing, I hurriedly looked around to see no one was around. It was just an excuse to look away. The sincerity in Elias's eyes was too much. Especially since his words made me think of someone else. Persistence was never an attractive quality in a guy. Not to me. Not until one persistent asshole fought so hard to break down all my walls, and this other asshole in front of me wasn't him.

"Please, Brittney," Elias stepped closer. "Just consider it."

"Consider what?" I hissed under my breath. "You said it yourself. You're moving away."

His lips pressed together before he said, "But I don't have to move alone. I want you to come with me...."

***

The meeting room was nestled in the far back corner of the hallway. It had two entrances; one from the dean's office and the other in the rarely used hall Elias and I had met in. For obvious reasons, I asked Elias to go the opposite way, leaving me to go in alone.

Mr. Jones was sitting at the long table on one side as several members of the committee were sitting opposite him. The school's dean was sitting at the head of the table, making small talk with my lawyer until they noticed I had walked in.

"It's good to see you again, Miss Brewer," the dean said in a much cheerier mood than I expected.

"Yeah," I murmured, already feeling uncomfortable. "Um, you too."

His smile turned apologetic. "I'm sorry for the formalities of everything, but the school would like to officially put this entire ordeal to rest."

"I understand." I took the seat beside my lawyer, trying not to let my anxiety show too much. Glancing at the people in front of us, all there to judge whether or not I was a slut, it became increasingly hard.

Elias soon arrived through the other door, and I had to try my hardest not to look his way. I wasn't sure what sort of expression I should have when looking at him, so decided not looking was best.

"You okay, Brit?" Mr. Jones patted my hand clenched on the arm of the chair.

I smiled tightly, then nodded. I know he wasn't convinced.

"There's no need to be nervous, Miss Brewer," one of the old men sitting across from me explained. "We've been discussing this matter over the past few days with Mr. Jones here, as well as Professor Miles. I think we all have a good understanding of what happened."

I couldn't resist an urgent glance at Elias. He was sitting back in his chair, completely at ease. I know he said he took care of this, but I still didn't know how simply quitting and taking a job elsewhere could fully solve the issue with me.

Elias returned my gaze, giving nothing away with his friendly grin. He sat up straighter than said, "See, Miss Brewer? I was interviewing for jobs all across the country recently, including one in California. A few weeks ago, when there was still snow on the ground here, I took a trip down to the Bay area. I kept my snow tires on without thinking, and ended up having issues with all four just before reaching Oregon on my return. I had stopped in a small town to get them fixed, and as coincidence would have it, it turned out to be your hometown."

I already knew all of this. Well, not about the job search. I thought he had simply come to see me.

"The mechanic that worked on my car was someone I am sure you are acquainted with, seeing as you are dating his brother."

All eyes turned to me. I subtly nodded. "Was dating, but yes. You're talking about Mike Finley's shop."

Elias smiled more than he should have when I corrected him, but continued on with his telling of the story. "Correct. Mr. Finley and I talked for a while, and I discovered your connection with him. I may have made an offhand comment about you being my favorite TA. I deeply apologize if that was taken out of context when it reached your ex-boyfriend's mother's ears."

That was how Elias took care of this. He lied and twisted the truth enough to appear as something innocent. Everything just sounded like a misunderstanding, even to my own ears. It amazed me seeing how easily it came to him. Lying was like his second nature.

"If only your tires had blown just a few towns over," I murmured. "This whole thing could have been avoided."

He held my gaze longer than necessary and said, "Indeed. If only..."

Mr. Jones coughed, then looked my way with a pointed stare. I averted my gaze, realizing I was letting too many emotions towards my former professor show.

"Let me get you some water." The undergrad holding the student body chair on the committee poured a glass of water from the pitcher in front of us and offered it to my lawyer. Mr. Jones accepted it gratefully as his fake coughing fit subsided.

Right as he took a drink, the doors to the conference room burst open, banging loudly against the wall.

"Brittany!" The last person I would ever expect to see on any university campus was panting heavily in the opening.

Mr. Jones spewed water all over the table, straight across to the poor guy that handed him the glass. The dean and other committee members were momentarily stunned. Elias was a mixture of surprise and irritation.

Me. I was too confused to know exactly how I felt.

Why the hell was Chris here?

Chapter Thirty

Chris

This fucking school is too damn big. How many fucking parking lots could there be? How the hell can I not find Adrian's big ass trailer with all these tiny hybrid fart boxes around?

"There!" Izzy pointed to the travel trailer in the distance.

"What the fuck. How was I supposed to find that?" It was tucked in the corner of the stadium lot. Nowhere near the academic buildings.

"You could have called him." Izzy rolled her eyes. "Or let me call Missy."

"Missy doesn't know I'm here," I reminded her. "No one does but Adrian."

"And my mom," Izzy reminded me with a grin. "That's why I'm here."

Izzy drove up with me to help Adrian with the kids. Or at least that was what she said. I know it was more because she was team Brit and wanted to make sure I didn't fuck this up. She's dealt with my mom long enough as her daughter-in-law to have a different kind of empathy towards the woman trying to break all ties with me and our small town.

Brittany can leave our town in the fucking dust for all I care. She wasn't leaving me. Not without a Finley-sized temper tantrum and all the groveling I could muster.

My truck tires screeched as I tore across two lanes to the stadium parking entrance.

"Geez, Chris. I'd like to get there in one piece."

"Well, I'd like to just fucking get there."

She gave me one of her looks. "Watch it, Finley."

I pressed my lips together to keep from saying some smartass. Izzy was the type to slap me if I pushed her too far. It's been a long few hours of me whining in the car. She's almost at her limit.

I've been at my limit. I just want my girl back.

I came to a sudden stop beside the travel trainer, barely making it out of the cab before Izzy swung at me.

"Adrian!" I yelled, ignoring Izzy's complaints about me stopping too fast.

The shades for the window moved, and I saw Adrian's eyes through the slits. Then two different sets of screams erupted from inside the camper.

"Damn it," Adrian pushed open the door. "I just got them down." Quinton was screaming in his arms, and Landon trailed behind him.

"Am I late?!" I looked around for some sign of Brittany.

"Well, yeah! What took you so long? The girls have already left with dad."

Damn it. I raked my hands through my hair, pacing back and forth.

"Geez. You woke them up. You come help get them back to sleep." Adrian glared at me.

"I can't! I got to go find Brit."

"Well, she's in her meeting. You'll have to wait for her to be done."

"Already?" I looked at my watch, groaning at the time.

"What do you mean, already? I told you when it was. It's not my fault you're late."

"It's not my fault you parked this hunk of junk so far from the school."

Adrian looked at me coldly as his youngest continued to scream. Izzy hurried to take the baby and grabbed Landon's hand before leading them back inside. The crying stopped instantly, followed by giggles as the music for a kid's show filtered out of the open door.

"This hunk of junk is brand spanking new. Asshole. And if you had half a cent in that two-bit brain of yours, you would have followed the signs for RV parking when you got here. Look where the hell I parked." He waved his hands at the extended spaces. "An idiot would have figured that out."

"Call me an idiot, then. I was too desperate to get here."

"Alright, idiot. Now that you're here, you're going to have to wait. She will be done soon."

I groaned, going back to pacing the concrete. "Fuck! I wanted to go with her."

Adrian sighed. "Yeah. Me too, but it sounds like she should be fine without your testimony."

It wasn't so much my testimony I was worried about giving. I was more worried about that asshole, Professor Dickhead, being with my vulnerable girlfriend during such a critical time. What if the asshole asked her out to coffee or something after they were through, and then she leaned on him for support?

The entire drive here I had fifty-million bad scenarios involving that prick and my girl running through my head. This was my desperate attempt to get her back, and I would not let that meeting happen without me.

I rushed over to Adrian and grabbed him by his shirt. "Where is the meeting at?"

He looked down at my hands, then looked pointedly back at me. "You looking to start something, Finley?"

"I'm serious, Adrian! Where is she?!"

Adrian looked ready to punch me. I would let him, as long as he told me where to find Brittany.

"Hey. I got it," Izzy said, waving around her phone from the open trailer door. "Mom told me she was in the Dean's meeting room, then I just looked up the school map online."

"Oh, Iz," I let go of my future brother-in-law to go hug my sister-in-law. "You're a freaking genius."

She rolled her eyes. "I know. Let's go. I'll lead since you suck with directions." She then looked at Adrian. "Quinton is asleep in his swing and Landon is almost passed out with his hand in a Pringles can."

"Uh, thanks?..." Adrian wiped the wrinkles from his shirt. "You're seriously just going to barge into Brittany's meeting, though?"

"Of course we are," Izzy said confidently as she grabbed my sleeve and started leading me to the campus. "We can't let that witch of a woman win."

"You really don't like my mom, do you?" I snickered as she continued to pull me along.

"Does anybody?"

"I guess not." I can't even stand to be near mom anymore.

Izzy looked back at me with a wicked grin. "Be sure to say that when you burst in there, guns blazing. It definitely wasn't your smarts Brittany fell for. It was that Finley tenacity."

"Is that how Mike won you?"

She threw her head back and laughed. "Oh, yeah. I sure as hell wasn't planning on getting permanently tied to Scarlet Finley's son. If he didn't drive me freaking insane every day until I agreed to date him, I might have run for the hills too."

"I'm telling him you said that."

"Oh, he knows. Why do you think he was so supportive of me coming with you? Now, let's put your endless persistence to good use and win back your girl."

The building was clear on the other side of this huge ass campus. We should have driven, but Izzy said she couldn't stand being in the truck with me for another second and quickly vetoed going back.

When we finally got to the building, both of us were panting from walking so fast. Izzy pointed ahead to a pair of old oak doors.

"That's the room."

"Finally!"

I pushed ahead, then opened the doors with no reservation.

"Brittany!"

My eyes raced to find her. Mr. Jones spit water across a long table with a bunch of stiff guys sitting around it. When the water settled, mostly in some young dude's face, I saw her. Looking beautiful in her surprise.

Her eyes were wide, her mouth open in total shock. She took a worried glance around the room before looking back at me. Then her eyes went to a specific person sitting close to me.

My lip curled in disgust. I didn't notice the dickhead himself just a few feet away from where I stood. He looked more polished than before. No matter how much you polish a turd, it's still a piece of shit. This piece of shit was glaring at me like my very existence was a hinderance to him.

I feel the same.

"Excuse me," an old man at the end of the table spoke up, looking appalled. "This is a closed meeting, young man. I'm going to have to ask you to leave."

"I ain't leaving." I glanced angrily at the dickhead, then back at my girl. "I'm not going anywhere without her."

"Chris," Brittany looked worriedly at the old man that spoke. "I don't know what the heck you're doing here, but now isn't a good time."

"Oh, it's the perfect fucking time. This involves me, too."

"No, it doesn't," Brittany argued.

"Yes, it does." I wasn't leaving or relenting. Not in front of the prick trying to steal my girl away. "This has everything to do with me."

Dickhead coughed loudly. "Why don't you speak with her later? You're interrupting a meeting to decide Miss Brewer's fate."

That damned professor and his fucking scowl were already pissing me off.

"Shut up, dickhead. This doesn't concern you."

The other stiffs gasped or showed their discomfort, but my Brittany was barely hiding her smirk behind her curled fingers pressed to those juicy lips. The upper lips. Not the other juicy ones that were just as kissable.

"Who are you?!" The older guy sitting at the head of the table openly gawked at me.

"Me? I'm the man she loves." I waved a hand at my girl.

Brittany scoffed. "We broke up," she muttered.

"Nope." I shook my head once. "No, we didn't."

"I clearly remember breaking up with you, Chris," she said carefully.

"I don't remember agreeing to it!" I snapped back. "You're not breaking up with me. We're still together right now, and I'm not going to let my girlfriend lose her degree because of my shitty mother."

The old guy at the head of the table tilted his head back and said, "Ah. Your mother must be Scarlet Finley?"

"Not anymore." I pointed my finger at Brittany. "After what she did to my girlfriend, I disowned her."

"I'm not your girlfriend."

"Hush, babe. Adults are talking." I looked at her sternly.

Her mouth dropped as she scoffed. I felt the tinge of pride for making her react like that.

"Chris," old Mr. Jones gave me a cranky look. "This is highly inappropriate."

"I agree! My girl shouldn't have even had to get a lawyer for this highly inappropriate situation. Why didn't anyone call me? I would have told you exactly what happened. Instead of tying yourself up with this shit, you should sue my mom."

"Sue her for what, exactly?" Another old man sitting across from Brittany and Mr. Jones asked.

"For being a conniving bitch," Izzy said from behind me.

The old guy at the head of the table looked at her. "And who might you be?"

Give it to my sister-in-law to smile sweetly in this room full of stuffy old men. "I'm his sister-in-law. Isabelle Finley. I've had to deal with his witch of a mother since I married his brother."

"The one that owns the mechanic shop?" The random young dude asked.

"Yeah," Izzy perked up. "How'd you know?"

The dude pointed a finger at Professor Dickhead. "Professor Miles mentioned it."

"Ah," she looked incredulously at the dickhead. "Are you the genius that had snow tires on in spring?"

Professor Dickhead smiled stiffly. "I am. Though, I'd like to point out that there was still snow on the ground here during that time. We were expecting another freeze."

Izzy lifted her chin. "Seems your mistake caused misfortune for quite a few people, huh?"

Professor Dickhead folded his fingers over his chin. "It would appear so."

A man with a spread of papers before him tapped the end of his pen on one. "So you can confirm that there is no merit to what your mother, Scarlet Finley, accused Miss Brewer of doing?"

"Merit," I scoffed. "The only thing, my girlfriend- "

"Ex-girlfriend."

"Hush, darling. I'll get to you in a minute. The only thing my girlfriend is guilty of is taking the heart of a handsome man with a shitty mom."

Izzy touched my arm and came forward. "Scarlet is a delusional mess with a complex towards her sons. I've taken the brunt for years, but the situation with Brittany and her youngest just set her off. Don't put any credit into her words. Her son himself is here to tell you she's crazy, and as the wife of his brother, I can attest to that too."

The old dude at the end of the table pursed his lips, then nodded once. "Alright then. I think we've heard all we need to hear."

My eyes were on Brittany, watching for any sign of relief. Instead, she looked nervous and vulnerable, holding my gaze.

"So, the matter of Brittany's degree?" Mr. Jones prodded.

The old dude smiled kindly at the lawyer. "I see no reason to prevent Miss Brewer from graduating this spring, as she planned. This matter is closed." He then looked at Professor Dickhead. "Unless you have more to add?"

"He doesn't," I interjected before the dickhead could open his mouth. "So, you're done with my girl?"

Dickhead looked annoyed, but the old dude chuckled. "Yes. We're done here."

"Good," I huffed.

Marching towards Brittany, she looked up at me in confusion until I stooped down and lifted her by her legs, tossing her over my shoulder. She let out a loud yelp, then started punching her tiny fists into my back.

"What the hell are you doing, Chris?! Put me down!"

"I told you I'd get to you later, darling." I smacked her ass, causing her to yelp and cuss loudly. "It's later."

Chapter Thirty-One

Brittany

"Put me down, Chris! I'm serious!"

"Hush," he smacked my ass again.

I was freaking mortified. People were staring as he strode through the quad with me hung off his shoulder like a bag of cement.

"Why are you such an asshole?!" I screeched, pounding furiously on his lower back. "Do you have any fucking idea what you just did?!"

"Yeah. I retrieved my stubborn ass girlfriend."

"I'm not your girlfriend!"

Smack

"Ow, you dick! Quit spanking me!"

"Quit giving me reasons to."

Gritting my teeth, I seethed at his arrogant attitude. Seeing him suddenly appear at that meeting was funny for a second, but the humor is gone. He can't just come in and upturn my life after I've made my decision. He can say what he wants. I'm not changing my mind.

"If you don't put me down in the next three seconds, I'm going to scream."

"Go ahead, honey. Wouldn't be the first time I made you scream."

"Gawd, you're such a vulgar jackass!" I pounded my fist against him.

"Only because you frustrate the hell out of me."

"Then put me down!"

Smack

"No."

My ass was probably as red as my face.

"Where the hell are you taking me?!"

"You'll have to wait to find out."

"Missy and Dad are waiting for me!"

"I'm sure Izzy can handle them."

I let out a frustrated screech. Kicking my legs only made him squeeze them tighter.

"This is kidnapping." I gave up trying to fight my way free. I was going to have to reason with him. "My brother's going to kick your ass when he finds out."

Chris scoffed loudly. "Who do you think invited me?"

My mouth dropped in surprise. Not that he could have seen my surprise since I was dangling behind his back.

"You're lying."

He laughed humorlessly. "I'm dead fucking serious."

Adrian invited him? Why? How?

"There's no way."

"Still don't believe me?" Chris shuffled his hands, so he was holding me with one arm. Then he pulled his phone from his phone.

Seconds later, I heard ringing on his loudspeaker.

"Hello?"

"Adrian. Tell your stubborn sis you invited me here."

"What?!"

"While you're at it, tell her to quit punching me in the ass."

"What the hell are you talking about? Is the meeting over? Did you get there in time?"

I punched Chris in the ass one more time, then yelled, "What the hell, Adrian!"

"Brittany? Hey! How'd it go?"

"Are you freaking serious?! How do you think it went?!"

My brother paused for a second. "Did they pull your degree?"

"Nope," Chris answered for me. "I got there right in time. Old dude said she's all clear."

"Hey, good job! I knew you'd be cleared." He paused, then asked, "If you won, why do you sound like your undies are still twisted?"

"BECAUSE YOU-"

SMACK

Holy shit. This mother effer just spanked me with his phone on speaker with my brother.

"I'm gonna have to let you go now." Chris yanked the phone away. "Gotta get her undies untwisted."

"Hey, you fucker! That's still my sister! Don't you fucking-"

CLICK

"Geez." Chris shook his head while pocketing his phone. "You Brewers got violence in your veins. Never a calm, rational, 'how you doing' type of conversation with either of you, is there?"

Clenching my fist, I started punching his butt. "Hey-" Punch, "Chris-" Punch, "How-" Punch, "You-" Punch, "Doing-" Punch, "You-" Punch, "Asshat?"

He sighed dramatically. "I've been better. I have a feeling things are about to look up."

"You'll be looking up from your grave if you don't put me down."

SMACK

I kicked and threw my fist at the same time, acting manic with fury. "WILL YOU STOP THAT?!"

SMACK

"What was that? I couldn't hear you over your twisted undie behavior."

"I swear, Chris. I'm going to-"

I didn't get to finish that sentence. Chris pushed open a door and aggressively dropped me to my feet. As I was fighting my hair and huffing in exasperation, Chris pushed me back against a wall, then grabbed my wrists to anchor my hands above my head.

"What?" He looked me dead in the eye. His gaze was piercing, just inches from mine. I felt prickles all over my skin. "What are you going to do to me, Brittany?"

"I'm going to curb stomp your- Hmph..."

Chris slammed his mouth to mine, halting all words. My muffled protests died down as his tongue invaded my mouth. My body bucked against his to push him off, but that just egged him on more.

When he finally pulled away, I was left in a daze.

Chris smiled smugly. "What was that? Something about a curb?"

My anger resurfaced. I fought off the butterflies in my chest to snap, "You fucking assh- Hmph..."

He did it again. This time, he pushed the weight of his body into mine, imprisoning me in his embrace. I bit and fought, trying to hold on to my anger....

But it was futile. Chris always had a way of overwhelming me with his persistence. In seconds, my groans of fury turned into mewls of pleasure. Instead of biting him, I moaned as he sucked my bottom lip into his fevered mouth.

Our tongues were invading. Our teeth were clashing. There was so much violence and hunger... But it felt so good.

The passion continued for so long that I didn't know what to feel anymore. I made up my mind to leave him. Leave everything. I was going to start anew where I could keep my walls up to keep myself from falling into despair again.

Then here comes Chris. Like a fucking whirlwind, tearing through my meeting and breaking down every wall I put up.

I couldn't do this. I shouldn't do this.... But I wanted this so badly it felt like I would die once our lips broke apart.

Damn it.

Tears began to burn behind my eyelids. It wasn't until a sob choked me that Chris broke our kiss to stare down at me with concern.

"Hey. Hey... Why are you crying?"

"I'm not!" I turned my head away.

Slowly, he let go of my wrists to tenderly grasp my chin. Then he forced me to look back at him. I was too weak to fight his persistence any more.

"Baby..." He softly wipes the moisture trailing down my cheeks. "Don't cry."

"I'm not crying!" I said stubbornly.

"Okay." He cracked half a smile. "I get it. You're not crying. There's just wetness randomly leaking from your eyes."

"It's the dust," I said as I tried to look away again.

His hold on me was firm. There was no winning against him.

"Damn dust," he whispered, cupping my face with both hands.

The tears wouldn't stop. My conviction had been firm, but then it crumbled with a few ass spankings and smartass remarks.

"You're such an asshole," I sniffled.

His answering smile was gentle. "I know."

"You ruined everything."

"I know." He leaned in closer.

I took a shuddering breath, then said, "I'm still pissed at you."

He laughed softly. "I know, baby. I know."

I scoffed half-heartedly. "You think you know everything."

"Oh, not everything, baby. I just know that I'm not letting you go."

I shook my head. "That's not your choice."

"Sure it is."

"I broke up with you."

"Psh. Yeah. No, you didn't."

"I clearly remember I did."

"Well, you don't know me very well then." He rested his head on mine. "I don't take no for an answer."

I let out a mix between a choke and a laugh. My tears were not relenting.

"No," I shook my head. "No, you don't."

"That's right. So, why did you think you'd be able to get rid of me just like that?"

"Because I have to, Chris!" I said in full frustration. "I can't do it! I can't live there anymore. I'm not staying in that town after what your mom did. I'm... I'm moving away."

"No," Chris set his jaw stubbornly. "No, you're not."

"Yes I am," I cried. "I can't," I sobbed, shaking my head vehemently. "I can't live there. I already wrapped everything up to leave.... Including things with you..."

Chris's eyes were wide with panic. "Then sue my mom!"

"It's not just your mom." I looked away shamefully. "That rumor will never go away. Everyone will always remember."

"Then sue everybody!" Chris took a step back, raking both hands through his hair. "Sue me if you have to!"

"No, Chris," I shook my head again. "That's not going to fix anything. I'm leaving. I have to."

"Leaving to go where, Brittany? Where the hell are you going to go? Your family and everyone you love and that loves you is there." He came just inches from my face again. "Including me."

I could smell his musky cologne mixed with the scent of his antiperspirant. He smelled completely like Chris, the blue-collar worker and best friend of my brother. I don't think I'll ever miss our small town, but I will miss this scent. The scent of Chris. Everytime I catch a whiff of Old Spice Swagger or Acqua Di Gio, I'll think of him. I'll miss him.

He just told me he loved me. This will be the lasting memory of us. The moment he begged me to stay, but I told him no.

"I'm leaving, Chris," I said firmly, using all my strength to halt my tears. I restored as much of my defenses as I could. I couldn't break again. "I'm sorry, but I have to."

Chris's bottom lip jutted out. He looked down at the ground for a long time before looking back at me.

"Is it because of him?"

"Huh?"

"Him," he seethed. "Professor Dickhead. Is that why you're leaving? Did he put some crazy bull shit in your head before I got there?"

I pressed my lips together, reluctant to answer. But I knew I had to. It was the only way Chris would let me go.

"Yes," I rasped, looking away. "We talked."

He let out a deep, guttural sound of disapproval. "You talked? Talked about what, exactly?"

Here it comes. This was going to ruin us for good.

"He quit for me," I said in the lowest of voices. "He covered everything up and resigned from his teaching position. And...." I hesitated. "And he took another position in Chicago... And he asked me to go with him."

I didn't think Chris's face could get any more furious, but I was wrong. My stomach dropped seeing his enraged expression.

"No fucking way." He snarled through his teeth. "There is no fucking way."

Chapter Thirty-Two

Elias

"Oh, Chris." The woman that had accompanied that barbaric man shook her head shamefully, pinching the bridge of her nose. "Those Finley men. They're a different breed."

Dean Leonhart chuckled softly in response. "Zealousness must be a family trait. My sympathies, Mrs. Finley."

The woman waved her hand dismissively. "My husband is the tame brother. Chris is the most extreme when he gets hooked on something."

Leonhart smiled fondly. "The young man must hold great affection for Miss Brewer, then."

"Well." the woman shot a glance in my direction. "He's not giving her up. I know that for sure."

She was speaking directly to me. Little did she know she and her brother-in-law had nothing to worry about. Brittany made that abundantly clear before the start of this disaster of a meeting.

"I'm sorry again for the way my brother-in-law barged in here. He just wanted to make sure you guys knew how full of crap his mom is. I hope this doesn't negatively affect Brittany in any way."

The man leading the ethics committee closed his folder and set it off to the side. "This issue is closed. Miss Brewer already finished with her classes and will graduate in two months. As long as her partner's passion remains off campus in the future, there will be no more actions taken.

Considering how that man just tossed Brittany over his shoulder and hauled her from this room, I had my doubts he would hold in his passion until they were away from the school. Brittany's voice of protests could be heard until just seconds ago. It irked me to no end, but what could I do? She refused me. Completely.

...And she never was that animated in our relationship. Ever. If I were to lose my mind and try tossing her over my shoulder, she wouldn't have had half the reaction she had towards him. Even on our best of days.

The woman's phone rang. She looked down at it, then her face twisted in annoyance. "Seems I'm needed. I'm sorry again, gentlemen, and I hope you have a good rest of your day."

"I'll walk out with you," the lawyer said in an exhausted tone. "Rick will want to know what happened."

With a small wave, she left with Brittany's lawyer, leaving all of us to ponder over what had just happened.

The head of the committee suddenly chuckled. I know we came into this meeting knowing that it was going to quickly come to a close, but I never imagined the catalyst to the report would casually walk in and stir up another storm. I almost feel sorry for that young woman."

"Do you?" Leonhart leaned back in his chair. "I'm rather jealous. I don't know if I would have ever had the courage to do what he did."

"Normal men can't act like that," the young man representing the student body grumbled.

"I suppose not," Leonhart said. "That's probably why I am jealous."

Jealous didn't even touch how I was feeling, but I tried to conceal my emotions behind my stiff smile.

The committee said their goodbyes to the dean before they went about their days. This was just a minor incident to them; an amusing story to retell later. None of them were aware of how I put all my hopes into today.

Gambling was never an interest of mine, but I took a gamble by resigning and calling my ex-father-in-law for one last favor. Brittany would never lose her degree or have her future put in jeopardy. I wouldn't allow my mistakes and poor decisions to hurt her more than they already had.

I loved her. I truly did. But now it was time to let her go. It was time to move on.

When it was just Leonhart and I left in the room, I finally let my demeanor change. I left my shoulders sag and my back bent as the weight of my broken heart crushed my spirit.

Leonhart was watching me. He spoke directly with my ex's father. He probably knew the truth about what happened between Brittany and myself, but he didn't let it show until this moment. There wasn't repulsion or contempt in his gaze. Just pity.

"That must have been difficult to witness."

I pressed my lips into a thin line, reluctant to attest to the pain I felt seeing another man lay claim to the woman I was in love with.

"Miss Brewer said they broke up several times. She doesn't seem like the type to be pushed around. Maybe that young man will get a good beating and let her go?"

I snorted at the idea. "It would take a lot more than a beating to make that backwoods bumpkin to get the sense to leave her alone. She's far above his station and he knows it."

"I imagine so," Leonhart chuckled lightly. He then sighed as he asked, "Did you truly love that girl, Elias? Was she worth giving up your career for?"

I remained quiet for a long stretch of time, considering his question. "I guess you know the truth to this all now?"

The corner of Leonhart's lips curled into a half-hearted smile. "Once you placed your resignation on my desk, I pieced what I could together."

"Brittany did nothing wrong," I reiterated, wanting to be sure she would remain out of trouble.

"I'm aware. I spoke to all of her other professors. They had nothing but great things to say about her ethics and integrity. There wasn't a single negative pertaining to her character."

I nodded along, knowing there wouldn't be. I was the only blight to her entire educational career. "I wanted to be sure you understood she wasn't.... entangled in these circumstances in order to get ahead. I never gave her a grade she didn't earn."

"I understand." Leonhart nodded his head. "A woman that used provocations to get ahead would have no reservations about doing it here. She just doesn't fit the profile. Even if the allegations were true and you and Miss Brewer were in that sort of relationship, for her, it would have been nothing more than genuine affection. That's why, despite having my doubts, I would not punish that girl for your mistakes."

My mistakes. Everything truly was my mistake. One honest conversation and I could be planning my future with the sunshine of my life. Now, I'll have to weather the storm until a new ray of happiness finds its way through.

***

Chris

"No fucking way. There is no fucking way."

Was she really trying to feed me some bullshit that she was choosing that dickhead mother fucker over me? There was no fucking way.

"You should head home," Brittany mumbled, averting her eyes to the ground. "We're done."

"Bullshit," I spat.

"Excuse me?" She raised her eyebrow at me. Her eyes were swimming. I could tell by the way she was biting her lip she was lying to me.

"You're not going to Chicago."

Her eyes widened. "Why wouldn't I be-"

"You're not going anywhere with that dickhead." I stepped closer to her. She took a step back. "You're not going near that dickhead again."

The sadness drained from her face, replaced by sudden anger. "Who the hell do you think you are to tell me what to do? We broke up, Chris Finley. I broke up with you. You can't just-"

“You didn’t do shit.” I took another step. She backed up once more until her back was against the wall. “All you did was piss me off.”

“Excuse me?!”

“You heard me!”

She pressed her chest against mine, standing tall with her little butt chin lifted defiantly. I met her challenge, not backing down either. The heat between us was electric. I could almost feel the charge of angry electricity zapping through my veins and sending shivers down hers.

“You’re an asshole,” she seethed. Those pretty lips of hers were distracting, all full and begging for my teeth to munch on one.

“An asshole is better than a dickhead.”

“That’s debatable.”

“It’s really not.”

Our breath was mixing. Our faces were so close I could taste her. I licked my lips in anticipation. Her eyes diverted to the movement. And that was all the invitation I needed.

With furious force, our mouths collided. Her nails scraped against my neck and my hands were squeezing her flesh.

How the hell did she think she could lie and feed me some bullshit about her choosing the dickhead? She couldn’t kiss me like this if she wasn’t still mine. That was for damn sure. She wasn’t going nowhere.

Her legs locked around my waist. My hips were grinding into hers. I didn’t know where the hell we were, but I was about to fuck her against this fucking hall. I was going to drive my point across until the whole damn campus heard her screaming my name.

“We....” She tried to catch her breath, giving me a chance to scrape my teeth along her delicious jaw. “We can’t do this...”

“Shut up,” I growled, having enough of her damned mouth.

“I’m serious, Chris.” She tried to push against my chest, but moaned when I anchored my pelvis to hers to keep her in place.

"Say you're mine."

"What?!" she gasped. "Are you serious right n-"

"Say it." I bucked my hips into hers again and grabbed her wrist to grip it against the wall so she'd quit trying to push me away. My tongue danced on the sensitive flesh beneath her ear. "Say you're mine and I'll let you go."

"No, you won't!" She tried to push her bottom half to buck me off. All she did was harden my resolve to keep her right where I had her.

"I swear I'll fuck you right here if you don't say it."

"Chris!" She bucked her waist again and tried to suppress her moan. "Seriously. Classes will get out soon! This hall will be flooded with people."

"I guess you better hurry up and tell me you're mine and you're not leaving me."

"That's way more than what you said before."

"It's not."

"It is!"

As if on cue, the doors closest to us opened, and people's voices began to filter out.

"Fine!" Brittany hissed. "I'm yours! I'm fucking yours! Let me go!"

"Say you're not leaving me." I stubbornly kept her pressed in place. A group of girls leaving the classroom nearest us giggled, but I kept my eyes trained on the stubborn woman kicking her heels into my ass. "Say it and I'll put you down."

"Fine! I'm not leaving you, you asshole! Happy now?!"

I smiled triumphantly. "Not entirely, but I will be soon."

"What the hell does that mean?"

"You'll see."

There wasn't a chance of hauling Brittany again. I barely managed to grab her hand as she stormed away the second her feet hit the ground. People were watching us, and I know Brittany hates being the object of rumors. Maybe I shouldn't have pushed her, but she shouldn't have pushed me with that shit about her dickhead professor.

"You weren't serious, right?"

She didn't turn to look at me as she muttered, "About what?"

"About going to Chicago." Going to Chicago with him.

She was silent for a long time, walking hurriedly in a familiar direction. She was heading for the travel trailer.

Eventually she asked, "Does it matter?"

"A bit. Since you're mine and all, and you promised not to leave me."

"I didn't promise."

I stopped short, forcing her to stop with me. "Uh, do you want another spanking?!"

"Chris!" she hissed, looking around to see who had overheard. "Shut up!"

"No. Say you promise."

"Fine!" She tugged on my arm. "Can we go?"

I let her pull me along. I should probably shut up, but just couldn't. "You didn't answer me."

"Fuck! No! Are you happy now?!"

"Not entirely," I said again.

"I'm going to hit you."

"I'll wrestle you," I muttered.

I could almost hear her eyes rolling. I was pushing her. I know I was. There was some kind of raw energy buzzing inside of me, keeping me from behaving. I hadn't touched or even seen Brittany in too fucking long. It was like my body was trying to soak all of her in and make up for lost time. Even if she wasn't ready for me just yet.

I just had to open my mouth one more time....

"Did the Dickhead really ask you to go with him?"

Her hand twitched. I knew what she was going to say before she said it.

"Yeah. He did."

That was it. That was all I needed to hear for my anger to take over again. Playful Chris was gone. Punisher Chris had awakened.

With a primal grunt, I bent forward and circled my arm around Brittany's waist. I lifted her thrashing body and had her over my shoulder in seconds.

"Hey! I'm not fucking doing this again!"

"Shut up," I smacked her ass. I could see the RV and my truck up ahead. Missy, Izzy, Rick and Hailey were just getting there. Adrian opened the door for them, then caught sight of Brittany and me. He looked confused, then irritated. The Brewer siblings had the same look of annoyance. It made me laugh, knowing Brittany and Adrian were probably making the same expression right now. I could see Brittany's face right now, since it was just above my ass, but by the obscenities she was yelling, it's a safe bet to say she's annoyed too.

"What the hell are you doing to my sister?" Adrian asked once I reached my truck.

"Teaching her some manners." I smacked her ass one last time before tossing her in my passenger seat.

She slapped me across the face. "I told you to quit fucking spanking me."

"I told you to quit giving me reasons to!"

"Chris," Missy said gently, touching my arm. "What are you doing here?"

"He invited me." I lifted my chin to her husband.

Missy looked back at him with one of those mom looks. I probably just got Adrian in trouble.

"I'll be dealing with you later," Missy said to him. She then turned back to me. "Chris, this isn't the place. Brittany already made her decision. You can't just-"

"She promised me," I interrupted her.

"Oh, jeez," Brittany groaned, grabbing her head and looking away.

"Promised you what?" Missy asked.

"To stay with me forever."

"I did not!"

"Yes, you did!" I shouted back.

"Where are you taking her now?" Rick was the one to ask.

I looked back at Brittany. "To talk. Unless you want to talk here in front of them?"

Her eyes narrowed, and her jaw set in a hard line. "You're a fucking headache."

I scoffed. "I'll get you some aspirin."

"Brittany," Rick leaned over me to look at his daughter. "Do you want to go with him?" His face said everything his words didn't. He was ready to take her from me if she gave him the word.

Brittany stared at me with so much scrutiny, I was scared she'd actually chose to go with him. Thankfully, she made the right choice.

"I'll talk with him." She lifted her chin. "We're just going to talk."

I couldn't help but smirk. "Yeah. Just talk."

Talking was the only thing we didn't do. We spent the entire drive to the motel shouting at one another for everything under the sun. She cursed me out for everything from my mother to the way I brushed my teeth. Apparently, I leave an unnatural amount of toothpaste in the sink when I'm done. I don't even know where the hell that argument came from.

I bitched about her meeting with the Dickhead alone, and about her saying she was leaving our small town. She wasn't leaving shit. I don't give a shit what my mom says. We're suing her and Brittany is staying where she belongs. At my side forever.

By the time I got the key and got into a room, we were both wound up so tight we just snapped. All that aggression turned into primal lust. Our clothes were on the floor and I had her sprawled on the questionable bedspread in minutes.

"Fuck!" Brittany screamed out. "Fuck, Chris!"

I laughed as my tongue dove deep inside of her. My lips closed around her clit, sucking lightly on the sensitive nub. Her legs shook around my neck. Fuck, she tasted so good. I craved her the entire time we were apart. Now that I had her, I was devouring her pussy like a starved man.

"Chris!"

Her back arched off the bed. The flood that followed was barely enough to quench my thirst. I needed more. I drove into her throbbing, tight hole with my tongue, lapping and licking until her spasms slowed. Then I sat back on my heel to admire the mess I made of her perfect cunt.

"Mine," I growled, spreading her lips wide. "This pussy needs me, Britt. You and I both know it."

"Shut up and fuck me."

"I can get off just staring at this." I rubbed my fingers through her sticky mess, then smoothed it over my rock-hard dick.

"Asshole," she sneered, sitting up to push me back, so I fell backward on the bed.

I hissed as she sucked my dick into her warm mouth. The way she always knew to tickle the head with her tongue had me going wild. My balls tightened painfully each time.

When she lowered her body over mine, her pussy swallowing my cock, all I could think about was how perfectly we fit together. How could she ever leave when we were obviously made for one another?

As she rocked her body on top of mine, I watched in wonder at her expression. She was taking what she wanted from me, grinding to find that perfect spot. Her head sagged back, and her mouth opened into a small "o". I knew she found her sweet spot when her thrust became more focused. She was circling in fevered spurts, clenching her cunt onto my dick.

Grabbing her hips, I began to hammer into her. I met her thrust for thrust with punishing force, making her scream. Her body convulsed, shaking until she lost all control. I had her. I was holding her in place, making sure her orgasm didn't stop until I wanted it to.

This was a reminder of who she belonged to; who I belonged to. We were made for each other. I don't know a better way to prove it. A drunk night of ecstasy almost a year ago was what made me realize it all. It made me see past the wall of being my best friend's sister. Maybe now she would get it into her head that it wasn't a drunken mistake. It was the beginning of everything for us. I needed to break that wall down for good.

Our passion lasted hours. The only light in the room was from the streetlight filtering in through the cracks in the curtains. When we finally collapsed, it was only because I could give her any more. I had defiled every inch of her body. She did plenty of damage, too. I was bleeding and bruised from her nails and teeth. We were both a sweaty mess.

"You're not leaving me, baby," I whispered as I held her close. "I'll never let you go."

Her silence was heavy, causing me to hold her tight. I could barely see her face, but I could tell she was crying. Her teardrops cooling my chest confirmed it seconds later.

"I love you, Brittany," I whispered, kissing her tears away. "I'm not letting you go anywhere without me. You're my girl."

Her tears became sobs. Brittany buried her face in my chest, and I held her as she got it all out. That was how we both fell asleep. Emotions and bodies were raw, and my heart was on my sleeve.

....Then in the morning when I woke up, I was alone. Alone in a seedy motel room, my heart was gone. She disappeared while I dreamed deeply of the future I wanted with her.

Chapter Thirty-Three

Missy

"I'll be in the next room," I whispered into the dark hotel room. "Call me if you need me."

"Okay," Brittany said meekly.

I hated this for her. Getting a tearful call in the middle of the night to pick her up outside of a cheap motel was the last thing I expected when Iz told us what had happened.

"He wants me to stay, Missy. I can't… I can't stay in that town, and I can't hurt him any more…"

I understood what she felt. I'd run away from my small town too. When there are too many painful memories gathered in one place, it's hard to remember the good. Distance and time were the only thing that made me look back on my childhood memories with fondness.

Scarlet was just the straw that broke the camel's back. Brittany endured too much in her hometown. I wish Adrian would see that and quit making this harder for his sister than it needed to be.

Adrian was sitting in a chair when I went back to our room. Rick messaged me, saying my husband had gone to look for me in the trailer where Rick was sleeping with the two older kids. I snuck out, saying nothing to Adrian, not wanting to argue about this anymore.

By the look on his face, we were about to argue, anyway. At least I got Brittany before he could stop me.

"Where have you been?" Adrian was clenching an empty bottle in his fist. Quinton must have woken up while I was gone.

"Out," I muttered, turning for the bathroom.

"Out?!" Adrian hissed, pushing out of the chair to follow me. "Fuck, Missy."

"Hey!" I exclaimed in a whisper. "Don't you start! I'll fight with you tomorrow."

"No." He closed the bathroom door, then pressed up against me. "You're going to fight with me now."

I narrowed my eyes at him. "Quinton's sleeping."

"I know. I'm the one who put him back to bed after freaking the fuck out that my wife wasn't here."

"I'm a grown adult. I don't need your permission to go out."

"No, but the least you could do would be to answer your damn phone."

We stood in a tense stare-off, neither one of us backing down or giving in. After almost a minute, I huffed, "The kids will be up in a few hours. I'm going to bed."

As I turned for the sink, Adrian grabbed me by the waist and jerked me back around. He pinned me with his hands on either side of my body on the counter.

He pressed his face close to mine. "Where were you?"

He wasn't going to let this go.

With a roll of my eyes, I said, "Brittany."

His groan told me that was the last thing he wanted to hear.

"I told you to let them sort this out themselves."

"And I told you to quit pressuring your sister into doing what you want."

"What I want?! I want what's best for her!"

"No, you don't! You want what's best for you!"

"That's not fucking true. She's family. She doesn't need to move away from where she belongs."

"Distance will not change who her family is!"

"No, but it's sure as hell not going to be easy to help her if she's far away."

"She managed just fine while at college."

Adrian scoffed. "If that's the case, why are we here?"

This jerk. He just wasn't getting it. "You can't control your sister's life. She needs to get away, and there isn't anything you can say to me that will prevent me from helping her."

Adrian's expression remained fierce.... Until it wasn't. His vulnerability showed through. His shoulders sagged forward as anxiety filled his eyes.

He hung his head, resting it on my shoulders as he let out a shuddering breath. He was hurting, too. I felt the tension in his shoulders when I hugged him close.

"I'm scared, Missy. I'm so fucking scared for her."

"You shouldn't be. She's an adult."

"She's my sister!" Adrian rasped. "It's my job to protect her."

My poor, overprotective husband. He's struggling to let go.

Gently, I grasped my husband's anxious face. "Your job is to protect our kids. It's protecting me."

His eyes narrowed. "That's a little hard to do when you run off without telling me and do a shit job answering your phone."

I chuckled softly. Smoothing the worry lines on his handsome face with my fingers, I whispered, "I'm sorry. I should have answered my phone."

"Or woken me up. I could have gone."

Laughing softly, I shook my head. "Nope. She explicitly said she didn't want you to go."

Adrian snorted. "That's rude."

"Almost as rude as inviting her ex-boyfriend to her hearing."

Adrian averted his eyes sheepishly. "I didn't invite him. I just mentioned to my friend what was going on...."

"Uh, huh?" I smirked, knowing exactly what my husband was trying to do. As much as I liked Chris for Brittany, I knew he couldn't undo the damage his mother caused. Our town will never feel like a safe place for Brittany again. If Chris was set on staying, there was nothing we could do. It was a losing game. They were both going to get even more hurt the longer they held on.

"He loves her," Adrian whispered. "He really does, Missy. This wasn't just about keeping her with us."

"I know," I sighed. "Even Chris wouldn't remain that persistent if it was just a passing attraction."

"He barged in on a fucking meeting with her dean," Adrian snorted.

"It doesn't get more committed than that." I pressed my lips together, trying to choose my next words carefully. "Brittany loves him too. That's why she's letting him go."

"That doesn't make any damn sense."

"Maybe not to you." I rested my chin on Adrian's chest, staring up at him.

"If she loves him and he loves her, I don't see what the problem is," he muttered.

"The problem is, she is an adult, so stop meddling. You don't have to understand, but you need to respect her choices."

Adrian groaned, "You sound like a broken record."

I sighed, not wanting to argue any more than we already have. "Please, Adrian." I wrapped my arms around neck, holding him to me. "You've got your hands full with me. Let your sister go."

He rested his head on mine, closing his eyes with a frustrated grunt. "You're a pain in the ass sometimes."

I chuckled. "I'll let you have your hands full of my ass whenever you want."

He opened one eye. "Promise?"

"Do I need to promise? You'll get what you want, anyway."

"Fuck yeah, I will," he huffed. He grabbed my butt and lifted me to the counter as I let out a surprised yelp. "Quiet." He nibbled on my ear. "You're going to wake the baby."

I smiled to myself before mustering up the meanest look I could and pushing him away. "So you promise?"

"Promise what?" His eyes were unfocused, already lost in his lust.

"Adrian!" I grabbed his face, forcing him to look at me and not at my cleavage. "Do you promise to leave Brittany alone? No more interjecting what you want in her life?"

Adrian's jaw set stubbornly. "Fine," he huffed. "Now, quit nagging and get on this third leg."

He didn't give me a chance to say anything more, but I took note of the fact there was no sincerity in his agreement.

***

Weeks later...

Brittany

"The movers will be here soon," Missy said, rearranging my travel bag for the tenth time.

She keeps coming back with hands filled with snacks. She thinks she's being sneaky, hiding them in the side pockets of my backpack. I'll get a text after they drop me off at the airport telling me about her hidden surprises.

I'll let her have her fun. I'm going to miss her too.

The past several weeks have been a whirlwind. Finding a job and a new place to live has taken up all my focus and energy. I was grateful for the constant distraction. It kept my mind off other things.

I finally landed a teaching position in Santa Monica. A private STEM school hired me to teach first grade starting next fall, and I'll be working over the summer for their summer program.

Missy, deep in her mother-hen persona, has been traveling with me to help get everything done. She's been my rock through everything. I wouldn't have been able to do this on my own.

Adrian has surprised me. I thought he would have put up more of a fight about me leaving, but he's kept his opinions to himself.

The morning after.... After my meeting with the school, I expected him to berate me about my decisions, but he kept his mouth shut. He grumbled a little every time Missy and I would fly down to LAX, especially the times we brought all the kids with us, but he didn't do anything to stop us. He even went down with Missy a few weeks ago to finalize on a vacation property.

Missy found a fixer-upper between my new job and the beach with an apartment over the garage. I'll be living in the apartment while the house is being renovated, or indefinitely if Missy has her way.

They're finally finished with the renovation of the house they bought me here. They listed it a month ago and accepted an offer last week. Today is my last goodbye to the place.... and all the memories in it.

"Mama! Don't forget this!" Hailey came running out the room that was meant to be hers, holding one of her books. "Aunt Brit reads it to me sometimes."

"The movers will pack it up with the rest of your stuff, baby. She doesn't have any more room in her bag."

Hailey puffed out her cheeks. "That's cuz you keep stuffing it with snacks."

Missy gave me a sheepish glance. I couldn't help but laugh.

"Bring it here. I think I still have some room in my suitcase."

Hailey's mood lifted as she hurried over to me and helped me put the book on top of all the clothes Missy neatly folded in my suitcase. My method of just shoving everything in wasn't pleasing to my anxious sister-in-law. I've been told more than once to just stand back and let her do it.

"I get to go to your summer camp with you. Right, Aunt Britt?"

"You're all signed up and paid! You can't back down now," I answered, trying to match her excitement.

Hailey enrolled in the programming course at my new job for two weeks, then she's coming back for an art program for the last two weeks of her summer vacation. My brother did kick up a fuss about that, but Hailey threw a big enough tantrum followed by a week of silent treatment until he gave in.

Life was changing. It was changing fast.

I finally graduated. It was a bitter-sweet feeling. I'd worked so hard for my degree. I thought I would feel remorseful being done with school, but being on campus again left a bitter taste in my mouth.

Elias was there, but it was like we were strangers. As I walked across the stage to shake my department head's hands and receive my diploma, Elias didn't give me any more congratulations than any other student in line. His last words to me were, "I wish you well," which I reply with, "you too."

That was it. That was the end of my chapter with Elias.

I held no more resentment. No hateful thoughts were running through my head. I genuinely wished for him to be happy while also being content with the fact we would probably never see one another again.

Elias was the least defining moment of the entire ceremony. Being handed the expensive piece of paper worth four years of hard work and tears wasn't what caused the sweet sense of relief to consume me.

The thing I would look back and remember most about graduating would be what happened as I looked over the crowd before descending the stage steps.

Chris.

Chris had come. He was standing against the railing on the stadium bleachers, right at eye level. Even with thousands of people in the crowd, I couldn't have missed him.

His proud smile and the sad look in his eyes made my heart ache. I nearly stumbled down the stairs from the pain of seeing him again. I wouldn't admit it to anyone, but I wanted to see him, just one more time.

After the ceremony was over, he was gone. My eyes never stopped searching for him, even as I stood amid my family congratulating me. Dad told me later that he saw him leave and asked if I had invited him.

I hadn't. I haven't talked to Chris since that night....

And now I was moving. That would be my last memory of Chris's face. If I let myself think too much about it, I begin to drown in remorse. I wish things could have been different, but I know we could never go back to the momentary bliss we shared when he broke down all my defenses. What walls I had built back up were shattered on that night....

I wasn't okay. I kept trying to act like I was, but I really wasn't. Not even fucking close.

Maybe it was a blessing neither of us reached out to the other in all this time. Eventually, I want to be able to wish for his happiness too, even if it's not with me.

The movers came and packed up the meager belongings that weren't already in moving boxes. Most of my stuff was still packed up from the initial move, but Hailey's room had to be packed. There were random things scattered throughout the house, and once those were boxed up, that would be it. This door would be closed for good.

"Uh, ma'am." One mover came out with a bundle of something in his hand. "I found this in the bathroom closet. I was about to pack it, but it's pretty dirty. I didn't know if you wanted it with your clean stuff."

I took the grungy fabric from him, holding out the wrinkled mess to see what it was. It was a shirt, but not one of mine. It was Chris's, dirty and stained with all kinds of plaster and grime from his work.

"It was wedged between a basket and the wall. Looks like you missed it on laundry day. It's kinda trashed, anyway. Want me to just throw it away?"

I could smell Chris in the fabric. His cologne mixed with the scent of his deodorant and sweat. It was unmistakably him.

"No," I whispered, bundling the shirt back in a ball. "I'll take it. Thank you."

Missy was currently in her minivan with Quinton, nursing him as the movers worked. Adrian and dad took the other kids and just went to grab pizza for lunch. With no one to watch or judge me, I opened my carry-on and crammed the shirt in there, taking out most of the snack to make room. I couldn't bring myself to throw it away. I couldn't just let it go.

After a picnic of pizza on the floor with everybody, Adrian loaded up what was flying with me down to LAX in the back of my dad's truck, then we did a final walk-through of what was supposed to be my home.

Memories of pizza and beer, and the persistent man you would never leave, haunted me as I looked in each room for the last time.

"Let's go, kid," Dad said, hugging me and kissing the top of my head.

"I wanna go too," Hailey pouted as we all walked out the front door for the last time.

"We talked about this, Hailey," Missy said in her mom-tone.

Hailey glared up at her. "You talked. I still want to go."

"Sorry, baby girl." Dad ruffled her hair, earning him one of Hailey's glares. He just laughed. "I want some time with my little girl before she jets off."

***

Missy

"It's not fair!" Hailey yelled, kicking her feet into the back of her chair. Tears were streaming down her rosy cheeks. "Why can't we go too!?"

"Yeah! Go!" Landon yelled with sympathy sobs.

Adrian was talking with the movers, still holding our sleeping five-month-old in his arms. I'm glad I didn't take the baby to load in the car too, or we'd have three babies screaming right now.

"Hailey, your grandpa wanted time alone with your Aunt Britt. He's not going to see her next week like you are."

"I don't care! I want Aunt Britt!"

She was so heart-broken that her aunt was leaving. We all were. Hailey had her father's inability to hold in her emotions. If she went with Rick to drop Brittany off, it would have just made it so much harder to say goodbye.

"Aunt Britt?" Landon looked around, seeing that Rick's truck was gone. I don't think he fully understood what was happening yet. He just knew everyone was sad. "Where Aunt Britt?"

"She's going to the beach," I said in a cheery voice while reaching back to wipe the snot off his face. "Do you want to go to the beach and play with Aunt Britt in a couple of days?"

Landon rubbed at his eyes and nodded his head. "Dog-dog."

He was talking about the corn dogs you get near the Ferris wheel on the pier. Food was always the answer for the kid. I opened up a pack of apple slices and handed them back to him. He smiled eagerly, his Aunt Brittany long forgotten.

"It's not fair," Hailey said again, crossing her arms and looking out the window.

"It isn't fair, baby girl. I know."

I didn't want Brittany to leave either. As much as I demanded my husband to leave his sister alone, I was regretting holding him back. I know it was the right thing to do, but it's surreal that she was actually gone.

Saying goodbye was different than when she would go to school for semesters at a time. I always knew she was coming back. She's not coming back any more. This was final. Our small town would never be her home again.

"Mom?" Hailey said in a calmer tone, her voice sounding stunned. "W-what's he doing here?"

"Who?"

I looked at the moving truck, and my jaw dropped. Chris was getting out of his truck. Boxes were piled up and tied down to the bed. Adrian was looking at him expectantly, waving his hands at the boxes while saying something to the movers.

"Oh, no," I murmured. "You've got to be fucking kidding me."

"BEEP!" Landon yelled, then giggled.

"Mom, why does Mr. Chris have lots of boxes?"

Adrian glanced towards the car, meeting my eyes for only a second before he shamelessly looked away.

Chapter Thirty-Four

"What did you do?!" I hissed once Adrian and I were back home and alone in our room. "What the hell did you do?!" I pushed against his chest aggressively.

"Getting rough already, huh?" Adrian pulled me against him. "I'm up for it. Hailey can handle the boys for a minute."

"I'm serious, Adrian! We talked about this. I thought you understood-"

"The only thing I understand is that you want what's best for her. I got that, Missy, but I never agreed to just release my sister into the unknown."

"The unknown? She's not even leaving the state!"

"I know, but she's still going to be alone down there. How was it for you when you left home and were alone in a new city?"

I lifted my chin. "I managed just fine."

"Did you?" Adrian scoffed. "Baby, you dated a fucking psychopath that tried to kill you, then you ran away again to come here." Adrian pulled my tense body closer to him, wrapping his arms tightly around my waist. "Tell me falling in love with me didn't fix everything for you?"

I muttered, "It gave me a constant headache. That's for sure."

Adrian chuckled, then rested his head on mine. "You fixed everything for me too, baby. I was a lonely, jaded man before you and your thick hips swayed into my life. I mean, I was still incredibly sexy. There wasn't a finer handyman in town."

"There weren't any other handy men in town," I mumbled.

"But that's besides the point. You built my broken life back up. You were my missing piece, and I know I was yours. Love fixed us, and it's going to fix my sister, too."

"You make it sound so simple."

"Because it is." His nose glided down mine and his eyes gazed back at me. "She made her choice. I'm accepting it. Just like you told me to do. But Chris deserved the chance to make a choice, too."

I twisted my lips. "You're... annoying."

He chuckled, a wide grin breaking his face. "I'm right, aren't I?"

"I don't know," I muttered stubbornly. "If she calls me crying, Adrian, so help me..."

"She won't," he murmured, pressing his lips to the corner of mine. "I know my sister."

"Even so, she-"

"Hey," Adrian pressed his finger to my lips. "Your job is to worry about me now. Let my sister go."

I stubbornly set my jaw. He just laughed and kissed the tension away from my face.

With a defeated sigh, I asked, "What is Chris going to do in Santa Monica, anyway?"

Adrian's eyes sparkled. Smirking down at me, he said, "I told you I found a guy to start the renovations in the new house."

***

Brittany

The drive would have usually felt long, but today it was unbelievably short getting to the airport in Redding.

Dad was emotional, trying to cover up his sadness with bad dad jokes. At one point, as he was laughing to himself, I reached out my hand with a fond smile and grabbed hold of his. We rode in comfortable silence; him squeezing my fingers as I did the same.

Then his phone rang at an annoyingly high level when we got past the mountains and into a service zone.

Dad gave my hand one last squeeze before getting his phone blaring in the cup holder. As he glanced at the screen, a look of irritation crossed his face.

"Who is it?"

"Not anyone I want to talk to," Dad muttered. "That's for sure."

He clicked it off before dropping it back in the cupholder. It wasn't even a minute before it started ringing again.

Before he could silence the call again, I picked it up to see who it was that got my dad so angry.

'Scarlet #8'

"She got another number?" I asked, silencing the phone for him.

"Seems like it," dad growled. "I've been advised not to block this one and keep any messages she leaves as proof she isn't taking the court orders seriously."

I had to take a different course of legal action against Scarlet for what happened. She found out about potentially being sued, and instead of doing the reasonable thing and apologizing, or simply stop running her mouth, she got louder with her complaints against me.

A week after I was cleared of her allegations by my school, she showed up on my doorstep with her pastor. She went completely mental when I refused to answer. I told her through the doorbell camera to go away and leave me alone, but she must have interpreted that to mean rip up all the flowers Missy carefully planted in my flower beds and throw them all over my porch.

Her holy messenger, who she brought to probably perform an exorcism on me, was the one that called the authorities on her. Now there are real charges filed against her, and a restraining order. She'll receive nothing more than a slap on the wrist.... if she can quit acting like a douche.

Her harassment has turned towards my dad now. Dad had to block her number many times.

I'm not sure what the crazy lady even wants. She fucking won. Chris and I ended thanks to her. I was leaving town for good. It was like she took a sharp turn into crazy town instead of rejoicing or gloating.

Iz told me she and her kids are keeping their distance from Scarlet now. Maybe she's lashing out thinking I'm the reason. I overheard Iz telling Missy that Chris cut her off, too. I couldn't bring myself to ask about him or where he was now....

"Did you ever find out what her problem was this time?"

Dad pursed his lips, his eyes tensing in their corners. "Can't say for sure. The woman is just crazy."

My eyes narrowed suspiciously. "You look like you know and don't want to tell me."

Dad shrugged. "Can't say."

"Dad..."

He sighed. "Just forget about the hag. Not like she can bother you anymore."

"I know," I muttered. "It just bothers me. I don't understand why she's still being a bitch."

"That's just Scarlet. That's why only dogs like her."

Because dogs don't know any better. If I was a dog, I'd bite her.

When dad pulled into the small airport, all thoughts of Scarlet left my mind as the realization this was it sank in. Anxiety made my chest tight.

I was leaving home for good.

"Now, you be careful in that miserable city on your own," dad mumbled, hugging me tight outside of the airport. "I'll be coming down with Rose in a few weeks."

"I'll miss you, dad," I whispered, trying to keep my voice from shaking.

This was it. This was my last goodbye to my dad before setting out on my own.

"Miss you too, kid," dad grumbled, then kissed the top of my head. "Love you."

"I love you too."

***

"Group three, now boarding at gate number..."

This was it. With a heavy sigh, I stood and slung my bag over my shoulder. They were calling me.

I'd devoured the sandwich, and granola bar Missy left in my bag. The bar at the Sky Room was tempting to help settle my nerves and curb the sudden loneliness I felt, but I chose Missy's snacks instead. Eating was safer than drinking at times like these.

Now that sandwich and granola bar were turning in my stomach. Maybe alcohol would have been better after all.

"Enjoy your flight, Miss Brewer," the flight attendant said brightly as she handed me back my boarding pass.

"Thanks," I muttered with much less enthusiasm.

Adrian booked my flight for me and got me a seat in business class. I was one of the first people on the plane. No one was seated around me yet as I slid into my window seat.

Unzipping my backpack, I carefully pulled out what had been on my mind since the loneliness sank in.

Chris's shirt was in a tight ball, the perfect size to use as a pillow. After pulling up my hood, I stuffed the shirt between my head and the window. The scent instantly brought me back to times when I felt no loneliness. The man the shirt belonged to wouldn't ever give me a chance to feel lonely. If he were here right now, he would try to get me to the bathroom to join the mile high club or pestering me about in-flight meals even though it's only an hour flight.

Maybe that was why I felt so off about leaving. I thought I was ready. I thought I would be able to do this without any regrets, but smelling his grimy shirt made endless regrets come rushing in.

I should have told him goodbye. I just left that night. No warning. I didn't even leave a note. There wasn't a final moment between us. Things feel unfinished.

I thought I was avoiding an argument. All we did was fight and run around in circles. I thought leaving after all that passion would leave me with no regrets, only one last unforgettable memory.

That was only half true. I regret not seeing him one last time. But now it was too late....

"Is this seat taken?"

My eyes snapped open at the familiar voice beside me. I was hallucinating. That was the only explanation...

Only I wasn't. When I looked up, the annoyingly arrogant smile on the man who had been taking up my every thought was beaming down at me.

"Excuse me, miss lady," Chris said, nudging my foot, which was a centimeter in the leg space of the seat beside mine.

"C-Chris?!" I gasped. "H-how?..."

"Can you hold this for a sec?" He dropped a shopping bag in my lap without waiting for an answer. "These too." He had a drink carrier in his other hand with two coffees in it.

I held his stuff in a daze, watching with my jaw to the ground as he shrugged off his backpack and put it in the overhead bin. He sat in the seat beside me, buckling himself in and fully adjusting the belt before looking at me again.

"Thank you." He lifted the drinks from my hand and the bag from my lap. Then he sighed as he settled in, pulling out a book from the bag. 'Dating After 50 For Dummies'. He pulled one coffee out before handing the other to me without even looking up from the book.

"Chris, what are you-"

"Shh, I'm reading."

I eyed the title of the book again. "Dating after fifty? Seriously?"

"It was the closest thing they had," he said in an exasperated tone, dramatically turning the page from the title page to the table of contents.

"Closest thing to what?"

"Hmm. I don't want to tell you yet."

"Yet?"

"Yet." He nodded with his eyes on the page. "I'm looking for the chapter on what to do when your girlfriend runs off in the middle of the night without a heads up."

I scoffed. "You think you're going to find the answer in your little yellow book?"

"Maybe." He shrugged, then took a long sip of his coffee before eyeing mine. "That's going to get cold."

"I don't want fucking coffee, Chris. I want to know what the hell you're doing here."

"Here," he groaned, handing me the shopping bag. "I got you a book, too."

'Communication Skills For Dummies'

"Are you-"

"Fucking serious?" Chris finished my sentence. "As a heart attack. Go ahead and look through that for me." His eyes zeroed in on the shirt balled up against the window. "Interesting pillow."

My face burned as I grabbed the shirt and tried to shove it back in my bag.

"Uh, uh," Chris stopped me, grabbing my wrist. "Is that what I think it is?" He took the shirt from me, un-balling it with a look of astonishment. With a dry chuckle, he muttered, "Well, will you look at that?"

"Give it back, asshole," I reached for it, but he lifted it higher than I could reach.

"Why? It appears to be one of mine."

"Fine," I hissed, looking around at the curious eyes all around us. "Then put it away."

"What are you going to lay your head on, then?"

"You think I'm going to be able to sleep now?" I whispered heatedly. "Chris! What the fuck are you doing on this plane?"

He shrugged. "Isn't it obvious?"

My heart hammered, and my mouth filled with extra moisture, forcing me to gulp loudly.

Chris smiled crookedly. "I'm flying to LA for work."

I don't know what answer I was expecting, but it wasn't that. "Work?"

"Work," he nodded. "Seems my old employer needed someone to help fix up a vacation house he purchased down there."

Adrian. No wonder he volunteered to get my tickets for me.

"My brother put you up to this?"

"Up to what? Working?"

"Don't play stupid. I don't know what you're planning, but I'm not moving back. No matter what you say or do, or whatever weird book you read." Even if my heart was hammering just arguing with him like this again.

"Good! I ain't moving back either. You know how much of a damn hassle it was to get my stuff to fit in that moving truck with yours. We had to arrange your couch three times to get the door to shut."

"My couch? What are you talking about?"

"Your movers! It was a damn hassle. Had to tip them a little extra, even though your brother already did. My tool box was heavier than it looked."

"Wait." I held my hand out. "You had my movers put your stuff in with mine?" I shook my head fervently. "What the hell is going on?!"

"Ma'am?" A flight attendant came to our row, giving me a pointed look. "I'm going to have to ask you to lower your voice. You are disturbing the other passengers on the plane."

"I-"

"I'm sorry about that," Chris said sweetly. "My girlfriend here is just stressed. You know how moving goes. Is there any way we could get a little something to help her calm her nerves? I can mix it right in with her coffee and it should shut her right up."

"Chris!" I growled.

The flight attendant chuckled at him, then gave me a less favorable glance. "I'll see what I can do."

"Thank you so much." Chris then smiled at me. "Drink your coffee and read your book."

I narrowed my eyes at him. "I can't believe I was missing you just a few minutes ago."

"Were you?" He perked up. "Instead of that drink, wanna sneak off to the bathroom with me and-"

"Chris," I hissed, slapping his chest. I ducked down in my chair, hearing giggles and chuckles around us.

"Later then." He winked at me. "I got some reading to do, too." He then opened his book back up, running his finger down the table of contents page. "Let's see. Where do I find how to force my uncommunicative girlfriend to become my fiance and move in with me, all in one day?"

My mouth dropped open when he pulled a small box from his pocket and set it in my lap.

"Here. Can you hold that for me until I find the answer? It may take a minute. Go ahead and put that on for safekeeping."

He made a show of leafing through the pages of his book while stunned tears spilled from my eyes. He couldn't be serious. This had to be a dream.

"Open it," he whispered.

I looked back at him, and his eyes were on me expectantly. I slowly opened the velvet box, then choked on a sob, seeing the diamond band nestled inside.

"You... when did you...."

"Shh," he hushed me, then lifted the ring from the box. He took the coffee from my hand, setting it on the ground before slipping the ring into place. Everything felt surreal. It wasn't until the surrounding people erupted into cheers that it hit me I wasn't dreaming. This was actually happening.

"You're my girl, Brittany Brewer, soon-to-be Finley. Did you really think I was going to let you live a life without me?"

"You asshole," I rasped through the tears, then quickly brought his face to mine.

I could taste his triumph in his kiss. His smile wouldn't leave him, even when his lips were intertwined with mine.

"I love you," I gasped between sobs and kisses.

Chris smirked, then whispered, "I know."

Epilogue

One Year Later....

Chris

"And.... it's sent!" Clapping my hands, I let out a victorious whoop as I circled around the mailbox. "Whoo!"

"Was it really that hard to mail a single package?" Mike asked me with a shake of his head.

I laughed dryly, scratching the back of my head. My brother didn't know what I had just sent to our mom.

"Let's go, or we're going to be late," I muttered, walking back to my truck.

"Man." Mike shook his head as he shut the truck door. "I can't believe you finally talked her into this. I thought she was going to jump cities again when you brought it up at Thanksgiving last year."

"Eh, she was just flirting with me," I smirked. "It's a game she likes to play."

"It didn't sound like she was playing to me."

"You just don't know her very well."

"Whatever, dude. If Izzy told me to guide myself through a table saw for calling her my fiance, I would have cried."

I laughed at the memory. Brittany was reluctant to tell her family about my proposal. I kind of just took it upon myself to announce it when her family and mine were all gathered again for the first time since we moved. Brittany wasn't happy, but she came around by Christmas.

We're eventually in wedding planning mode now, or at least she is. Every time I try to involve myself, I get shut down by all the women in our families, not just Brittany.

"Hey, what was it you two were yelling about last night?" Mike asked as we coasted down Ocean Avenue.

"You heard that?"

"Everyone on the block heard that."

I pursed my lips, reluctant to tell him. "I was just trying to help plan the stuff she's been stressed about, but got shut down again."

"Oh, shit. What did you suggest now?"

"You say that, like my ideas are always bad."

Mike huffed. "I heard you tell Brittany it would be cool to have a nacho bar during the ceremony."

"Missy was talking about how she was craving nachos all the time! I thought I was making a helpful suggestion."

"She's pregnant! She won't be by the time you get Brittany down the aisle. If you can manage to not make her run away again before that. So, what was it you did this time?"

I tightened my grip on the steering wheel. "So, this dude I just hired is a member of a speed metal cover band and-"

"You didn't!"

I nodded shamefully. "Yeah, I might have hired him to play at the reception without asking first."

"Ha!" Mike fell forward with laughter. "What the hell were you thinking?!"

"That he was cheap and available."

"Oh, goodness, Chris." Mike shook his head, wiping the tears from under his eyes. "No wonder she didn't want to marry you."

"Hey, douchebag. I thought it was a valid suggestion."

"It wasn't," Mike chuckled. "So, what are you going to tell your friend?"

I bit my lips, looking at him sideways.

"What?"

I sighed, then said, "So, you know how you're supposed to plan my bachelor party?"

"Yeah?"

"Well, I told him we'd hire them to play for that instead."

"Live music for a bachelor party? How the hell is that going to work?"

"I don't know! I panicked. I couldn't think of anything else to tell him."

"Tell him your fiance said no!"

"Yeah, but he looked so bummed."

Mike snorted. "Yeah, not gonna happen, man. I'm not hiring a band, let alone a speed metal band, to play during a poker game. Just pay him a cancellation fee and call it good."

"I can do that?"

"Jeez," Mike laughed. "No wonder Brittany won't let you plan anything. Just be happy she's marrying you and keep your mouth shut."

"I'm trying," I said with a wide grin.

Brittany was marrying me. It was a hard road to get here, but finally, I don't have that pit in my stomach wondering when I'm going to be able to call her my wife.

Moving down with her wasn't as easy as I thought it would be. Adrian hired me to help remodel his vacation house down here, but that wasn't truly a full-time gig. I was managing the renovations being done by a construction company, but had to find another way to make a living in this busy beach town.

The good thing about this area being all uppity and full of money was that there were endless needs for blue-collar workers. With Missy and Adrian's help as co-signers, I managed to buy out an auto shop which has grown a lot in the past couple of months.

Brittany started her teaching job, which she loved. I'll drop lunch off to her sometimes and she always has this brilliant smile on her face.

As hard as it was to leave our old town behind, I'm glad we did. Brittany has never been more vibrant and free than she is down here. It's a different vibe being in a crowded city like this. I could walk down the highway in my underwear and no one would bat an eye. I'd be on the news and be the talk of the town for months if I did that back home.

I've also gained a new love for surfing. I did it a few times as a kid, and on vacations and stuff, but there was something different about having the ocean at your backdoor.

Brittany and I have continued living in the apartment above Adrian and Missy's vacation home, but Brittany was unaware we were about to move into the main house. I've been working on buying it from them, and plan on giving it to my bride as a wedding present soon.

"So, did Brittany really tell you that you could invite mom to the wedding?" Mike asked.

"How'd you hear about that?"

"She told Izzy."

I cringed, thinking about the package I just sent our mom. "Yeah, but I'm not going to."

"What?" Mike looked at me, confused. "I thought you just mailed her an invitation?"

"Nope. I, uh, mailed her something else."

"What?"

I laughed nervously. "Uh, I'm sure you'll hear about it, eventually."

I haven't talked to my mom since confronting her about what she did to Brittany. I had her blocked on everything. I sent her an email soon after the night Brittany walked out on me, telling her how much she hurt me and the woman I loved. She had forced me to choose between her and Brittany, and I chose Brittany.

That email caused my mom to lash out harder at Brittany and her family, solidifying my decision.

Mike was the only person in regular contact with mom, and even that was just to check on her once a week. Iz and their kids don't even see mom anymore. She screamed at Iz one time for taking sides with the Brewers, and Mike put his foot down and said no more.

Brittany may have offered to invite mom, but I would not give mom the opportunity to put a strain on our relationship again. I just mailed mom a letter wishing her the best, along with a little yellow book that's been sitting on my bookshelf for the past year.

When we finally got to the venue, I pulled my truck into the spot beside Brittany's car. I saw Adrian's truck and Roseanne's mini-van nearby.

"Party's here!" I shouted as I walked in, finding our families in the back of the restaurant, along with our work friends and the few extended family members that managed to make it.

"You're late," a sinfully sexy Brittany took long strides towards me. My eyes raked down to her cleavage. "Eyes are up here, buddy."

"Oh," I grinned. "There they are," I teased her, cupping her face and giving her a chaste kiss. "Hi."

She laughed, all hints of annoyance gone. "Hi. What took you so long?"

"Sorry. I was showing Mike the shop. He hadn't seen it since we fixed it up." I leaned in and whispered in her ear. "And I also had to mail off that book."

Brittany gasped. "You didn't!"

"I did," I chuckled. "Mom should be getting 'Dating Over 50 For Dummies' in two to five business days."

"She's going to lose her shit," Brittany said in total amusement. "Did you send her the wedding invite too?"

My eyes softened as I shook my head. "No, and I'm not going to."

Brittany tilted her head. "Why not? I thought you were considering it."

"Because," I pulled my fiance close to me, "I moved on with my life, and it's time she does the same. I only have the capacity to make one woman blissfully happy, and that's you."

"Blissfully happy, huh?" Brittany giggled. "When does that start?"

"Oh, you got jokes now?" I growled, swatting her ass playfully.

"Hey!" Adrian yelled at me from across the room. "Knock that shit off!"

"BEEP!" all three Brewer kids yelled together in unison, making everyone chuckle.

"Do it again," Brittany whispered in my ear. "Or do you need me to give you another reason to?"

"Mmh," I hummed, grabbing her ass and giving her a deeper kiss than before.

Adrian began shouting, but there were cheers and hoots and hollers, too. It was our engagement party, and I was going to grab, spank, kiss, or do whatever I damn well pleased with my girl's ass, and any other part of her all evening. Adrian could just kiss mine.

I broke down too many walls to get to this blissful point with the woman I love. No one was going to stand in our way ever again.

"I love you, Brittany, soon-to-be, Finley."

Brittany smiled like a radiant goddess up at me. "I know."